# A FALLING OF ANGELS

## W.T DELANEY

# A FALLING OF ANGELS

## W.T DELANEY

*This book is written as a tribute to the men and women of our Military, Special Forces and Security Services*

# FOREWORD

*From DannyMac*

I am honoured to have been asked to provide a foreword for A Falling of Angels. Doubly so, as I have been assured by the author that I am the principal model for his character Danny McMaster, that wily, world-weary veteran of so many hair-raising campaigns and stirring exploits. While my operational background could be said to reflect certain aspects of McMaster's, his achievements and breadth of experience far surpass my own modest efforts in the fields of counterterrorism and, to a lesser extent, counterintelligence. Nevertheless, I feel qualified to say that, while A Falling is manifestly a work of fiction, it contains much that is true about the secret (and largely silent) struggle being waged, by people like McMaster and his colleagues, against the murderous religious fanaticism that afflicts so many Western countries today, and that shows few signs of abating in the foreseeable future.

WT Delaney, is a seasoned veteran of many operational theatres both during and after his years in the Corps of Royal Marines, He has drawn upon his considerable experience and expertise to paint a vivid yet wholly plausible picture of the challenges faced daily by the military, police, intelligence and security agencies of many countries, with the UK and USA, all very much in the van of this vicious and bitter war. For war it undoubtedly is, whether fought in the deserts of the Near East, the concert halls of Manchester or the back alleys of east London. The derring-do of Delaney's covert operators, and the scale of the threat that they work so hard to neutralize, may seem to the lay reader to be on an altogether super-heroic plane but reality is not very far behind. The grim fact confronting the West is that actual terrorists, combining a medieval mindset with ultra-modern technology and sophisticated know-how, are increasingly bent on mounting ever more 'spectacular' attacks on those who, in the sewer of twisted theology, are deemed unfit to co-exist. A Falling of Angels is a rattling good yarn, but a terrifyingly sinister and persistent truth pervades it.

## DM

# PROLOGUE

*Scotland*

Samantha had never seen a dead man shot before, but she knew there was a first time for everything.

She was driving the black V8 transit van while still slightly shocked by the whole experience with the bullet-filled corpse rolling within a hermetically-sealed body bag in the back. Taff looked over his shoulder at the blood-filled plastic and checked his watch and frowned.

"How long have we got?"

"An hour, maybe," Sam said. "That was the most bizarre night shoot ever," she said in a hushed voice checking the rear-view mirror.

"Yeah," Taff said, as he checked out the cargo again as it rocked slightly in the dark recess at the back of the van.

"Fucking bizarre."

The interior lights were blacked out, but he could just make out Pat and Scotty either side of the bag, trying to anchor it with their feet. The shape of the ever-vigilant Jimmy was framed by the glimmer of moonlight coming through the rear windows as he watched the Scottish countryside swiftly vanish behind them.

The team had just left a British Army rifle range in the Scottish county of Angus. It had been an unsettling experience even for the battle-hardened. The gory violence of the resolution still shocked them even though they knew it was essential to the plan. The Americans had provided the body but didn't say how they got it, and despite the American Liaison Officer's burning sense of urgency, the unfortunate FNUSNU (Forename Unknown, Surname Unknown) had still taken a full two days to properly defrost.

The team secretly hoped he had been a bad guy before his demise, but whether or not he had deserved his post-life firing squad, the 'cousins' at CIA had kept him on ice anyway. This particular package reclining in the darkness of the V8 transit van had died an unrecorded death, nearly a year before in unknown circumstances. Not that the way he died meant anything, the most important things were that he was of a similar height, weight and blood group of the target and that his death had left his body without any visible cause of death. The SAS had the task of delivering the body to the range and then preparing it. It was a strange sight as the four burly blades from G Squadron, dressed in spectral white coveralls, wrestled with the long-dead FNUSNU into his new clothes as if they were changing a uniform on some, particularly uncooperative Action Man toy. They cursed and muttered the odd joke, laced with dark humour, as they dressed the corpse in the same type of clothes last spotted by the cameras outside the target's safe house. The body now possessed some newly fabricated false documentation identifying it as the objective.

It was the strangest shooting that Samantha and the team had ever seen. The SAS guys had positioned the newly prepared but now limp body on the hundred-metre point as the ultimate 'Figure 11' target and then walked back to prep the weapons that they would use later on the operation. The gunfire momentarily stunned the silence, and weapons' flashes lit up the dark as G Squadron SAS pumped numerous high-velocity rounds of various calibres into their newly dressed and thawed-out target.

They paid particular attention to his face.

2

# Chapter One

*Two Months Earlier*

Samantha was back. The overpressures of a high-velocity round thumped and cracked over her head. She was in Afghanistan near a dusty shithole town called Sangin. She smelt the cloying dust as the sun's heat belted down on her blonde hair. A rivulet of sweat trickled across her face. Her head still rang from the explosion of the IED that had detonated just five minutes before. She had felt safe then. Smiling and happily chatting to the guys in the back of a British 'Wolfhound' armoured vehicle. Five minutes later and now she was fighting for her life. Her cerulean blue eyes blinked as they tried to focus.

Sam was alone, she was isolated and she was scared. Her mind raced as she tried to assemble some sort of plan to get her out of the shit. The falling pitter-patter of fully expended rounds from a Taliban RPD machine gun kicked up a random pattern in the dust just in front of her. She tried to merge herself into her only protection, the rusty metal of a long-abandoned Russian personnel carrier left over from a previous Afghan ambush.

CLANG!

A big 12.6 Dushka round impacted with a loud chime as it ripped through the hollow shell of the old war machine. She heard the tortured scream of the metal as the armour-piercing round tore through the thick steel only inches from her head. The volume of incoming rounds increased as the enemy began to guess her hiding place. The incoming fire was more accurate now; it was more spaced and more deliberate. There was no friendly fire to keep the Talibs' heads down. They had time now, and as the accuracy increased, her chances of survival faded. She looked down at her empty M4 carbine. The weapon's breechblock was now held to the rear as if begging for ammunition and the gaping chamber still smoked slightly from the eight mags she had cycled through it as Sam waited for the weapon to cool. This was bad shit and she only had one thirty-round magazine left. She would save that for when they came for her.

She pushed her final mag home and felt it click into position. She slammed the cocking lever forward and sent a fresh round into the empty chamber. This was the last of her 5.56; she laid the rifle on its side, in the dust, chamber up. She reached down with her right hand to reassure herself by quickly grasping the pistol grip of the Sig 228 that nestled comfortably into the space where her gun belt met her body armour.

She would wait for them. Maybe she would die?

But she would take some of the fuckers with her.

She reached into the pocket of her combat trousers and pulled out her last two L96 grenades. She pushed the splayed pins together on both and partially tugged at them to ensure they would work when needed.

They were in the open now and the first two fighters were in plain sight and only fifty yards away. The younger Talib, maybe only sixteen, was crouching, looking intently over the open sights and barrel of his AK47, looking for her. He was covering, while the older one went forward. He was armed with a Russian RPD machine gun, it's bulk seeming too heavy for his frail-looking body. He glanced towards her and his expression of concentration changed into a grimace of burning hate. His brown decaying teeth framed a smile against his long white beard as he brought the weapon into his shoulder.

Sam was quicker; she aimed, got the sight picture of his centre mass and in the split second before the old man could depress his trigger finger, she smoothly depressed hers.

CLICK.

4

The dead man's click.

Sam froze. *FUCK!*

*I'm going to die.*

"FUCK! FUCK! FUCK!" Sam screamed.

"Sam, WAKE UP, WAKE UP!"

Sam heard the love and concern in Taff's voice as her present suddenly intersected and cancelled her past. She was immediately awake and focused. Sam felt the warmth of her husband's body pressed against her and knew that she was safe. She had just suffered another episode.

"Was it the same dream, kid?" said Taff.

"Yeah, Sangin again," Samantha said.

"It's strange, it's not the actual contact you think about. The thing is..."

Sam was silent for a second as she turned towards Taff and looked at the concern in his eyes.

"... I suppose it's thinking about what could have happened."

"Yeah, I know," Taff replied.

"I've had my fair share of bad nights."

Taff searched out and held his wife's hand. The dreams were more frequent now. He knew Sam was drowning in internalised suffering but he just couldn't seem to reach in and save her. He didn't know what to say. No matter how happy they seemed, the sadness and the death were always there.

"But you lived through it, Sam."

A single tear ran down Sam's right cheek.

"Yeah, but I'll always know that some of our guys didn't."

Sam closed her eyes and mindfully pictured the faces of the dead. There was a long, poignant silence. Sam opened her eyes and her glance became a vacant gaze. She was again somewhere else. As always, he felt a full loving connection to her and her inner sadness.

"It's been a long time since Four-Five Commando and Herrick Nine; maybe it's time to get some counselling for both of us. What do you think, kid?"

Taff already knew what the answer would be.

Sam moved lithely, cat-like, from the bed and walked across the room. He loved the way she moved, a cross between an athlete and a ballet dancer, in a fluid, smooth, powerful, but ultra-feminine way. They had only been married for two years now but it seemed that they had always been together. Sam looked over her shoulder and smiled.

"No, I don't think so, I have my own ways of dealing with it."

"Yeah, roger that, Sam, so I guess you're going to do some phys?" he said.

"Yep, train through pain to gain," she replied with her usual beaming smile.

Taff looked at the clock. It was six o'clock and there was still at least an hour to daybreak and his wife was just about to go for a run on her own. She liked to wrestle with her inner demons in her own way. The strange thing was, it was normal to them now, and that's how Sam dealt with it. On her own!

She had left her house and was soon running downhill along a rough gravelled track through a sparse area of woodland. Two old, moss-topped walls of local stone lined the track and constrained the thick undergrowth that threatened one day to push them over. A derelict cottage from the time of the Highland clearances peaked out from the woods. Sam always got a slight sense of foreboding as she jogged past this particular place; the locals called it 'The Weeping Willows' and it was said that some very bad things had happened there once. Soon the incline changed and she was running steadily uphill in her favourite part of the world.

The little tracks and country roads that wind through the Scottish Highlands always helped; they brought back happy memories. Her timed training run started on what the old wartime commandos had called 'The Dark Mile', a leafy tree-covered lane beside the stunning beauty of Loch Lochy. The route then wound its way, ever upward, to finish at Spean Bridge. The milky morning sun shimmered on the ripples of the loch's

6

dark, still, almost black surface. It was here, on these cold inky waters, where the early commandos had first perfected their small boat drills.

The road then rose steeply towards the bridge. She leaned into the hill and picked up the pace.

*Deep breathing, deep, calm and controlled,* she thought. *Just let the stress drain out of you.*

Incrementally, with every stride up the hill and with every respiration, Sam felt the emotional baggage from Baghdad and Afghanistan leave her. She relaxed into the pace as her mind wandered back to the last job in Iraq and all those other times where her duty to her country and her comrades had overcome her primal instinct to survive.

She considered what the years had brought; some heartbreak, some success and some loss. It was now over four years since the team had rescued Connor Cameron from the evil cradle of the *Daesh* in Mosul. The jobs with Hedges and Fisher still cropped up, although they were mostly of the usual security type. Meanwhile, in Iraq and Syria, the struggle against ISIS had continued unabated.

Sam sprinted to the top of the hill and stopped, panting for breath. The Commando Memorial was now just a short walk away; it was a time to take her usual moment for reflection. She stretched her arms upward and took in some deep breaths of the clean mountain air and looked across at the rugged beauty of the Highlands. The morning's hazy sun highlighted the jagged hills in a bright halo of burnt orange. The Commando monument was a large, dark silhouette against the mountains and what threatened to be a stormy sky.

The monument always managed to impress, inspire and comfort her. It had become over the years almost like her spiritual home. The three five-metre-high wartime commandos, sculpted in bronze, looked out over their former training grounds. The unique countryside had shaped and moulded fiercely independent men for centuries. The mountains and the dark, cold waters had also helped forge the men of the wartime Commando Forces. Her dad had loved it here; every year he would visit Achnacarry just to recharge what he called his 'commando batteries'.

Samantha then walked over to where the low-walled garden abutted the main memorial. She knew exactly where the small stone tablet was. She had placed it there when she had scattered her dad's ashes. It read:

Colour Sergeant Tommy Holloway
Royal Marine Commando
'In the mountains, with his mates.'

Sam smiled. That's where he wanted to be. He had brought her here many times when he was alive. They had run this route together just after she had graduated from Sandhurst, as a fresh-faced 'Second Lieutenant' in the Intelligence Corps. Sam had known commando types all her life. One of her earliest memories as a toddler was being carried on her dad's back, inside his old-school, camouflaged backpack, as he made his way into work. She had fond memories of being held aloft and entertained by mad Marines at Four-One Commando functions when her dad was a Corporal in F Company, or 'Fighting Foxtrot' as he called it. The Commando thing had sort of bound her life together. Her dad was forever quoting the Commando virtues and she often mentally recited them:

*Courage, determination, unselfishness and cheerfulness in the face of adversity.*

She had based her military career around them and still tried to live by them. She had served throughout her career as an Intelligence Corps officer in other units heavily seeded with commandos because although Commando Forces made up only three percent of the entire military, they provided forty-five percent of Britain's Special Forces. She also thought of the Para guys that she had served with; *they probably provide the lion's share of the rest.*

She had one more stone to find. She also knew where his tablet was. It was amongst the new ones dedicated to the young commandos that had paid the ultimate price in the latest Afghan war. She found it. There was a small inset photograph of a newly fledged Royal Marine Commando taken in his best ceremonial 'Blues' uniform with his recently awarded 'Green Beret'. The picture was already slightly faded. It was gradually losing its battle with the bitter Highland weather, the plastic covering was scratched and clouded, and this made the image seem even sadder. The tablet read:

Darren (Daz) Smith
3 Troop X Company 45 Commando
Killed in Action
Sangin, Helmand, Herrick 9

Sam looked at the young face that reflected out. It was full of strength and hope, and immense pride. She bowed her head and remembered this particular young bootneck. He had died on the Four-Five Commando Quick Reaction Force that had saved her after the ambush in Sangin. Sam closed her eyes and thought of him.

The day he died, she had lived.

They say the eyes are the windows of the soul. As Sam closed hers, another pair glimmering with hate observed her. The hunter had just located his prey. He had finally tracked her down. Now, there she was, framed in sunlight and trapped in the twin prism of his British Army binoculars.

# Chapter Two

The hunter dropped the binos, felt their weight on his neck and picked up the camera, framed the shot and activated the shutter. The girl now turned and stretched and ran back towards the bronze monument and was now out of sight. He waited for a while and checked that he was still unobserved.

*Everything OK.*

Now he needed to get back to his car; the job was done. He had the photos needed for the targeting pack. He quickly disassembled the Nikon D5 digital camera telephoto lens back into its velvet-lined storage tube. The small camouflage net was also shoved into his backpack. He picked up the book that had been lying next to him, the RSPB's *Handbook of Scottish Birds* by Peter Holden. It was always wise to have a visual clue to your cover story for any passer-by to see. He deflated and rolled up the camping mat he had used to shield him from the rough, sweet-smelling, Scottish heather, and got ready to walk back to the car.

He smiled as he placed on his old-type Ray-Ban sunglasses to shield his eyes from the soft winter sun and breathed in the fresh mountain air as he slowly descended the hill towards the car park where the Mercedes was parked. The car got a cursory security check, as he always did. He glanced into the passenger side and rear, checking for anything that he hadn't seen there before. He opened the driver's door and climbed in. He momentarily relaxed against the cool beige leather and reached for the cigarette packet on the dashboard, just above the sign that said in English, Arabic and Punjabi 'NO SMOKING' while again carefully checking the car park.

No new cars or people, things seemed the same.

He expertly tossed a Marlborough Light into his mouth, ignited it, and sighed in pleasure as he inhaled a long, slow drag and thought. He had been tracking the woman that had killed his brother for what seemed like a lifetime. Hate stretches time; it contorts it and magnifies its malevolence. It seemed strange, but the very openness of British society and the all-powerful Internet had made everything easy. 'Open source information' his computer instructor in Luton had called it. All these little pieces of the puzzle had come together over time to produce the definitive picture.

Her name had come from the press reports after Afghanistan under the lurid headline of 'The Angel of Death' where Captain Samantha Holloway of the British Army's Intelligence Corps had killed innocent Muslims in Afghanistan. The London firm of lawyers for the families called 'Lee and Day' had insisted that her name was made public. Her face had emerged from her wedding photos posted by friends, and her address had been gained by simply running her name through the local council's online portal. Every little success narrowed down her location.

The faraway beep of a car horn jolted him from his thoughts. He removed the Nikon from the bag and unhooked it from its black waterproof protective case. He put the encryption stick into the USB slot and used the camera's digital memory to choose which photos to send wirelessly to London. He waited for a return text message. His phone tinged; the images had arrived. He smiled and then deleted them from the memory. The camera now only showed his best attempts to catch the wild birds of the Highlands in their natural habitat. He removed the encryption device and replaced it in its hiding place at the bottom of the driver's seat and got ready to drive back.

He checked the rear-view mirror for surveillance as he pulled out of the car park, and again as he wound his way down the steep country lanes. He felt confident that he was safe. It was a closed-cell operation, he had insisted, and the team he would be using hadn't even been informed of its existence yet. The two operations should happen sequentially, the big one first and the smaller one. *He would enjoy the smaller one.* At that happy thought he took one deeper draw of the cigarette and stubbed it out into the overflowing ashtray.

*He hated Americans but loved their cigarettes.*

He flicked another one from the packet while cradling the steering wheel with his left hand. The last one, *I need more.* He checked the mirror through a haze of smoke as he indicated to access the dual carriageway to the motorway.

The rain had started falling and the automatic wipers flicked on. He pushed the entertainment button on the steering wheel and the local radio station filled the car's sound system. Nevis Radio was playing an old country and western song by Billy Ray Cyrus called 'Achy Breaky Heart'. He felt a sudden chill that just seemed to ripple along his spine but didn't know why. The music just disturbed him. It was everything he hated. He switched off the radio in an angry stab of his finger.

*Kuffar shit!*

# Chapter Three

*Night Duty, Task Force HQ, Vauxhall, London*

Ahmad glanced through the red folder on his desk. It was a meticulously written record of his relationship with his source. Even in Britain's twenty-first century agent handlers still had to keep written records for two very good reasons. Firstly, it was now required by a thing called PACE, 'The Police and Criminal Evidence Act', and was a legal requirement and secondly for a far more practical consideration, if the whole digital shebang were ever taken down by a cyber attack Ahmad could still access and record information using the old methods.

He always remembered the mantra drummed into him from his MI5 instructors.

*'Information doesn't become intelligence unless it is written down, recorded and processed.'*

*And after nearly two years the file was becoming quite heavy.*

It was also Ahmad's record of his personal relationship with Imran, Agent 3010, codenamed KEN and the MI5's most productive CHIS (Covert Human Intelligence Source) inside ISIS. It had all started on that cold day in Dover when Imran had driven down the ramp of a ferry and tried to return home, sickened and disillusioned, after a religiously inspired rampage through Syria and Iraq. The ex-jihadi had been given a choice by MI5.

'Either work for us or get banged up for war crimes as a Category 'A' prisoner in Belmarsh.'

When faced with the stark choice, the street-smart, ex-Luton doorman, living in Whitechapel had jumped in their direction. Ahmad opened the thin red cardboard cover of the file. It had two thick black diagonal lines clipping the upper right-hand corner. It simply said:

## TOP SECRET– UK EYES ONLY

A brief synopsis outlined the contents.

*Agent 3010, codenamed KEN, is a known ISIS member. He is a British citizen of Bangladeshi heritage. He was initially radicalised when on remand in Wandsworth Prison by Mullah Rahman, who was then the Muslim prison chaplain. The agent was initially recruited under duress in 2014 on his return to London after two years fighting for Islamic State in both Syria and Iraq. 3010 is a happily married man with two children, a boy 3 and a girl 5. He lives in Whitechapel in London.*

The file was full of such facts, contacts notes, and handler recommendations. There was also a box full of columns and signatures on the upper right-hand side of the file. Each person who looked at the file had to date and sign for it, no exceptions. He looked along the column. He recognised the current head of MI5's signature; he had read the file three times. There was also the iconic signature of the director of MI6's mark and date, just a simple 'C' in green ink that was barely legible against the red file cover. He had looked at it three times as well. His agent was an important asset and that is why the file on '3010' was so popular. Imran, agent number 3010, had provided vital information that had saved countless lives.

The file though was only really just a skeletal record of the source meets, the information passed and the subsequent successes. Ahmad, the MI5 handler, knew that it was not only a recording of information. It was also the bones of a much deeper relationship. He had now worked with Imran for over four years, and he knew him in much more depth than this simple file could ever record. The cherry red folder could never explain the complexities of running an agent like Imran. It was never going to be easy. He was a star source but also a very conflicted guy.

Ahmad had also learned along the way that HUMINT (Human Intelligence) was much more than just meeting a source and jotting down some case notes. A good handler needed to get inside his agent's head until he almost knew what he was thinking. Was he happy with the arrangement? Did he believe himself adequately rewarded? Or was he wound up, like some tightly coiled spring, ready to recoil back with extreme malice? Ahmad knew that a source handler had not only to empathise with his agent but he also had to understand his limitations and the severe emotional impact of his isolation. He needed to know his loneliness, his fears, and the incredible personal pressures that his secret life brought him. An agent like Imran needed to feel valued and be part of a team. He also needed to know that the rewards would always heavily outweigh the risks. Ahmad felt responsible for him and he knew something was wrong. He needed a rest. But as long as he was producing information that saved lives, he would continue working.

He sometimes felt his source's inner sadness and realised that he was suffering from some self-inflicted trauma from his former jihadi days. There was only one place inside this red cover for supposition or conjecture, and that was the text box at the end of the source report that said, 'Handler Comment'. As he scanned this important space sometimes overlooked by other eyes hungry for exploitable pre-emptive intelligence, he could actually trace his agent's downward emotional spiral, and knew that he needed help. 3010 was suffering, and he thought he might know why. *After all, if British soldiers could suffer from PTSD, why not a returning jihadist?*

Imran felt the young man's fear.

The Iraqi soldier was about the same age and he was kneeling in front of Imran's chest facing towards the camera. The soldier was bound with his hands behind him. Imran felt the last warmth of the evening sun on his back and looked at the prisoner's shadow interlaced with his own, overlaid together and projected onto the dirty yellow sand of Tikrit. He heard the young soldier's gentle sobbing in the moment just before he killed him. His victim's hope had gone completely now and he knew that the pain of butchery would signal his end. Imran looked down at the top of the man's head.

His left hand was placed on the prisoner's left shoulder, pressing him firmly in place. In his right hand was the combat knife. He felt the kneeling man's fear. It permeated slowly upwards through Imran's left arm until its icy coldness found space in Imran's very own soul. He looked along the line of prisoners waiting to die. They were all young Shia soldiers from the Iraqi Army. Only some were in uniform. Some were young, some old; some scared shitless but others defiant. Many seemed resigned to their fate, just like sheep waiting for the butcher's knife. Imran knew some would struggle, but all would die.

The time for the execution was approaching and Imran was nervous. An older jihadi brother had told him how to do it efficiently. The Mullah's speech was building to a climax. Imran waited, fearful but fascinated; could he do this? He placed the point of the knife, the serrated cutting blade, outwards, behind the man's windpipe in front of his spinal column. He remembered the older man's advice.

'Press the *Kuffar*'s forehead back with your left hand into your stomach, with your body firmly behind it. Stab the knife into his neck quickly just in front of his spine and slash the blade forward through his neck. Then you just need to saw through the rest of the neck to get the head off cleanly.

It's just like butchering a goat, brother,' he had said with a smile. But Imran was from London and had never butchered a goat.

The order arrived, and he cut. He smelt the metallic waft of fresh blood as he watched it jet onto the sand. He heard a terrible noise. The rasping and gurgling sound of the man who was still trying to survive through a gaping wound in his throat. The knife continued to slice through flesh and grate on bone.

The head was finally off.

He held it aloft by the hair for the cameras as ordered. Imran slowly turned the head to look at his victim's face.

*FUCK!* He recognised the bloodied face.

*IT'S ME!*

It was his face.

Imran screamed.

It was a dry scream – terrifying and guttural, like the rasping cry of the young man he had butchered in Iraq.

"IMRAN, Imran." It was his wife's gentle voice.

"PLEASE WAKE UP." His wife's concerned voice jolts him back from the hell of Tikrit.

He was back and safe in London.

It was always the same dream, but he could never discuss the horror of it with anyone. He couldn't share his nightmare with a therapist; it was locked inside him forever for a reason. He felt the guilt daily, and he would always bear the crushing shame of it. It was his burden until redemption. He was still inside an organisation that gloried in such violence and each day he was inside it, he hated it a little bit more.

*How the fuck did I let these murderous wankers into my life?* he thought.

*Why did I let them control me, use me, fuck me up?*

His fear of discovery further compounded the hangover of fear and hate that he had inherited from Iraq. Imran had worked as an MI5/MI6 covert source for four years now and living a double life came with the job. One part of him still had to be the old Imran, the pseudo-Salafist with criminal experience who pretended to play the war hero amongst Whitechapel's little bit of sharia law. The other Imran was a British husband and a father who would have loved to live a normal life.

Ahmad had explained to his agent the meaning of what the intelligence world calls 'the circle of knowledge'. A secret was only truly a secret when that 'circle of knowledge' was tight; simply put, the fewer people that knew something, the more secure that secret was. The secret he held was serious 'Need to Know'. As Imran had gained credibility within ISIS in London, the circle of knowledge had tightened. He was now accessing the deeper, darker secrets known by only a very few. This made life harder for him, Imran, agent number '3010' and also for Ahmad, his MI5 handler.

Imran looked up at the ceiling, closed his eyes briefly and reopened them and then tried to refocus. He felt the warmth of his wife's body next to him as she gently ran the delicate fingers of her left hand through his hair. His wife knew nothing; he could not share the horrors with her. He could not explain his feelings of isolation or his omnipresent thoughts about death that his double life was starting to bring him. It had been worse since he had found out. He had a secret to pass and he had to see Ahmad urgently. The problem was that the circle of knowledge was tight and they were looking for spies.

*It would be safer if I buried it, forgot it, or just ignored it.*

*But then I will be responsible for the carnage when it goes down. What if it was my wife and kids lying broken inside the carnage a suicide-bomb attack produces. Remember that last one in Iraq?*

He made up his mind.

*I need to meet Ahmad; I need to get this passed before the responsibility crushes me.*

# Chapter Four

*Baker Street*

It was evening time in London and it was raining. Danny McMaster slowly sipped a single malt whisky, untainted by either ice or water, while looking down from his office suite onto a rain-sodden Baker Street. He cradled his glass thoughtfully as he observed the small dots of glistening umbrellas weaving ad hoc patterns on the shiny wet pavements six floors below.

These were the people the Security Services were trying to protect. Each probably locked in their own thoughts and oblivious to each other.

A very few of the people below, *the protected*, could possibly comprehend how their lives could be changed in a single violent instant. The hustle and bustle of a vibrant city served as the perfect backdrop for his innermost thoughts.

*Perfectly ordinary people doing perfectly normal things.*

Danny looked back at a hectic couple of years for the security company he had founded with Kenny Hanrahan. They had developed the idea of 'Hedges and Fisher' on a long flight from Kabul to London. It had evolved from a hastily scrawled mind-map on an airline napkin to a going concern within six months. The British company's central expertise had developed over a thirty-year period during the ever-changing shadow wars with Britain's enemies. It had now been over four years since Sam Holloway's team had successfully snatched back the American hostage, Connor Cameron, from his dark suffering in Iraq. Danny poured himself another Laphroaig and smiled.

The operation had been a real shock for the Islamic State in Iraq, it had for the first time highlighted their vulnerability, and it had been great for the company and for Connor.

The hooded man's knife was about to slice through the hostage's neck as things had dramatically changed. Firstly, Connor, as an ex-Special Forces Commando soldier had decided not to cooperate in his own execution and secondly, at that precise moment, Sam Holloway and her team, accompanied by 300 furious and determined Kurdish Special Forces soldiers had imploded into ISIS's closeted existence to totally ruin their day.

The cameras were rolling, and the old Mullah's sermon had started to climax just as the team's explosive charges propelled the doors of their shuttered ideology towards them. The team's house assault and the Commando raid were timed to perfection. Connor was now free, and the company rewarded, and Hedges and Fisher was busier than ever.

He considered the last job. He knew the technical intervention by Sam's team on the London phase of the hostage rescue had saved countless lives. The team had conducted a covert entry of an ISIS member's house and jarked (bugged) six MacBook Air laptops. These laptops were now buried deep within the Islamic States' communications system. MI6 had called the operation 'Running Man'. It was now continuously collecting and transmitting data into a room inside the MI6 building at Vauxhall. Danny knew though that the problem had not gone away and the threat had only been slowed but not eradicated. He knew that a simple oversight, a missed link or a sloppy piece of surveillance work was all that was needed for disaster to strike anywhere on the British mainland. Danny was for the first time genuinely shocked at the extent of the threat. He had just read a secret report that outlined the actual attacks that 'Running Man' had prevented. It was a sobering document.

The operation had disrupted hundreds of plots at their inception and at least ten while in progress. These attacks ranged from an attempted kidnapping and beheading of a soldier to mass casualty bomb and gun attacks.

Danny, the old guard, counter-terrorist veteran, mentally quoted the Provisional IRA's boast after the Brighton bombing in 1984.

'Today we were unlucky, but remember, we only have to be lucky once.'

Death had stalked the streets below and had only been prevented by vital pre-emptive human intelligence, good old-fashioned tradecraft and a large slice of dumb-arsed fucking luck. One particular attack was only foiled by observation. A 'switched on' MI5 watcher had counted the number of female worshippers attending a Salafist mosque going in but when they emerged there was one black-robed figure too many. The watcher had then seen some obviously male footwear as one of these burkha-enshrouded worshippers climbed into a vehicle. After the reaction team had hit the car, it was found to contain firearms and pipe bombs. Two coach loads of schoolgirls were the intended targets. It was a close-run thing.

He looked down and observed the streets of London as they shimmered in a late outbreak of evening sun. In recent times, those rain-stained streets had become every bit as dangerous as the dusty alleys of Kabul and Baghdad. The threats had been easier to identify there and sometimes easier to deal with. The capital that Danny loved had transformed over the past ten years. Outside the areas that the Government controlled lay vast tracts where they only pretended to have control. Gun and knife crime now made some areas of its southern and eastern peripheries virtual no-go zones. Danny sighed; British society seemed to be transmuting into chaos in front of his ageing eyes. Violent crimes of all sorts had spiked through the roof. Over twenty-one young men had died this year, sixteen stabbed, seven shot, and it was only August.

*Some places in London were now more dangerous than Belfast at the height of the troubles and we had thousands of armed British troops trying to keep the peace there. But I suppose criminal drug violence is more acceptable to politicians than the political type.*

Danny had a different view from the mainstream; he knew that one type of violence sometimes morphed naturally into the other, in a sort of crime-terror nexus zone where political radicals used the violence on the streets to assist their own funding and agendas. Britain's prisons were now providing their own fertile recruiting ground for both Islamist and far-right terror gangs.

Wagner's 'Flight of the Valkyries' interrupted his thoughts as his mobile rang; he quickly looked for the caller. It was 'Fortnum and Mason', and the phone rang off. Danny understood that it was Tim Broughton, his MI6 liaison officer, trying to get in touch. He would ring Tim back on his encrypted line.

Danny rang the number, and Tim answered the phone.

"Hi, Danny, something's come up, we need to speak fairly quickly."

"OK, pal, where?" Danny replied.

"Let's chat at the club; I'll buy you coffee."

"What time?" Danny said.

"See you at 0900 hours tomorrow. That will give us time to set things up."

"Roger that, see you at the club at nine, old mate." Danny finished the call and deleted the caller from his mobile's memory.

The club was the 'Special Forces Club', and it suited their purposes; it was well away from the Government and the City and was situated in a quiet and expensive residential area of central London, where all the elegant Edwardian houses looked the same. It was also a place where hostile surveillance was easily identified. It was in a prosperous, well-heeled area of town, where outsiders tended to stand out. It was also a club where Tim and Danny were members so it fitted their regular patterns of life.

Danny arrived the next morning by taxi. He was dropped off outside on the main road and walked the last few hundred yards through the side streets towards the club's very ordinary-looking front door. He swiped his membership card and spoke into the intercom. The hall porter answered and pressed the automatic door after he used the latest facial recognition technology to check his identity. Danny pushed against the door, and it opened.

"Welcome, Mister McMaster," the porter said. "It's good to see you," in a gravelly Scottish burr, sounding very much like the ex-Para Sergeant Major he had once been.

"Good to see you, Tom," Danny said. He thought the old ex-Para, now in his late sixties, looked like an elderly, but still dangerous, attack-dog, which he probably was, Danny mentally confirmed.

"Has he arrived, Tom?"

"Yes, Mister McMaster, he's in the library, and you have it for an hour."

"Many thanks."

The library's door was firmly closed, a message to all SF Club members that a meeting was in progress, or at least about to start. Danny knocked, and the thick, ornate teak door was swung open by a smartly dressed Tim Broughton, the MI6 officer who had liaised with Danny and the team over the operation in Kurdistan. Danny always felt uniquely at home in the library of the SF Club. It had all the natural aromas that he associated with the best clubs.

A sort of fusion of leather, beautiful old books, whisky, and all with the ancient aroma of old cigar smoke.

# Chapter Five

It would only take an upmarket 'Sloane Street' crow just a few minutes to fly from the SF Club over a crowded city's skyline to a far less exclusive area of town, where the shiny roof of a dark red Audi A6 glistened in a late burst of sun. The car was parked outside a shabby tower block in South London. The man in the driving seat tapped the steering wheel in time to the low sounds of Capital Radio; it was his only visible sign of unease. George had been a surveillance operator for twenty-five years, firstly as a young man, as a special duties soldier in Ulster and now as a middle-aged one in A Department of MI5, mainly within the confines of the M25, the ring road that both surrounds and confuses London's motorists.

He had been in the Det in Northern Ireland at a time when it was one of the most effective anti-terrorist units in the British Army. The Provisional IRA had just called them 'The Men in the Cars' and they were an IRA man's worst nightmare.

Sitting next to him in the shiny Audi was his partner both in life and at work. Dorothy had been an Intelligence Corps Sergeant before she passed Camp One, the unit's extremely arduous selection phase. Over one hundred servicemen and women from across all the services had tried, and Dot was one of only eight to go operational in Ulster where she had hooked up with George.

She was dressed in a vivid red jacket by Vivienne Westwood and was running her fingers through her long auburn hair while observing what was happening behind her in the Audi's vanity mirror. She had also been an A Branch watcher for over a decade and had been in the shit before. She sensed that things could go very wrong, very quickly, in this little slice of 'not so' multicultural London.

George was dressed in a smart dark-blue cashmere overcoat, collar and tie and also jarred with his surroundings. His dark tweed peaked cap lay on the dashboard covering the ASP extendable police baton and the CS spray that might be needed soon. They had been rushed here at short notice from a task to cover a meet with an Arab source at Harrods and they were ill prepared to go 'eyes down' on a council estate in South London.

"We stick out like a pair of racing dogs' bollocks here, girl," he said.

"Yeah, we're dressed for Sloane Street and not..." Dot glanced at the name on the outside of the old block of flats, "fucking Frobisher Heights," putting an extra emphasis on the word 'fucking'.

She had studied architecture at university and knew the design for buildings like Frobisher Heights was inspired by one of the most famous architects of the twentieth century; the Swiss modernist had just called himself Le Corbusier, a man who thought that 'a house was a machine for living in'. The building was initially crafted in raw concrete and glass and must have looked magnificent when it first broke the skyline of a drab post-war London in the early sixties. It was now covered in a brownish, turd-coloured plastic cladding. High-rise buildings were meant to revolutionise the way people lived, and it had!

*Poor people could now be stacked vertically instead of horizontally,* she thought.

"An occupational hazard for the first guys on the plot, especially the trigger," replied the driver.

"Yeah, but at least we've just gone into the overtime rate," Dot said tapping her watch and changing her gaze into the passenger-side wing mirror.

"How long do you think we have got before we get pulled?" George added. Some local lads in the ubiquitous black lads' hoodies with matching red bandanas and expensive training shoes, glowered towards the car while trying to work out why it was there.

"Looking at those boys hanging about outside," she opened her handbag and checked the CS spray that rested there, "not very long." She rechecked the mirror. "It's just like West Belfast or Baggers (Bagdad)] in this shithole. They are trying to place us, see what we're about." There were now five young lads from the estate looking in their direction.

"They'll be thinking we're cops or some disgustingly middle-class couple trying to score some coke," she smiled. "Especially with a dodgy-looking old bastard like you in the car." She laughed.

"Roger that," he said smiling back. "I wish I had some coke," said George whimsically, "but guess what?"

"Yeah, I know." Dot knew it was one of George's oldest jokes. So they both repeated the punchline in unison.

"The bubbles get up my nose." Both quietly chuckled.

"But you're right though, this place does look like a war zone, and according to the news that's just what it is!" George explained, "The press call it 'the post code wars' more youngsters have been killed last year within a ten mile radius of this shithole than in Belfast at the height of the troubles." George shrugged. "But hopefully the props in the back will give us some cover."

" Yeah, let's hope" said Dot as she looked towards the little crowd of lads

The gang members continued to covertly observe the covert observers as they talked. The casual gathering though was more than just a group of teenagers chilling in the last of the summer. It was more like an emergency meeting and their chat was about making money.

Coco was leading the conversation. He was 'an older', the leader of the gang at the tender age of nineteen. He was bright, and street-smart, and this was his territory. He knew every inch of it, every tower, every road, and every back alley. This was 'Colt 17's' postcode. His gang ran everything here and also wanted to run everything everywhere else.

"What's happening to our supply, Skar?" It was a terse question, without emotion.

"It's that Paki crew in Luton, they're fucking us over, bruv."

"Explain, I thought you were going to sort it?" Coco was concise; it was both a question and an accusation. He fixed the younger crew member with a cold stare.

"They're putting the price up, some shit about lack of product." He turned his head away and he had seen what he was capable of; a sort of detached physical violence that scared him. He nervously reached inside his jacket pocket for a spliff as he grasped for the next sentence.

"They are trying to fuck everybody over, not just us. We need to show them that they aren't the only crew with knives!" He paused as he fixed the group with a characteristic hard stare.

"Or guns!"

The others shrugged in agreement. Skar pulled a spliff from his jacket pocket and lit it up. He was worried and Skar didn't do worried very well. He deeply inhaled a draw and let the sweet, acrid smoke drift into his mouth and nose. It was Kabul Black and the best, not that skunk shit usually sold on the street. He passed it over to Coco instead of an explanation.

"No, bruv, someone's got to think straight in this crew."

Skar nodded in agreement but kept pulling on the spliff anyway, coughing whilst exhaling.

"We are losing money." Coco scanned the faces of the C17 crew.

"And that isn't what we are trying to achieve." His face was impassive. The others knew the signs; the calm before the storm. The leader was always calm before he became extremely violent.

27

He had grown up in an inner city environment simmering with violence and knew how to look after himself, but his brand of violence was never mindless; it was always calculated and coolly focused; it was soulless; it was mechanical. He had spent all of his nineteen years living in Frobisher House and had been scrapping since primary school and he was as good with a knife and a gun as he was with his fists.

In any other environment, he would have excelled. His teachers had said that he was 'a very bright and intelligent pupil' but the academic path hadn't quite worked out. His real name was Richard Miller but he had got the nickname 'Coco' because he was always clowning around at school or maybe because of his light brown, half-Irish, half-Jamaican complexion. The other kids of a darker shade used to think his skin was the same shade as 'Coco Pops' breakfast cereal.

"You need to see them and discuss our requirements." The others had seen this side of the main man before. The slang talk was gone; the words became longer and more concise.

"You are the guy that set it up, so you have to fucking sort it." He smiled.

"We need to talk to other interested parties before we declare war on anyone, but the Luton crew must be instructed that they must start thinking of others, before others start thinking of them."

Coco's brain was as wired to unit prices, import, and supply routes as any of the stock exchange wankers living nearer the river.

Supply was about prices and negotiation and the Pakistani gangs on the outskirts of London were main suppliers of the opiates that gushed out of Helmand Province in Afghanistan. The heroin trade in London was run almost exclusively by the Pakistani drug cartels that were supplied by the Taliban. They had both the family contacts and the in-country infrastructure to move money via the Islamic 'Hawala' banking system that paid for the product and then in turn supported local Islamist organisations and allied politicians that provided the cover for their activities.

Colt 17 needed the gear so they could trade it with the East London Albanians who ran the allied cocaine trade. It was coke that made the big money in this part of the City. London's metropolitan elite enthusiastically hoovered it up as quickly as they supplied it. The Asian gang that was causing them grief was called 'The Gambino family' and they traded from Luton's Bury Park Estate.

Coco abruptly broke off the conversation and looked towards the car that looked both shiny and new and slightly overdue. It had been parked a hundred metres away from them for a little bit too long.

"Da red whip (car), what d'ya think?" He turned away from the car, again reverting to the local slang, although he said it slowly, almost like he was encouraging his fellow gang members to lip-read. That was because Tojo, the youngest, was oblivious to any outside sound. He was wearing a pair of 'Beats by dr Dre' wireless headphones and was nodding his head to some rap 'Drill' music that had been composed and posted on YouTube by a local lad who had been shot dead two months before. But he was a sharp kid and deliberated.

He removed one side of the Beats and made his risk assessment.

"Da po-po, feds (police), bruv, defo."

"Nah, bruv, dat old geezer is well past retirement age," said one of the other boys smiling.

"I'll roll by and suss 'em out," said Coco.

They turned their heads away from the suspect car while automatically pulling their expensive hooded jackets forward while looking down at their equally expensive kicks (training shoes) or 110s, called that because they cost over £110 a pop.

The feds were always trying to put plain-clothes pigs on the ground, so Coco knew all the telltale signs. The car radio handset left on the seat, the odd item of police clothing. He once caught

29

a cop writing his notes while he was looking at the flats. It was all part of living in what was called 'a gang hotspot' where you had to be smart and armed to survive.

*Well, at least in the drug business. You always carried a blade; the bigger, the better, and a gun on special occasions. Silly not to, the cops never searched you any more, anyway. Why wouldn't you?*

He walked towards the car with the slight swagger of an ex-top amateur boxer allied with the distinctive roll of the shoulders that inner-city London kids tend to favour. He glanced into the car and made an appraisal.

*Door locks are on. No obvious Fed shit knocking about. These two are not from around here. A child's seat is in the back of the car. An opened packet of kiddies' wet wipes on the child seat. Estate agent brochures all over the shop, that kiddie's book on the back window shelf; maybe I should warn these old people that this manor is not a righteous place for them to hang? Or maybe, they are surveillance, but just very good at it?* He had good reason to know there were people like that in town.

Coco looked back towards the car and tried to catch the driver's eye.

*Nah,* he had long since learned to notice the little things and say absolutely nothing, it could keep you out of trouble.

George had seen the young lad trying for eye contact and turned towards Dot and whispered.

"OK, standby, standby, he is going to try to chat."

At that exact moment, the pea-size earpiece concealed within his right ear sounded.

"George, this is Zero X-ray, your location two minutes."

"That's a roger," George said as he put the car in gear and indicated left to pull out onto the road and towards the junction at Red One.

Dot was first to spot the target vehicle. It was a new white Mercedes in dire need of a carwash.

"Hey Zero, that's us, we have, repeat, we HAVE, and moving, Red One to Green Two," she said using the radio brevity code. The chase was on and the hoodies from Frobisher Heights were forgotten as the Audi pulled out and the mobile surveillance was on.

He sauntered back to his friends with a smile.

"Nah, jam (relax), just some old whiteys in the wrong place."

"What's next, then?" Skar said.

"Well, no product to sell, thanks to your mates in Luton, bro, so I guess we go to make some money."

"Where?"

"St Pancras again?"

The group nodded ascent.

"Yeah, St Pancras Station, the gift that keeps on giving."


*Glasgow*


*At the Same Time*


The rain had stopped just as the Mercedes pulled up at the safe house. It was dark, not pitch, but urban dark. The shimmer of a Glasgow Corporation  street lamp reflected off a large puddle on the pavement. He flicked off the wiper and the lights and waited in the car to assess the atmospherics. The brutality of war had honed his senses in an almost Darwinian manner. Only those in tune with their immediate environment survived on the battlefield, so he never rushed in. He always assessed the situation first, waited, and observed. The house was a detached upmarket property in a predominantly Asian area of Glasgow called Pollokshields. It had the advantage of a large garden and enhanced security measures including a reinforced front door. Asian areas were always the best because the locals never asked too many questions while guaranteeing a constant stream of cousins, uncles and aunties from old imperial India to greatly aid anonymity.

He had chosen the safe house carefully. It was owned by a doctor who had gone back to Pakistan to get married. It was a large detached building with five bedrooms. It was also comfortably furnished and most importantly, it had superfast broadband. Short-term lets always attracted less attention; he had booked it on airbnb with a VPN registered in Lahore. This was the place that would serve as his base of operations. He would collect the computer equipment the next day.

Once he was satisfied with the location he felt in his jacket pocket for the keys. He checked the WhatsApp message on his burner phone and memorised the alarm code and approached the front door. The front garden was large for the area. A large scraggly hedge, once groomed, but slowly reverting to nature encroached onto the flagstone path. As he sorted the keys he examined the door. It was a reinforced double steel door designed to look pretty ordinary on the outside. The agency had emailed that it could only be opened by three different keys in sequence. The controller nodded in appreciation as the final middle key clunked withdrawing the nine different deadbolts from the concrete doorframe. The thought occurred to him:

*The doctor is a careful man, it's more like a drug dealer's door!*

He knew the reason why. Glasgow's drug problem was off the scale and burglary was one of the favourite ways the local junkies had of providing themselves just that one more hit of restless oblivion. He opened the door and quickly tapped in the code before the tenth bleep and hit the light switch. He immediately locked the door with the reassuring sound of the deadbolts clunking into the wall.

*This looks like the right place to organise everything from.*

It was just about perfect; he needed a place to work from, a place to think and a place of refuge from the *Kuffar* world outside.

He took out his phone and checked the broadband speed and smiled.

# Chapter Six

*London, The SF Club*

Tim Broughton looked older than when they had last met. The usually fit-looking man appeared physically jaded, his dark brown hair now threaded with the odd white strand.

"Danny," he said smiling.

Tim had recommended Danny and his company 'Hedges and Fisher' for Connor Cameron's rescue. Connor's father, Sir Ian Cameron, the London-based tech billionaire and industrialist had financed the operation. Private funding was now always necessary to get someone back. The twenty-first-century British Government no longer had either the finance or the inclination to 'send a gunboat' as in times of yore. Every government decision was weighed against its relationship with trade and status, and ultimately concerned garnering extra political bargaining chips with any rich Islamic dictatorship that cast its shadow over the free world. Woe betide any government minister that 'fucked up' another big arms sale to Saudi Arabia.

*It's a weird world* thought Danny as he smiled and shook Tim's hand.

"How are you, Tim?"

"Still surviving the stress, my old mate." A thoughtful look reflected across his face. "And that's why I've asked you here, Danny. But..."

He seemed to struggle for words.

"I need to ask you a question. Let's chat."

The MI6 man once again checked the door and then moved to his favourite brown leather Chesterfield sofa. He sat, looked up and gestured for DannyMac to join him. DannyMac glanced towards Tim and caught his gaze; he knew the man well and noticed the strain in his eyes for the first time. Tim broke the awkward moment of silence.

"How are things at Hedges and Fisher, old mate?"

"Good, Tim, we've just picked up a small contract with a Russian family over to buy a football club as a hobby. That's what a team is working on at the moment. We have another bid in with the Qatar Embassy reference the World Cup thing, if the damn thing ever happens." Danny smiled. "Seems against the grain to work for either, but needs must, mate, and after all, between them they sort of own most of London."

Danny frowned at that truism; *it's a strange world – the large investment funds own London and very little of the disposable cash is British, it is all petrodollars and the Russian Mafia and* then he was back in the present and beaming a smile.

"Just crack on and ask, old mate, we owe your organisation a few favours," he said.

"OK." Tim sensed his tacit support and carried on. "In short, we have a problem." Tim paused for thought and subconsciously ran his hand through his increasingly thinning hair.

"The Task Force is under pressure, Danny, things are changing. The new PM wants results and to sort out the Islamist terrorism problem almost overnight. There is a lot of pressure directly dropping down onto us since the Brighton and Liverpool suicide attacks. It seems that the *Daesh* has developed a new way of doing things. Everything now is directed almost by remote control. We only hear what's going on at the very peripheries, and then it's usually too late. Somebody new is controlling their operations, somebody technically advanced.

"We are bearing the brunt of it; the Task Force is sort of stuck between a rock and a hard place. We are wedged between 'Five' and 'Six', the ginger-haired orphan, belonging to neither, and getting shafted by both.

"Added to this we have another problem that's just emerging." Tim's eyes furtively scanned the room again as if even the SF Club wasn't safe enough for the next sentence.

"This is the thing, Danny, HUMINT indicates that ISIS is planning something big and we will need to counter it quickly and concisely."

Tim's brow crinkled a bit as he concentrated on delivering the final pitch.

"We need more operators, mate, we have no extra resources, we are recalling retired Special Forces every day." Tim looked away as if he was expecting a bad result. "I want to ask you, and some of your selected colleagues to work directly for us again."

Tim registered the genuine surprise on Danny's face as he prepared to answer. It was like the modern equivalent of having your call-up papers dropping through the letterbox. He leaned forward and cupped his hand under his chin and was quiet for a moment.

"I will have to ask my people you're interested in, but I will need details on pay, conditions, and the rules of engagement. This isn't a war zone but the enemy is the same. We will need assurances about the law and a get-out-of-jail-free card if things go noisy. Can you get your legal guys on to it before I brief my team?"

"Yeah, I completely understand, I will get them on it today. Once you have that, when will you know?" Tim said quickly.

"As soon as I can talk to them face to face, and off the Russian job," Danny answered. "What's the time frame for this 'Something big', old mate?"

"Not sure, but soon," said a worried-looking Tim. "But I need your guys ASAP.

We have something in play, we should know more tomorrow."

Tim's phone buzzed in his pocket. He removed the iPhone and quickly scanned the message. It was from Ahmad. The text said, *Meeting at Paddy's confirmed.* Tim smiled.

*I only hope he shows up.*

Ahmad gunned the Mercedes slightly as he left Vauxhall Cross. London's traffic always gave him time for reflection. The satnav said that the drive to the pickup area in Kilburn would take thirty minutes but he knew from bitter experience that at that time of the day you could easily treble that figure and that's only if you successfully avoided the occasional irate taxi driver or semi-suicidal bicycle dispatch rider. Minor accidents were common on this route and that was never a good way to start a pickup. The unusually slow and careful drive had its advantages though as it gave Ahmad time to mentally prepare for the pickup and debrief of MI5 agent '3010'.

Ahmad was still perfecting his craft and each source operation changed his preconceived ideas of what the job involved and also made him a more intuitive agent handler. Ahmad checked his rear-view mirror and saw the cover car, three cars back, changing lanes to join him in traffic. He depressed his radio switch and transmitted.

"Hello, Zero and all stations, that's me towards Green Three." Green Three was a road junction towards the Bayswater Road. The voice of the operations room sounded in his earpiece. "Roger that, Delta 3, that's you intending Green Three."

A girl's voice responded. "Roger that, Delta 3, this is Delta 1, towards Green Three and backing."

Ahmad glanced into his rear-view mirror and saw the white Audi blend into the same lane of traffic. He would now start his counter-surveillance loop. Delta 1 would observe his progress to check for hostile surveillance. He drove carefully, constantly checking his rear-view mirror while mentally noting the registration plates and colours of the cars behind him. It's one of the skills intelligence operators developed over time. It was now natural to read a number plate in a mirror image and quickly mentally check it against the list of vehicles used by ISIS in London. He pressed the send button again.

"Hello, Zero and Delta 1, this is Delta 3, towards Green Two and clear."

Traffic had slowed and Ahmad was once again stationary. He was still an hour away from the pickup of source 3010. He had arranged to pick up his source on 'Paddy's', one of the agent's prearranged walking routes. Paddy's started on the outskirts of Kilburn High Road and ended just before Shoot Up Hill. Ahmad had a great affection for London. It was the place that had given his mum and dad shelter from the worst excesses of Saddam Hussein at the height of his power. You could sort of trace the cultural inputs of London on that simple drive through it. A short trip through London's traffic confirmed its cultural mix.

The start of the journey was not far from the City of London, a bustling hub of upmarket white-collar commerce, and continued through Knightsbridge and the Bayswater Road until you then hit the beginning of the Edgware Road and the Middle Eastern influences. The rich London Arabs lived in Mayfair and at the top of the Edgware Road, not far from their very stable investments, as the very stability of the Middle East dissolved in front of their eyes. The ethnic mix then started to change as the Arab guys sitting around taking tea and puffing hookah pipes with girls in hijabs faded as the cultural landscape changed. The population became mainly Afro-Caribbean and hard-looking Paddy or Pole.

There was an edgier feel to the Edgware Road now. The buildings looked grittier, the paintwork on the doors and windowsills a bit more worn and faded. You could now see some rough-looking Irish pubs. He caught quick glances of the main ones: The Old Bell, The Kingdom and the Powers Bar. Although never much of a drinker, Ahmad's dad used to take the odd scoop in a pub called The Galtymore. It was a rough and ready 'Paddy boozer' that was closed now. *Probably one bar brawl too many?* Ahmad smiled as he thought about what his dad had once said.

*'It was the only place in London where it was nearly as dangerous as being a 'Peshmerga in the Mountains' against Saddam.'*

His thoughts went back to the pickup of 3010. Ahmad glanced in the rear-view mirror at the follow vehicle and depressed the covert radio button twice. He immediately heard the reply from his cover car in his earpiece – two buzzes of static – to confirm that they were approaching the pickup area, then!

BANG!!

"FUCK-FUCK-FUCK!" Ahmad shouted, as he braked hard.

The brake lights of the car in front had suddenly flashed on and he had quickly reacted. There was a loud squeal of tormented brakes and then the sickening crunch of plastic bumpers. Ahmad's Mercedes had mercifully stopped within a hairsbreadth of the old Toyota.

*Thank fuck for that, an RTA (Road Traffic Accident) on a run-in to the job is never good skills.*

Ahmad heard his cover car, a girl's voice again in his earpiece.

"Hi, Delta 3, you OK?"

"Yeah, roger that, no damage, but we have a quite serious RTA in front; add ten to the timings."

The cover car responded.

"Roger that – add ten."

Ahmad took his iPhone from his pocket. He quickly texted the brevity code for a delay to Imran's phone.

*Taxi late – add 10.*

*OK.* The reply came almost immediately and Imran would then delete the message. Ahmad checked the situation. There were two drivers, an elderly lady in an ancient Toyota Camry and a pissed-off-looking London black cab driver. They were exchanging insurance details while they waited for the police. At least the delay gave Ahmad more time for reflection.

He had run 3010 for over four years now and everything was going better than he could have expected. Imran had been almost the perfect agent and his information had saved numerous lives.

He had also demonstrated his loyalty by his involvement in the Hedges and Fisher hostage extraction. He had also shown his bravery by saving Sam's and Taff 's lives as they moved Connor from the 'Death House' in Mosul. The whole team could have died without his intervention. It had been a busy couple of years for his agent within ISIS.

*He needed a break,* thought Ahmad. *But he won't get one.*

An agent was only productive when inside a targeted terrorist organisation and in order to be effective he had to develop himself inside it, but as he got deeper and more trusted, a CHIS, a 'Covert Human Intelligence Source', also became harder to run. A good handler had to juggle priorities. An agent's personal security was important but that had to be balanced against the need to feed the beast, what the spook world called 'The Intelligence Cycle', with all the vital, life-saving information he provided.

Like many London jihadi types, Agent 3010, had a criminal past. It was what made his type of operator useful to the Islamists. Drug dealing and gang crime are always ideal jumping-off points for any covert activity and Imran was still involved on the peripheries of them. Things now were changing because as his agent's access increased so did his problems. Tim had always insisted on a bimonthly case conference at Vauxhall Bridge to discuss each agent's potential. The policy had paid dividends and Imran was now moving into the upper echelons of ISIS in London. Mullah Rahman and the main London-based guys trusted him and as a returning jihadi hero all the younger Muslim guys in Whitechapel admired him.

The extra income generated by his expertise as an agent also had to be explained. Ahmad had suggested an Uber-type limo taxi company specialising in the Muslim-only trade and it was going well. Mosque runs and wedding-party outings supplied its trade. Imran had set up the business from finance supplied by MI5. He now had four of his Islamist friends driving brand new Mercedes cars. Not by coincidence, these were the vehicles that were most used by Islamist circles in London and also allowed MI5 to bug and monitor their movements.

Imran's newfound wealth was derived from darker sources as well. He was one of the new breed of jihadist who operated both sides of the crime-terror nexus. ISIS was also powerful on the inside of Britain's overcrowded prisons and they had already tapped into a ready source of new manpower; disaffected young criminals now funded the organisation in the best way they knew how and street-smart Imran provided the link. As an old Asian street-gang member he still kept in constant contact with his former criminal associates. Young drug dealers, moped riding bag snatchers and burglars were all used to clandestine operations in London. Their recruitment inside HMG's prisons ensured the organisation with a pre-trained cadre of new blood that could reinforce the real killers returning from the caliphate.

It also gave Imran a steady supply of 'burners', stolen mobiles that when given a new SIM and used on encrypted messaging sites like WhatsApp or Telegram ensured operatives had a means of untraceable communication. Ahmad's agent was also very conveniently involved in the smuggling of mobile telephones for the use of jihadist prisoners, like the 'Beat the Boss J8', easily bought on Amazon. These cheap super-small mobiles and the stolen handsets were channelled through MI5's technical department before being plugged into the prison system.

The radio buzzed into life and disturbed Ahmad's train of thought. The other support car doing the reverse sweep broke silence; a military man's clipped voice with a distinct Yorkshire twang.

"This is Delta Two, that's X-ray Foxtrot and on time at plus 300. He's wearing black on blue and is clear."

Ahmad prepared for the pickup. A tingle of excitement coursed through his body. Imran or Agent 3010 had asked for this emergency meeting. He said he had something important to pass.

As Ahmad prepared to pick up 3010 another agent handler prepared to talk to his assets at precisely the same time. His agents were what ISIS called its crocodile units; the pre-recruited agents of destruction ready to return to their former host communities they had left to wage war on. It was a complicated set-up but it needed to be. He had five laptops, purchased or stolen from various places, all made by different companies, some used and some new. He had disabled the cameras and the Bluetooth connectivity and cancelled the security settings. Each machine was now effectively firewalled from the other to achieve what his lecturers had called 'Cyber Hygiene'. Each computer now represented a different agent using varying social media sites. An overflowing ashtray was perched precariously on the edge of the desk and the room already smelt of stale cigarette ash. The reinforced door was closed, the blinds were drawn, and the controller was working in the glow generated by the computer screens and feeling safe. The Londoner half closed his eyes, lit another cigarette, inhaled deeply, and as the nicotine hit his bloodstream thought back on his life of struggle and sacrifice.

He had joined the great jihad at eighteen to free himself from the unclean *Kuffar*. He smiled as he remembered a time when smoking was strictly *haram* in the caliphate. He had once broken the fingers of a young boy he caught smoking in Mosul. It seemed a hundred years ago but in only 2014 they had rejoiced after they had routed the Iraqi Army and raised their sacred black flag in victory. Things had changed since then. The physical remains of the caliphate had since been ground into the dust in the little Syrian oasis town of Badhuz near the Euphrates. Now the time to strike back was nearly here, and God had chosen him to strike where the enemy was weakest.

The Islamic States spiritual leader, Abu Bakr Al-Baghdadi, had chosen him to raise the black *Shahada flag* once again by making him the leader and organiser of what he had named the 'crocodile units', designed to slip back in and take the war to where the *Kuffar* felt safest. He had been gifted a unique place in the history of jihad because he was one of the first of the brothers to truly understand the Internet. He had studied and excelled at his university in Luton and then developed his skills by countless hours organising and recruiting the gullible online. Only he had overall control and only he truly appreciated the sacred responsibility that he had been given.

He had all the skills he needed to move from one social media site to another without being tracked, he was invisible and officially dead. This dead man was a ghost that would haunt the *Kuffar* until they all went to hell.

The sacred task was entrusted to him, and only him. The revenge for Badhuz was coming slowly, and each operation was now set in sequence, each action more daring than the last, until the blessed final attack when the full revenge for the defeat would be complete. He smiled. He was the only one of God's holy warriors that had been entrusted to plan operations that would span the globe over the next two years until ' Operation Eiqab (Retribution).

*And only I know all the plans. I have been blessed.*

He looked at the instruments that would make it happen, *Inshallah*; each laptop had the agent's name and his location on a range of different coloured post-it notes stuck to each screen. He had memorised the all-important activation codes. He checked the legend on the battered-looking Lenovo T440p. The Day-glo yellow note said *Youssef, Colombo*. The new Apple MacBook Air had another lime green note; it had two words, *Omar, Oslo*. When he contacted his agents they would think that the orders had arrived from where the computer VPN stated and a simple digital clock gave him the time at that location. The crocodile network spanned the world and formed an independent network of battle-hardened ISIS sleeper cells that had been trained, blooded in combat, and given their activation code words. The targets were only to be allocated at the last moment.

The final laptop was an old MacBook Air stolen from a house in Uxbridge nearly a year before. It had been data-washed and scrubbed and the VPN said that it was now in Germany. The Day-glo lime green sticker just said *London* and the operation name said *HIRJAH*. He quickly typed in the activation code and waited. The laptop tinged in recognition. He smiled, realising that his plan had started smoothly. He sent the WhatsApp address a non-descript-looking page from a pop-up advertising an English language teaching website. Hidden in the advertisement was a hyperlink to everything the ISIS ASU (Active Service Unit) needed to carry out the attack. The precise time, the high value target, and the way it was to be conducted.

He had designed the new security protocols, coded references, and closed groups using Telegram and ProtonMail only with multiple VPNs. The organisational circle of knowledge had tightened and they were slowly identifying the security problem they had in London. If one of the brothers was a traitor, the sequential extra security measures would find him and fix him. He waited for the acknowledgement barely daring to breathe and then TING, an emoji of a yellow smiling face with a broad grin filled the screen. The controller smiled as well.

# Chapter Seven

*Frobisher House*

As Coco supervised, the youngest member of the group carefully covered the black 150cc Yamaha Cygnus in shiny black with the old tarp. It was a smart bike that didn't look out of place in town. It used to belong to a courier service before they lost it. It was nippy enough and ideal for a bag or phone snatch and plenty fast enough to get away from the feds if needed. Coco always rode the bike, generally with Skar on the back doing the snatch; he was a great basketball player and had outstanding hand-eye coordination. Coco had been driving motorcycles and cars since he was fourteen, so his natural talent lay in that direction.

The only other guy they ever needed was a decent spotter, a guy who could quickly identify the stupidest people flaunting the most expensive items. Big rail stations were best for that, but you needed someone with an eye for making money to spot for you. He needed to make instant appraisals on the cost of anything worth stealing, a decent mobile maybe, or a designer handbag. Sometimes one of the older lads would lose the hoody, dress upmarket, and spot from one of the nicer hotels or coffee shops. No matter how well you planned it though, it was still a risky business, but generally the more planning you did, the better it went.

*Fail to plan and you plan to fail.*

Other known risk variables had to be considered. The feds were always a problem; the worst type being the plain-clothes type, but a good spotter could ID them. Then, more dangerous than that, there was a local crew called 'The Somers Town Boys'. Luckily Coco had boxed with one of their top chaps, so he always tried to give him a bell to run a trip into his postcode past him. It made sense, as it was only good manners and cost nothing, but the STB had their hands full at the moment anyway. They were fully at war with the Bangla knife gangs that inhabited Drummond Street and the mad Somalis further down the road.

Coco removed a black rucksack from his shoulders and opened it in front of the other guys and emptied the contents.

"Right, what did we jack (steal) today?"

He picked up a new phone.

"Hey, that's criss (new), an iPhone 8, bangin (great)," as he removed the SIM card and made sure it was turned off. "I'll keep this, bruv, mine is clapping (worn out)."

"Cool," Skar replied, eyeing a Chanel handbag that he had expertly snatched off the American tourist earlier. He knew his designer stuff; it was a black lambskin original in the quilted 'Chocolate bar' design with the distinctive gold chain and double C emblem in gold.

"This is at least a grand online," he said as he opened it and looked through the contents.

A passport, a London guide, a phrasebook, expensive Chanel make-up and a bottle of 'Chance Eau Tendre' perfume.

"Look at this, bruv!" There was another matching Chanel purse inside crammed full of credit cards and notes. "Result," he beamed.

"The cards will be blocked by now," said Coco, putting a slight dampener on his friend's enthusiasm as he counted the cash. His eyes lit up. "Two hundred in fifties, jackpot!" The money was in a clear plastic envelope from the 'Forex Money Exchange'.

"Jackpot, that's sick," he said while counting the rest of the contents in US dollars.

"A thousand!" They both smiled. The rest was easy; London boys did not need to take stolen goods to a 'Fagin' like fence anymore. Everything was sold on eBay almost instantly and the rest, like passports and credit cards, were passed onto specialists for a fee. Pakistanis always paid big for US passports.

"That was a pretty good day," said Skar.

"Yeah, I love St Pancras," Coco replied. "Let's have a repeat script pretty soon, bruv, sooner the better."

"Shouldn't we leave it for a while, boss? The local community cop says they are going to start using plain-clothes feds at all the stations."

"Nah," Coco smiled, "let's strike when the iron's hot!" He fixed Skar with a stare as if he was threatening his authority. The younger gangster looked away.

"Don't worry, I do the thinking, bruv, and I have the plan," he said as he walked to the entrance of the flats.

He got a face full of council-house lift as the doors opened with a cheery ting. It was the familiar smell of disinfectant and stale cigarette odour, with the slight after-smell of somebody's industrial-strength curry. No matter how many times his mum and the others cleaned it, it always reverted to that same stale stench within hours. The council didn't share the task; it wasn't on their need-to-do list. Frobisher House was old and depressing, but it did still have some decent families in it.

He entered the flat he shared with his mother after unlocking the steel mesh cage that entombed his front door. He had organised the fitting of it himself. Unfortunately, the drugs game produced addicts and those addicts had no fucking sense at all. Even Coco's refuge from the madness outside wasn't immune to robbery. He moved through the bright, airy space that sort of jarred with the dreary, standard London council dirty magnolia in the outside passage. He walked to the kitchen and looked out from the double glazing over his own little bit of London. He could see what was left of the old dock buildings.

Frobisher House wasn't the best address in town, but his flat overlooked a decent stretch of the Thames and had a vista that some of the 'Fortune 500' types at Canary Wharf paid big bucks for. He had stopped being a gangster as soon as he closed the door of the flat. He became someone different, a bit like those super-hero alter egos in the Marvel comic books he'd devoured as a kid. He always tried to end his street life at the door.

The apartment was immaculately clean, neat and tidy, and he always made sure he kept it that way. His mum was a shift worker at the local St Thomas's Hospital, and he ensured that she didn't have to face housework when she came home. She was the person he loved most. A good-looking Irish country girl from Kildare, whose gentle disposition hid an inner steel core, tempered throughout her forty years by life's disappointments. He knew that he was one of her most recent ones.

She had high hopes for him until he hit his teenage years. His glowing school reports and the photos of his boxing days were still dragged out for visitors on every possible occasion. She had been proud of him then, but not of what he had become. He could sometimes see the worry reflected in her careworn eyes. She was maybe just waiting for that police knock on the door delivering the news that no mother wanted to hear. Six people he knew had already been killed this year.

He opened the fridge and removed one of the microwave meals in a Tupperware box. A white sticker on the lid was written in his mum's neat hand.

5 minutes on full power leave to stand for one minute and stir and then another 1 minute on full. Be back at 8 tonight. Love Mum xxx

PS Apple crumble and custard top shelf.

She prepared all his meals during her only day off. Her love was both total and unconditional. One day he would look after her properly, hopefully before his run of luck ended.

*Everything has a beginning and an end, but some start points can only end one way.*

He realised that his life was slowly, almost inexorably, spiralling out of control. He tried to remove the thought from his mind as he moved through the neatly arranged living room and into his bedroom. His personal space was unlike anything a casual visitor would expect of a teenage gang member. A large five-tier bookshelf covered one wall with hundreds of books ranging from action-adventure to history, and philosophy. On the bedside cabinet lay his current reading material. It was Sun Tzu's *The Art of War*. His bookshelf, like himself, was conflicted. He was bright, and he loved to read and realised that most of the stuff he needed to know had been written already.

His MacBook Pro rested on top of his whitewood Ikea desk like it belonged there. He flicked it open and flashed it up and placed in the encrypted USB stick. He moved to the site and started tapping away. The message was short and to the point. He had been keeping tabs on the beardies upstairs but had very little to report. It was one of those strange anomalies of multicultural London that all the devout Muslim families preferred to live together on the eighth floor in a little bit of self-imposed segregation, for comfort rather than religious reasons.

He worked quickly to scan the passports they had stolen and sent them so they could go into the system before they were passed on to the fixer for sale.

*I hope that keeps Lou happy for a while. I wonder if I could find a way out with him.*

He wasn't worried about the feds. He knew that they didn't have either the resources or even the inclination to find a perpetrator in gang-related violence. It was only some young black kid killing another young black kid. He was just another problem less to worry about. People only actually got caught when they rapped about it on Facebook these days. You didn't need to be Sherlock Holmes to catch a murderer, just only had to look at gangster stuff on YouTube to find out who had pulled the trigger!

No, the cops didn't worry him, prison didn't concern him, but getting killed did. He felt that his time was slowly ticking away.

Coco subconsciously traced the knife scar on his left upper shoulder with his fingertips through the soft cotton of his tee shirt. The scar was thick and corded. He remembered the attack just outside on the road where he lived and a cold shiver ran down his spine. He increasingly sensed that his luck was being stretched each day he plied his trade. The on-going beef with the Pakistanis would only increase the pressure on him. He opened the desk, and there, glistening against the whitewood interior of the drawer was one of his options.

It was a Czech Army Skorpion VZ 68 machine pistol. It was probably the only way to get the supply problem sorted out. He was the main man, and he was the person that would be expected to sort it. He remembered a Sun Tzu quote.

*A leader leads by example, not by force.*

He slammed the drawer.

*How have I got to this deep? I'm going to murder somebody for drugs or get killed trying it. How much longer have I got?*

*I need to change my life while I still have a life to change.*

And then the thought came to him again; *I'd be safer in prison.*

The solution became blindingly obvious; he needed to plan something that was going to fail badly. He thought of what Skar had said about plain-clothes filth, and he smiled as he remembered something that Lou had said to him on his training weekend in Bedford. He had only ever been in touch online since then, but the guy had made a big impression.

*Remember all the P's standing for 'Proper Planning and Preparation Prevents Piss Poor Performance'.*

Although he didn't think that Lou would approve of what he was actually planning. And he wasn't going to share it with him. Another quote from Sun Tzu sprang to mind.

*Let your plans be dark and as impenetrable as night.*

He smiled; that's it.

*Plan to fail?*

It had been a long drive back to London for the controller and it was evening time as he navigated the last roundabout that said LUTON. This safe house was only a possible, and he felt unsure about its location. Even the satnav in the Mercedes seemed to express an element of doubt when it repeated the address of the Bury Park Estate. It was a rough area in a piss-poor Asian enclave that was known for its gang culture, but maybe that was one of its advantages? The police had long since given up responsibility for patrolling the estate and had even withdrawn the local community police officers due to police cuts, not that the local community policemen were anything more than a government sponsored sharia patrol anyway. The local Mullah liaised with the police and arranged for who got the job, which made sure that the area stayed white person and fun free. He indicated right as he looked for the house number.

Number 37 was a council built 1950s semi that had seen better days. It was a bit run down and very much like the rest of the street. The bonus was that the house next door was empty and newly fitted with council issue steel shutters and already tagged in green spray paint with the logo of a local Asian drug gang that called themselves 'The Gambinos'. On this occasion his street sense antennae let him down and he didn't see the problem until it was too late. He had seen five or six of the local lads looking towards the car as he had been scanning for the house number but hadn't picked up any hostile intentions, maybe because he felt quite comfortable in an exclusively Asian area. The small group of local hoods looked no different to any other set of gang lads from London's present inner-city crime wave. They all seemed to look the same and all dressed in the same fucked-up way with tight trousers that hung crutch low defying both common sense and the laws of gravity. The only difference with these guys and any of the others were the odd Asian additions to their bad-boy uniform. Black prayer hats, wispy pubescent beards and the odd Arabic *shemagh; the sort of thing you need in a hot country but a bit out of place in urban Britain* even the returning jihadi warrior thought.

He hadn't noticed another two who had been tracking his progress from the opposite side. They had emerged from an alley opposite a play park looking for a victim or maybe rival drug dealers. A sharp tap on the window brought his attention to a foot-long Zombie knife held by a hooded figure glaring hate into the window and shouting something loud and unintelligible. Objective Cyclone calmly pushed the car into drive and left. The knife guy connected a kick to the car as he sped away.

He smiled and reached a decision.

Maybe this house would work quite well. ISIS reigns where chaos rules. Ungoverned space was good for business.

# Chapter Eight

*Kilburn*

Ahmad's plan was going well as he spotted his CHIS casually blending in with the early evening crowds and discreetly checking for any surveillance. Kilburn was chosen as 3010's pickup route for a reason. It was one of the only predominantly working-class areas of North London that was still truly multicultural. It was a mixing pot of many imported races but had the advantage of not being owned by any of them. It was like an ethnic free-fire zone where big burly Irish and Polish guys rubbed shoulders with Jewish shopkeepers and Turkish kebab shop owners. They eyed each other warily observing the world from their own perspective cultural box. It wasn't a friendly place and it was not at all picturesque, but it was the sort of place where a stranger did not stand out and Imran was definitely a stranger in this part of town. It was all concrete, glass windows, and fading paint, with lots of litter scurrying around in the light breeze with a general look of neglect. As Imran moved along the crowded pavement the faces reflected lack of interest rather than hostility. No one knew him here, so it was a good place to meet.

3010's tradecraft had improved as much as the information he provided. Years of constant 'on the job' training had created the almost perfect spy. Imran was dressed in normal English street gear; an old pair of G-Star jeans and a faded bomber jacket. It was never a good idea to flaunt your new found wealth in this part of London. Imran checked his reflection in the plate glass of a Paddy Powers betting shop as he checked for hostile surveillance. He pretended to compare the odds in the newspaper he held. His phone vibrated twice, the signal for a hundred metres to pickup. He casually glanced over his shoulder as Ahmad started to pull the Mercedes over and his tradecraft kicked in. He hailed the car with the paper *The Kilburn Times*. It was held in his right hand and this confirmed his ability to meet. This was his 'no-comms' signal for abort; if he had held it in his left hand it would have meant that the pickup was compromised and his handler would have driven on. The Mercedes pulled up by the pavement. Ahmad hit the door-locking switch, and Imran opened the door, and quickly slid into the plush grey leather of the passenger seat.

"Hi, bruv, what's happening?" said Ahmad with a smile.

"Fucking lots, old mate," replied Imran in his cockney Asian twang. Ahmad noticed a concerned edge in his agent's voice.

"What have you got for me?"

"Not a lot of time, and this." Imran handed Ahmad a USB thumb drive.

"This is the latest on EMNI (ISIS's Foreign Intelligence Service) and the Mullah's last contact with them. It has the expected times and methods for the arrival of the guys coming back. One team, four fighters at least, or maybe two or even up to three teams, and details of the safe house locations they've been considering."

"Well done," Ahmad said, while pocketing the thumb drive.

"Does anyone know what the returning guy's mission is?" His agent looked towards him, his sharp, dark eyes mirroring his concern.

"No, no details yet, but I think the Mullah knows." Imran paused. "The word has gone out that something nasty is on the way in and there's going to be a number of highly public homegrown attacks to pave the way. Nothing too sophisticated; mass stabbings of the public, maybe driving a lorry into a crowd like in France in 2016. It's just to distract you guys until the teams with the big missions arrive."

Imran stopped. His eyes betrayed his concern.

"Three of these lads are nut cases, they have had their training and they're back. One of them is a young lad from my manor. He went on jihad six months ago and he still talks to his family and they still talk to me. This thing that's getting planned, it will be very heavy. The word is..."

Agent 3010 looked genuinely worried. The awesome responsibility of his recently acquired knowledge was weighing him down. He needed to tell Ahmad what he knew before the knowledge mentally crushed him.

"It will be big attack, very fucking nasty, and it'll be on a high-profile target."

There was a temporarily stunned silence in the car, as Ahmad started to comprehend the enormity of the statement.

Ahmad looked at the agent who was fast becoming his friend.

"Oh fuck, that is bad," he said.

"And one other thing that could mean something," Imran continued, "it looks like one of the cars is being used by the Fat Man." The 'Fat Man' was a disparaging coded reference to the Islamic States', London-based main facilitator and religious head, Mullah Rahman. The agent turned towards his handler. "And he hasn't mentioned it to me, bruv. That's a bit worrying, don't you think?"

"Any ideas why?" Ahmad said, as he checked the rear-view mirror and maneuvered the car back into the thickening traffic.

"I think it's probably one of his many family business-type matters, he has relatives all over the shop. Most of them paid for by interested Wahhabi donors from the Gulf States. They are supposed to be 'safe houses' but they could just be used for his rather large extended family. One of the houses is in Glasgow. You have the location on the USB stick. I've checked the mileages on the cars. One is way out. It's the black Mercedes." Imran reached inside his pocket and pulled out a compressed piece of what remained of a packet of chewing gum and palmed it to his handler.

"Here's the registration and VIN number."

"Excellent work, Imran." Although Ahmad knew that praise was an essential ingredient in the handler/source relationship he was genuinely impressed with the extra little bit of sensible tradecraft.

He smiled. "How much time have you got now, mate?" he said while again checking the rear-view mirror.

"I've another five minutes, and I got to be outta here, bruv, I have a meeting with the Mullah. He is panicking and getting more hyper every day."

Ahmad quickly pulled into the inside lane and about 200 metres to his front he spotted the emergency drop-off point, the entrance to Kilburn Tube station.

"Is the station OK for you, mate?" asked Ahmad.

"Ideal."

"OK, mate, when can we have a proper meet? What about Mo's place tomorrow, same time?"

Mo's place was a walking route at a place called Ruislip in West London that Imran had memorised at a previous debrief.

"You up for that?" Ahmad chirped.

"No, mate, no time, they are all over security at the moment. Something has spooked them, something big is happening and they are looking hard for security breaches, so I can't afford to fuck up. I will phone you. We might have to resort to Sayeed's place."

Sayeed's was another brevity code for a more technical DLB (Dead Letter Box). Sayeed's place was an ordinary, ancient-looking brick, in a Victorian red-brick wall in a Whitechapel back alley. The tattered old brick was actually some electronic wizardry that stored data wirelessly and instantaneously transmitted it to any device synced with it. Imran only had to be near the brick to squirt the data in and Ahmad could collect the data wirelessly later.

"OK, I'll drop you off in two."

Ahmad depressed his radio switch twice in quick succession and his cover car answered through the bean-sized receiver in his ear. A clipped and concise girl's voice in a London accent said,

"Roger that, Delta Three, you are going for early drop-off."

Ahmad pressed the switch twice to confirm.

Ahmad weaved quickly through the evening traffic. The Mercedes pulled up smoothly outside Kilburn High Road Station and Imran opened the passenger door and with a cheery, "See you later, bruv," he was gone and had melted back into the throng outside the station. Ahmad immediately assessed the situation.

"Hello, Control and all stations, we need to RTB (return to base) immediately. We have a time-critical product that we need to action." The girl in the cover car immediately responded and quickly pulled in front of Ahmad's Mercedes.

"Roger that, I'm fronting you."

Immediately followed by the armed security car.

"Yeah, this is Delta Two, we're backing."

One of the two former SAS guys in the blue Jaguar XF behind the handler's car checked the regiment issue Sig Sauer assault weapon resting against his leg in the footwell of the Jag. It was his job to make sure the information got back safely and this state-of-the-art silenced assault rifle was the ultimate guarantee of success.

"Roger that," said Ahmad as he tapped the accelerator slightly to carve the Mercedes through the thickening London traffic.

He thought about Imran. He had seemed worried about the increased security measures that ISIS had adopted: *was he a suspect? Had his training been thorough enough? Could he protect himself during an interrogation?*

Imran was thinking like an operator as he walked towards the station and blended into the rapidly increasing crowds. It was ideal dropping off in the rush hour; it was hard to follow anyone in a crowd. He remembered snippets of his tradecraft training. He could hear Ahmad's voice in his head:

*'In a crowded environment, hostile surveillance will try to pick you up at a choke point. Maybe at an entrance, an exit, or at other natural places that channel the flow of a crowd such as a ticket turnstile.'*

Imran almost unthinkingly checked for a hostile follow as he made his way into the station. He stopped briefly and looked in the newsagent's window and pretended to read some small ads while checking for surveillance in the reflection. He was looking for what intelligence tradecraft calls 'a double sighting' where you've identified a hostile follow because you've seen someone more than once. The trick, as Ahmad had explained, was not to concentrate on the obvious but look for an identifying feature that is a constant, maybe something physical or distinctive. Imran had learned to remember such features by instantly scanning a suspect from the shoes upwards, to his, or her, head. It could be something as simple as shoes that were scuffed in a particular place. It had to done quickly though, as too much scrutiny also attracted attention.

*Especially in a tough-arsed Paddy-Black area like this.*

As he checked the reflection a group of hard-looking young lads eyed his back. A mixed group, some white, some black, and all threatening in an unspoken sort of way. They clung together in a tribal collective and they all possessed that hard look that can be seen in the eyes of poor working-class kids in any town or city in the UK. The normal, impassive, dead-eyed, 'I don't give a fuck' stare that told you that they were protecting their own urban shithole or what they called, in London, their 'manor'. The look had acquired another element since the last suicide bombing in Liverpool. Imran's Bangladeshi heritage was not an advantage in this part of town; the extra element in the impassive stare was a glint of undisguised hate. Imran looked away; as in other parts of this great metropolis, a cursory glance in the wrong direction here could get you stabbed pretty easily. He checked the time; he had bought himself a Rolex Sea Master watch.

*But maybe this is not the ideal place to flaunt it?*

He glanced back at the glowering youngsters. They naturally thought of themselves as predators not victims. Imran covered his watch with his cuff, and a thought crossed his mind.

*I suppose we are all divided into winners or losers, predators or prey. It's strange that in some parts of London you can easily start as one and very quickly, become the other.*

Imran's phone pinged. He quickly glanced at the Telegram message as he made his way to the ticket barrier. All the brothers were using Telegram now. It was a simple system that even the thickest of the 'brothers' could use, and the encryption was superb for their purposes. The message was from Mullah Rahman. The simple coded reference meant that he wanted to see him. Imran would know more then. The Mullah would no doubt let him know when London's latest predators would arrive in town.

# Chapter Nine

The three vehicles threaded their way through London's traffic making slow progress back towards Vauxhall. The other MI5 operator, a pretty female in a bright blue hijab was supplying Ahmad's front cover.

"That's us at Blue Three-Two," she said.

The blue Jag with the two ex-blades (SAS men) responded as they shadowed behind Ahmad's Ops vehicle.

"Yeah, roger that."

The only sound in Ahmad's car apart from the low drone of Capital Radio was a series of spot codes from the girl in the hijab. It frequently popped into his earpiece always confirmed by the blade's voice in the rear car usually saying,

"Roger that."

The ethnic map of London reversed itself on the route in. Kilburn, the hard-edged working-class area of the Irish and the Poles faded as they returned along the Arab end of the Edgware Road. Soon they were at Marble Arch and back into the suited and booted parts of the City. London's lack of cohesion had always struck Ahmad as strangely familiar. The political elite in Britain paid lip service to the utopian idea of a thriving multicultural metropolis. The truth, as he saw it, was entirely different. It was more like scattered pockets of monocultural ghettos that existed entirely separately just like a series of different tribal areas in the Middle East.

But hey, maybe it was only him who saw it that way!

As a Kurd, he fully understood how family, ethnicity, and religion could become the ultimate refuge against outsiders, but as a proud Brit, who had once served, and who was still serving his country, he found it sorrowful. People had been allowed to fester in their own self-induced ghettos. It was the shameful over-arching spirit of political correctness displayed that had allowed the sharia law enclaves to be condoned, cordoned off and even encouraged. The Government had 'bottled it', in cockney parlance, and just ceded control. He thought of his own upbringing in Bermondsey twenty years before where integration was a prerequisite for survival. The only extremists then were probably 'the Treatment', the ultra-violent supporters of the local football team, Millwall FC. Things had now really changed since the jihadists had started to drift back into London. Attitudes had hardened a little after each atrocity and that made things difficult for any law-abiding Muslim to lead a normal life. Modern Britain was being drip-fed hate on a daily basis. Ahmad's thoughts were interrupted by a buzz in his earpiece.

"That's us, at Red Three," the lead operator said.

The final section of a route was usually considered the most prone to compromise. It was almost impossible to change the established routes in and out of central London and the only comforting covert cloak was the sheer amount of traffic.

As the three cars jostled amongst a multitude of other vehicles and towards Vauxhall Bridge, Ahmad transmitted.

"Hello, Zero Alpha, this is Ahmad, your location in ten."

"Roger that." Ahmad recognised Tim Broughton's voice as the brutalist architecture of the SIS building hove into view. Ahmad smiled, as he thought, *not very secret at all.* It looked like a giant Mayan Temple by the Thames, clad in cream-white stone and glistening in a sickly shade of green tinted glass. The location of MI6 was well known and that's why the Task Force never used it. Ahmad heard the front cover car.

"That's you clear to the front," said the girl in the hijab.

"That's you clear to the rear, and we're backing." The hard-sounding male voice of the ex-SAS man responded in a sort of gentrified Glasgow accent.

The joint MI5/MI6 Task Force headquarters was at an undisclosed location near both organisations in what was left of the commercial parts of London's Docklands. The unit's garage was below ground. A covert camera monitored his progress as Ahmad pointed the Mercedes towards a steel and concrete ramp and descended towards the entrance. The car stopped and the electric underground garage door opened. It was a dark, cavernous old warehouse with parking spots. The lights flicked on.

He parked the car on his spot and swung open the driver's door. Another job had just finished and its three Operational vehicles, two saloons ( a new Renault and a tattered-looking BMW) and a Post Office van were being stripped of their covert cameras by the unit's technicians. The warehouse was always busy. There was always either a job going out or one coming in. None of the parked cars would have ever appealed to a mythical super spy. No James Bond Aston Martin DB5s here, just shit-looking regular cars.

The garage was packed with small saloons from different ages and types ranging from the ubiquitous Ford Focus to mid-price, mid-range stuff, like Peugeots and Renaults, and even the odd small van. An operational car had to look normal; it needed to fit with its surroundings. The Mercedes that Ahmad was driving would have attracted the wrong attention on one of London's warzone estates but it fitted perfectly the profile of the smarter parts of London's Edgware Road. As he turned and closed the car door, he heard a cheery, "Hello, mate, you have a good op?"

It was a guy who had trained with him as an intelligence officer. He was wearing a dirty black unkempt-looking hoody and dirty grime-encrusted jeans accessorised with scuffed white trainers. He was a team leader 'watcher' from MI5's A4 department.

"Yes, Paul, and you, bruv?" said Ahmad.

"Yeah, sweet," Paul said with a smile, displaying a missing tooth from a childhood rugby injury.

Ahmad smiled back. Paul was bright; he had a two-one from Oxford but still enjoyed mooching about the shittiest parts of London just following a target. They had lived together in the same safe house during driver training when Met police instructors tested them on their driving phase. The stress of hurtling around country lanes at 120 miles an hour while trying to do a 'commentary drive', where you had to actually narrate your death defying journey to your instructor while hurtling around country roads at breakneck speeds had bonded them as 'friends bound by fear' as Paul had once said. A4 was an impressive outfit. Constant operational development and practice had made them one of the best surveillance outfits in the world and presently, with returning jihadists cropping up all over the shop, they were without doubt some of the busiest people in MI5, or what insiders called simply 'Box 500'. Tim, Ahmad's boss, now always had two A4 teams attached to the Task Force to cover HUMINT operations.

Ahmad passed in front of the body scanner and waited for the lift from the car park. It stopped automatically at the work floor and the lift doors glided open. He looked into the hall camera as he made his way quickly to the transmission room. He approached the shiny stainless-steel reinforced automatic doors. He stared into the iris scanner with his right eye and quickly punched in his pin and the solid, airtight, hermetically-sealed door opened with what sounded like an asthmatic breathing in.

Ahmad stepped inside and made his way to one of the computer stations. The door swished again and sealed itself behind him. Two other task force handlers looked up from their desks. A petite Asian girl was at the same desk as a large Afro-Caribbean guy. The Asian girl was still shrouded in a black silk abaya minus her niqab.

"Hi, Ahmad, how goes the war?" she said.

"Good, Fatima." Both agent handlers worked on the recruitment side of the house.

"And yours?"

"Fucking excellent," Fatima replied as Lou laughed.

Lou was a Londoner from Willesden who was an ex-Marine Commando and a DHU guy (defence HUMINT handler) in Afghanistan before he joined Box. His hair was crazily dreadlocked and he wore a baggy Bob Marley tee shirt under tension from his muscular frame.

"Sorry. It still cracks me up when you swear, girl."

"Well, working and living with you, Lou, you halfwit," Fatima flashed back, "get fucking used to it," while smiling broadly.

The two handlers had worked together for two years and were partners both at work and in life. There was always some banter in the 'binner'. The handlers knew the office as the 'binner'; nobody knew why, probably a throwback to the old FRU days in Ulster. It was a large room with modern-looking desks, comfortable chairs, and computer terminals. The only difference between this place and any other office space was the actual level of security it afforded anything transcribed or decoded within its confines. It was effectively a firewalled space and was sealed from the outside world both physically and digitally. Any material worked on in this room stayed entirely on the highly encrypted Task Force server. This is where the agent handlers compiled their source reports.

"Anything from CORKSCREW?" Ahmad asked the pair casually. There was a furtive glance between the two as Lou batted the question.

"No, CORKSCREW is comms-dark for a while, but once he's in touch, we will run through your RFIs (requirements for information) with him."

"Thanks, Lou." Ahmad flashed a smile. "It's appreciated, mate. I will copy you in to my latest report once I've tapped it out. Something big is happening, buddy."

"Yeah, thanks for the heads-up, mate," said Lou, almost absentmindedly, as his computer screen pinged and a name he recognised flashed up.

Although Lou was a close friend, Ahmad knew the way the game was played. They both worked within the Thames House firewall but Lou had only attached status within the task force. Agent handlers were funny about what they even actually disclosed to each other. The circle of knowledge was always more effective the smaller it was.

Lou and Fatima were breaking new ground in source handling procedures. They ran both their recruitment operations and their sources online and on the same social media platforms that they had snared them on. The system had its advantages and they ran some decent cyber sources and CORKSCREW was one of them. He was a young, tech-savvy person, who reported on the present links between inner-city crime and terrorism. Like many, he lived in and around the Islamist groups that had morphed into the prisons and the drug gangs. Persons of interest on the edges of the interface made excellent 'eyes and ears' sources reporting on anything that they thought unusual or on any rumours that they picked up on the street supplied by unwitting sub-sources, and an anonymous Facebook address or a WhatsApp number was the ultimate, simple, and safe way to report it. It was sort of like cyber spying, with all the advantages but with very little of the actual risk of personal contact with your agent or handler.

*I suppose that's the future of source operations. Young people feel safer in the virtual world; after all, that's how ISIS ran their recruitment. The only problem is that there is very little face-to-face contact where you can probe that inner part of the handler-source relationship. How do you check an online source? What if the person you are in touch with is just another bored teenager in a darkened bedroom with an over active imagination? Verification for that particular type of source can only be assessed by results, and even then, can it be organised misinformation to throw you off the track? I prefer a face-to-face agent. Where human interactions can be assessed. Maybe?*

Ahmad turned to his own computer and supplied a thumbprint, and the desktop buzzed into life. He removed the USB stick that Imran had supplied and plugged it in. He scrolled down the content on the stick. It consisted entirely of ISIS propaganda and back issues of the ISIS magazine *Dabiq*. The same shit the organisation spewed out for the consumption of its followers. It was Imran's digital cover story just in case the thumb drive was ever seen by any of his Islamist mates. Ahmad then typed in the encryption code and then in an almost magical way, individual words highlighted themselves in bright orange throughout the text. They then dissolved, spiralled, swirled, and then re-emerged. The text formed itself, slowly, word by word, until it finally became readable. It was Imran's imbedded text document.

Ahmad's eyes widened. *This is intelligence gold dust.*

Ahmad worked quickly to finish his report. All Security Service intelligence reports were standardised. A report always started with the agent's source number and codename and it always ended with the handler's recommendations for exploitation. The same standard format was used for any report; the only difference was the urgency given to the dissemination process.

This would be a TOP SECRET report marked URGENT.

Imran, Agent 3010, had done an excellent job. Ahmad now had a start point and the possible dates for the arrival of the four-man ISIS ASU (Active Service Unit) and three possible safe house locations, two in the London area and one in Glasgow. Ahmad finished the report with his recommendations. He now had everything needed for a successful surveillance operation.

His fingers moved in a blur as he quickly typed into the box provided.

*Agent 3010 has managed to establish when and where an active ISIS ASU (Active Service Unit) arrives in our operational orbit. The handler recommends that a specialist unit be nominated to gain close control of this group. It is recommended that the monitoring team have the ability and clearance to address any life-threatening or imminent danger to the public.*

Finally, Ahmad graded the report Alpha 2. A Security Service report is graded from Alpha 1, for those considered the most accurate, to Foxtrot 4, for those considered the least. Ahmad had graded the report Alpha 2, which meant he thought the report was RELIABLE (A) and (2) probably TRUE. This was the second highest intelligence grading you could give a source report. Ahmad thought carefully before he pressed the send button. The burden of responsibility weighed heavily on him. A terrorist group was arriving determined to carry out a mass-casualty attack only measured by the number of innocents they killed, the fanatics' 'metrics of madness'. *The more you kill, the more recruits you attract.*

He knew that it would be safer to kill or capture them on arrival, but these were, after all, only the caliphate's disposable cannon fodder. The task force needed to identify the actual control element and that was in deep cover cloaked by an Islamist cover story of charities, Saudi-funded Wahhabi mosques, publicly funded research groups, foreign intelligence agencies, and protective local politicians. They needed an experienced team that could cover all the options from surveillance to the ultimate sanction. They also needed people who were unencumbered by links to the Government but who would still act in the public interest when required.

Most importantly, they also needed people who could make the right calls outside the strictures of current legislation. He paused and considered the problem.

*Maybe Hedges and Fisher? Tim would decide.*

He nodded to himself and pressed the send button.

*Lanesborough Hotel, Park Lane, the Next Day.*

Sam was in the shower when the phone rang. A security circuit usually starts with a phone call from a friend that can lead to money and success or in some circumstances life-changing injury or death. It was always important to know your key skills and the limits of your capabilities. The job they were working on was at the lower end of the spectrum; a Russian oligarch and his family were on a shopping trip to buy a Champions League football club. It was not the ideal time to take a phone call because Taff was in the shower with her. She looked across from the shower door to check the number. The incoming call said 'DannyMac'.

*A call worth taking.*

She smiled, and pressed the green button.

"Hi, Danny."

"Hi, Samantha, what are you up to at the moment?"

"Just got a break from the Russians and enjoying life for a brief moment," she said.

Taff scowled and whispered from the shower door.

"Well, at least we were," he whispered.

Sam flashed a serious look back to Taff and continued.

"Why, what's up?"

"I have a possible change of task for you two, can you get to see me?"

"When?" said Sam.

"Can you make a briefing tomorrow?" answered Danny.

"Not until the late afternoon," Sam said.

"We have the wife shopping before her guys take her to the airport – it's death by Harrods until then." Taff slapped a wet part of Sam and she nearly dropped the phone. She flashed him the 'behave' look.

"Who's the client?" she asked recovering her composure.

"Can't say on this means but it's vastly more interesting than your current task and it's the same crew as the last foreign job."

Sam's voice brightened at the thought and she needed no more convincing.

"Where and when?" she said.

"Dominic's at six, if that's OK." Danny used the brevity code for the company safe house in Essex.

Sam looked across at Taff, who was covered in soap suds and giving Sam the 'Who the fuck is that?' look.

"Yeah, I will check with Nigel and get back to you."

"Roger that," said Danny.

Sam, naked, soapy, and still wet, wriggled her way back through the small shower door. She moved in front of Taff, pressed back slightly and felt him hard against her lower back. She then wriggled some more as he kissed her neck.

"Don't tell me, Princess, that was Danny," he murmured.

"Yes, Nigel, we've got a job," she whispered as she turned to kiss him. "But, before we talk about jobs, you've got a job to do first," she added.

"I'm on it," said Taff.

# Chapter Ten

*Next Day, Harrods, Knightsbridge*

Sam looked around and assessed the risk of something happening in the extremely busy and upmarket department store, and came up with the answer, *Maybe no risk at all!* After all, this was London, not Kabul, and she was part of a close protection team that included Taff, who looked impressive with his muscular frame squeezed into a Savile Row suit and he was teamed up with a massive ex-Spetznaz Close Protection Officer who looked like he'd been quarried from Siberian stone. He was a really good guy though and spoke five languages, including English in a funny sort of London mockney accent and he was tuned in to that same, uniquely dark, ex-Special Forces comedy wavelength shared by his British colleagues.

It was just another typical day at Harrods, just the same as the others and to a close protection operative the shopping equivalent of Groundhog Day. Samantha and Taff had finished late and shared one bottle of wine too many and another 'shop till you drop' experience with the beautiful Russian's wife, Czarina, was not what she needed.

*That coffee and Panadol have not quite kicked in and things are a bit fuzzy!*

Sam knew that it was at times like these that things go badly wrong. Sam took a deep breath and concentrated her efforts. Pickpockets and bag-snatchers made a good living in high-end department stores. Customers with money magnetically attracted London's criminal class. Such a seemingly minor incident would inflict severe reputational damage on both herself, Taff, and of course Hedges and Fisher.

This sort of job was exactly the other end of the security spectrum to the hostile end of the 'circuit' but in some ways it could be just as stressful. London had become an increasingly difficult place in which to look after the super-rich, but the Russian family had made it an easier proposition by arriving with a large retinue of their own security staff and drivers. Sam and Taff only supplied the local knowledge and acted as liaison officers to make sure things went smoothly. In another three hours they would drop the family off at the signature VIP lounge at Heathrow to the waiting Sukhoi 100 private jet that would whisk them back to Mother Russia.

The chance of an organised hit on a client was always a possibility. The super-rich sometimes trampled other super-rich on their way to their first billion and oligarchs and gangsters have long memories. This job though had paid well and had so far been plain sailing.

Sam snapped out of her thought and concentrated again on the task in hand.

The main thing was making sure that the beautiful wife didn't severely injure herself by coming off the escalator by the Egyptian staircase in those *ridiculously high and frankly dangerous, but gorgeous, Christian Louboutin shoes*, thought Sam.

*Only eight hours to go and we'll see what Danny has got to offer.*

*Later, Outside Heathrow Airport*

Sam checked her rear-view mirror and pulled into the fast lane on the M4 after the drop-off of her Russian clients. As she indicated she also checked the types and colours of the following vehicles in an almost involuntary manner. Taff was sort of doing the same in the passenger mirror. She smiled as a thought crossed her mind.

*What an average married couple we are. We can't even drive down the motorway without worrying about hostile surveillance.*

The drop-off had gone according to timings with the big Sukhoi 100 private jet rolling in spot on time. Even in the civilian world the Russians always worked to finite timings.

"That was easy money, and even on schedule," she said.

"Yeah, not too stressful." Taff glanced again in the offside passenger mirror. "I have a theory that the further north you go the more likely you are to adhere to timings. The Russians are like the Brits in that respect. When you are freezing your arse off, you like people to be on time, yeah?"

"Yeah, roger," Sam smiled. "Succinctly put, Nigel, unlike that Qatari lot we had last time."

"Yes, that was dire, all waiting about and constant references to the risk management school of *Inshallah* (Arabic for God willing). Glad to be taking a rest from CP (close protection) for a while."

"So, if not CP, what do you think the job is?" Taff said.

"Not sure, DannyMac didn't say, Nigel." Sam glanced across. "He just said that it would be, to quote him, 'a bit more interesting'."

"A CT (counter-terrorist) task I PRESUME," he said loudly, deliberately using an intelligence officer's most hated word. She glanced towards Taff and smiled.

"I presume so, but..." And then they both repeated together as the familiar chant inculcated from Chicksands:

"Presumption is the mother of all fuck-ups." They both laughed.

"We'll know that if Ahmad or his boss, Tim, are at the briefing," Sam carried on, "then that's a sure fire combat indicator of a government task."

"He's probably too busy with his 'Brussels', Sam." Taff used the British Army rhyming slang for an informer. In the early days of agent handling PIRA (the Provisional IRA) had called informers TOUTS and as Brussels sprout had rhymed with tout the expression had stuck in the army's handling units, like the old FRU (Force Research Unit) or its later iteration JSG (Joint

Support Group). Sam glanced across at the gently smiling Taff.

"I'm not sure the Security Services use that term, Nigel."

"I think you might mean his CHIS (Covert Human Intelligence Source)," Taff winked.

"Yeah, roger that, CHIS, I suppose MI5 is the most PC organisation there is these days. They probably don't use the Ulster terms."

"No, probably not," said Sam.

"Not that political correctness ever worried you, oh husband of mine."

"Yeah, that's a big roger, Sam," he smiled. "I find it a bit fucking frustrating, to be honest," he said, still with a rising inflection on the 'honest' in an exaggerated Welsh accent, which he saved for such occasions.

As Sam glanced across to the big reassuring lump sat next to her a quizzical look played across her face.

"What are you thinking about, Sam?"

"Oh, just thinking, Nigel."

"I hope it's about me, kid."

"More than you realise, husband of mine."

"Are you thinking what I hope you're thinking?" Taff said softly.

"Yeah, I suppose I am," said Sam, fleetingly thinking of the night before.

"Well, pull over, gorgeous, and let's get started," Taff replied.

"Work first, fun later," said Sam. "I'm just recovering from last night and

the hard shoulder of the M25 is not the ideal place to relax."

"It's not my hard shoulder I'm worried about, Sam."

"Enough of that, Nigel, we have a job to do," she said with a smile. "Protection of the realm takes preference over poorly timed, and unasked for, vehicle-based, sexual procreation."

Taff laughed, "Sometimes I forget that I'm married to an ex-Int Corps Rupert."

"Yeah, well you are, Nigel, so get used to it," said Sam.

There was a moment of silence in the car as the first of the rain started to fall and the automatic wipers swished on. Sam looked thoughtful. The gentle pitter-patter of rain got progressively heavier. The wiper blades now beat harder in response and provided Sam with a tempo for her inner thoughts.

Supposition again! She also supposed that she had never been so happy. She had the man that she needed and they lived together in a place they both loved. There was only one other thing that could complete the happy cycle of life they now led, and that was a baby, but maybe they were not in the right occupation to even think of that?

Sam's smile faded somewhat. Outside her seemingly happy existence, she knew that the more comfortable she felt, the more guilt she had to endure and then the old demons from the past would start to claw at her a bit more often. She sometimes experienced an intense guilt at just being alive, when other comrades hadn't made it. How could she ever be a normal loving mother? She was trained to kill without a second's thought. When working, she was a focused military machine, and when she wasn't, the ghosts of the dead pulled at her and dragged her back to Iraq and Helmand.

Sam was beginning to realise that the life that she had chosen for herself would always claim payment. She had started to understand that she only truly felt alive in that unique space between life and death only experienced on the battlefield. She also realised, sadly, that she would only ever be free of it, when she had pushed things too far. Taff glanced across to Sam's glazed expression; he sensed her feeling of helplessness.

"You OK, Sam?"

Sam snapped herself out of it.

"Yeah, good, no problems, Nigel."

Sam smiled quickly and she was back in the present.

Taff knew that he sometimes lost the Sam he loved in the dark depths of her own thoughts. She would never talk about it. She would never share her secret worries with him.

*I am losing her,* he thought.

Sam indicated right at the satnav's command and started the run into the meeting place. Two minutes later the woman's voice said, "You have arrived at your destination."

The company safe house was Edwardian, detached, expensive, and like any other in that part of London. Sam pressed the key fob and the electric gates swung open. The BMW crunched its way along the gravel drive until its headlights glittered onto the immaculately painted black door. It stopped with a final crunch of stones in front of the house.

"Here we are then, the start of another epic adventure," Sam said brightly, glancing across at Taff.

"Yeah, roger that," he said.

"Here we go again."

"Hopefully not with so many mad bastards trying to kill us this time."

"Yes, Nigel, but somehow I doubt whether they would have sent for us unless there was a chance of a modicum of incoming involved."

Sam used Taff's correct name.

"Yeah, but, as a family business, it's what we do," Taff said smiling gently. A thought flicked across his mind.

*What a fucked-up business to be in with someone you love.*

They left the car and walked to the front door. Taff rapped the big brass horseshoe-shaped knocker. The door opened, and Danny beamed a smile. He shook Taff 's hand and gave Sam a fatherly hug.

"Are the dynamic duo ready for another task?" he said addressing them both.

"Maybe," said Sam and Taff almost in unison.

"Depends on what you need and what you are paying," said Taff.

"A real professional's answer," Danny replied.

"Hopefully we will all know more after the briefing. It's all new to me as well!"

Danny led the pair into the large open-plan living room where all the members of the original hostage extraction team were seated. Pat, Scotty and Jimmy Cohen looked up and smiled as they entered the room. They each greeted the pair with the sort of warmth known only to those who have bonded in combat. The questions and quips followed thick and fast.

"You're getting fat, Taff," said Pat.

"More phys, fewer pies, old mate, the new wife is feeding you up too much."

"Cheeky fucker," said Taff, rising to the bait.

"You look as radiant as ever, Samantha," said Scotty. "Why you married that ugly Welshman, I will never know."

Taff replied with a beaming smile.

Jimmy Cohen walked across from the far end of the room where he had been helping Ahmad set up his presentation.

He shook Taff 's hand and gently kissed Sam on the cheek.

"Great to be working with you again, guys," he said warmly.

Jimmy was a wiry-built ex-Para who vaguely resembled 'Brains' from the kids' TV series, *Thunderbirds*. Jimmy brushed his glasses onto the top of his head and smiled.

He was a Londoner and had joined the IDF (Israeli Defense Forces) after serving in the Parachute Regiment's Pathfinder Unit. Jimmy had more recently retired from 'The Shin Bet', the Israeli Security Service. Jimmy Cohen was the team's technical expert and was one of the best in the world. These were the three original team members that had helped free the US hostage Connor Cameron as he was about to get murdered. The mad dash to Mosul, with the ever-present fear of imminent death, had made them the ultimate team. They were the very best at what they did.

Pat Patterson was a stocky ex-SAS warrant officer with a prematurely lined face that was attached to a hardened body forged by ten years in the Parachute Regiment followed by another twelve in the SAS. Pat had been in the military grinder since he was fifteen. He had joined as a junior leader after a life in the care of Doctor Barnardo's. The army was the only family he had ever known. He had been on the circuit for four years and always at the sharp end. He had promised his wife and kids that this would be his last job; maybe...

He was sitting next to Scotty, the same age, mid-forties, but looking younger. He was medium height and a fit-looking guy. He had been a Royal Marine Commando, an SBS Special Forces soldier, and a member of the DET or 14 Intelligence Company, the codename given to the British Army's specialist surveillance unit that had operated in Northern Ireland during the troubles. Scotty had just retired from military life as a Major in the Special Forces of the United Arab Emirates based in Dubai.

There was another face they all recognised. Sam looked towards where Ahmad Talibani was standing to the left of the PowerPoint screen. Ahmad was the MI5 agent handler that had supplied the vital HUMINT-based intelligence that had ensured the last mission's success. Ahmad strolled towards the group and warmly exchanged greetings. He was dressed in a well-tailored dark grey business suit and wearing a fresh white shirt and Intelligence Corps tie. Introductions over, Danny spoke.

"Ahmad is again our Security Service representative for this project. He will first explain the situation and then tell us how we can help."

"Thanks, Danny," he said and then looked towards the screen and depressed the PowerPoint's remote control.

"Gentlemen and Sam, this is a TOP SECRET briefing and therefore covered under the Official Secrets Act."

He spoke clearly and confidently with a London accent.

*Just the right sort of guy to be an intelligence operator* thought Sam. *He is ideal for the role.*

Ahmad was of Kurdish descent and he had lived in London since he was a toddler. He spoke fluent Arabic, Dari, Punjabi and, of course, Kurdish. Not too tall, nor too short. He had that Anglo-Middle Eastern look that seamlessly bridged London's culture gap. His short hair and neatly cropped beard looked ordinary, and with a few props he could pass equally well for an Arab, a Punjabi, or even a lost Spanish tourist. He had the ability to blend into the background whether he was working in Whitehall or in the monocultural back streets of Whitechapel.

He removed a laser pointer from his right-hand jacket pocket and pointed it towards the screen. Ahmad glanced quickly around the room at his comrades; he knew he was in good company.

"I will give you an outline of the problem and will take questions afterwards.

"Intelligence indicates that an operation involving a mass-casualty type attack is in the planning stage. The plan at the moment is internal to the ISIS organisation known as EMNI. EMNI is the closest equivalent that the Islamic State has to a Foreign Intelligence Service.

"We have information that this is to be done by an ASU (Active Service Unit) returning from Syria."

Ahmad turned and clicked the remote.

The PowerPoint screen behind him flashed and displayed a picture montage of four men of Asian appearance.

"Gentlemen," said Ahmad, "we think that this is just one of the teams that are now on their way back. I stress, one of the teams, as we also assess that there could be several."

The projected image showed the suspects in a semi-formal head and shoulders pose. Their names were clearly displayed beneath each face.

"These photos have been given to us by the VSSE (State Security Service) in Belgium.

"They come from forged identity cards seized in a raid earlier this month. We believe that these are the men selected for an attack against the UK." Ahmad lit up the men individually with the laser pointer. A small red dot focused on the first.

"Ali Abdul Karim, age twenty-three, an ex-petty criminal of Pakistani heritage radicalised while banged up (imprisoned) in Wandsworth by our old mate Mullah Rahman."

Ahmad smiled an unhappy, sardonic smile.

"Who, believe it or not, was employed by Her Majesty's Government as a Muslim prison chaplain. Ali arrived in Syria on an aid convoy organised by Action Aid Syria and went jihad for two years, and he was last reported at an EMNI training camp near Raqqa."

The pointer flicked to the next guy.

"Mohammad Al Tahir, known as 'Tadge', age twenty-seven, is a Londoner and another ex-con and a former member of Luton's Asian gangland community. He was also banged up in Wandsworth in 2010 for drug offences and once again he met Mullah Rahman inside.

"He is a former street gang member from a gang called the Gambino family, who with some other Muslim gangs have cornered the heroin trade in parts of London. He was once accused of drug-related murder but acquitted when key witnesses disappeared. He left London and has spent the last two years running amok in Syria and Iraq."

The pointer changed and highlighted an older looking man.

"This is the team leader. His name is Ismael Al Bakker, although most people call him 'Sharka'. He's originally from Bradford and is of Pakistani heritage. He was a taxi driver and got involved as an aid worker. He's probably the most deranged of the four. He's forty years old; he's been with Islamic State since the beginning. He is thought to have organised the bomb-making training in the EMNI camps. He's probably a mass murderer already. He is an ultra-religious type, as you can see from his forehead's contact with his prayer mat. This guy is the unofficial Mullah of the group." The red dot then pointed to the last photo on the montage.

"And finally, Rahim Akhtar Amadi, the youngest cell member. He's a young man from Whitechapel. He disappeared from home before his eighteenth birthday and we believe he was trained at the same camp before the fall of Raqqa. Pay particular attention to this guy, as we believe that he's possibly the suicide bomber.

We believe that he will always travel with 'Sharka'; it's common practice to keep the cannon fodder company once they're trained, just in case they lose their resolve. As you can see, he is called Mohammad Al Bakker on the ID card; they are travelling as father and son."

Sam could feel a definite tingle; the hair lifted at the back of her neck.

*This is the most serious threat the country has faced.*

She had known after Paris, Manchester and then the horror of Liverpool that another mass-casualty attack in Britain was an evens bet, but now the odds had changed. Without ground to hold ISIS now had the means and the people to deliver it.

"What assets have you in place?" she asked.

"That's slightly better news," Ahmad replied.

"We are still getting some results from RUNNING MAN although the product is diminishing. We also have some other technical means and we've also got well placed HUMINT at all levels of the Islamic State in London and this is where he thinks the next attack is coming." Ahmad pushed the button for the PowerPoint and a detailed Google Map image of St Pancras Rail Station filled the screen.

"We believe that the ISIS Active Service Unit is on its way to London and this is the way they hope to slip in."

Sam exchanged glances with the other members of the team. All had that same knowing look. Intelligence briefings were always on the optimistic side and a bit like a pre-match pep talk but reality was sometimes a bit different. The intricate jigsaw of information painstakingly pieced together from a complicated overlay of agents and assets was sometimes just plain wrong. Or the details could be spot on when reported, but change completely by the time it was meant to happen. Collective years of experience waiting for the bad guys to arrive had taught them a hard lesson. An intelligence briefing was not always right.

After all, terrorists are only people and sometimes people just fuck things up; they lose car keys, get lost on route, or just change their minds. Irregular warfare sometimes leads to irregular and unexpected results. The guy who is tasked to drive the suicide lorry bomb forgets to fill it with fuel; the mortar bomb is dropped into the tube the wrong way up. Sometimes shit just happens and that changes how things work out.

A bit like how things had worked out in the so-called war on terror.

Sam was momentarily lost in thought. The Blair and Bush doctrine that provided the logic for the wars she had been involved in had failed in every way.

Firstly, you couldn't force liberal democracy in the Middle East with a bomb run or at the point of a bayonet. Secondly, if you did, at the cost of British lives and treasure, you just might replace it with a system that was more corrupt than the one that existed before you started trying to change it.

*Sam and her guys had fought and some had died in those wars.*

She wasn't bitter, soldiering after all was her chosen job and she had loved it, but she also knew that things had gone drastically wrong.

She did not buy the accepted British Government doctrine: 'We must take on Islamic extremists over there to prevent the poison arriving in our own countries.'

Well, that theory had worked out really well, hadn't it? All the places she had fought in were now back under Taliban control. For a British soldier who had served in places with strange names like Sangin, Nad E Ali, Marjah and Gharmshir, the places where her friends had died sounded like a roll call of despair.

The Islamist version of the madness seeping out of Iraq and Syria was unlike anything stirred up in Afghanistan. The Taliban were nationalistic in intent and only interested in running things in their own sharia law-based and flyblown emirate. ISIS was, and is, different, it has global ambitions, and as the enemies of the Islamic State finally closed in to destroy them, the Security Services were beginning the results of what they called 'Raqqa Scatter' or the 'Badguz effect'. As strange as it sounded, as Islamic

80

State lost ground it became less vulnerable. It had so far set itself up for the ultimate fall by holding territory.

Any conventional enemy is easy for western forces to fight, it's what they are trained to do, but the game was changing now. As ISIS was being beaten on the battlefield it was morphing into an even more virulent form, a global asymmetric type of warfare. War hardened jihadists were returning to their original host countries hidden within the throngs of refugees their own evil ideology had produced. They were returning to the western-based sharia shitholes they came from looking for revenge.

She realised the Islamist mindset.

To a returning jihadist, a member of the British public was not even human. The ideology dehumanised anybody who was not a fundamentalist Muslim and London, Paris, Manchester and Liverpool and any other city in the West were just target rich environments for these returning murderers.

Like other western liberal democracies, the British Government had no procedures; no plans, and no laws to deal with them. Her team had been pulled in because the normal taps for manpower were all but exhausted.

The blood of all those soldiers soaked into dusty shitholes in Iraq and Afghanistan had been wasted as the Government allowed the same twisted ideology to flourish in its own cities! Now mainland Britain was a target. What a waste.

# Chapter Eleven

*St Pancras Rail Station, a Week Later*

Sam's tired eyes blinked and again looked up at a bank of TV monitors fitted to the far wall of the hotel room. The room was a suite; it needed to be just to house the technical kit and equipment. Her eyes had been permanently glued to the screens for an hour observing the main station concourse. It was rush hour, and hundreds of people, isolated within their own personal thoughts and oblivious to each other, rippled across the station like a multi-ethnic wave of humanity. It was only at times like this she realised the hopelessness of their current task. How could you stop a returning jihadi when the very openness of British society was the gaping chink in its armour?

Sam and the guys were part of a protective surveillance set-up. St Pancras Station was a strange mixture of architectural styles ranging from a red-bricked Victorian Gothic to ultra-modern. A series of wrought-iron ribs supported a glass roof that towered above the main concourse and dwarfed the thousands of commuters scurrying around like matchstick men in an old Lowry painting. It was a vast area to cover with fifteen platforms over two levels and 200,000 people a day used it. It was big, busy, and a hard place to keep safe because it was also linked to London's Tube, rail, and coach systems. The team had been tasked to provide a security screen to protect the public with help from only two teams of MI5 watchers and twenty armed policemen from the Metropolitan Police's specialist firearms unit, SCO 19. Sam's team of contractors was providing a four-man reactive cell as part of the set-up. The team was stood by, fully armed in civilian clothes and waiting to go but they had been waiting for a week.

She was not just people watching; she was trying to detect anything strange or different. Suicide bombers sometimes gave telltale signs indicating intention. Sam knew from experience that in iraq they usually ritually purified themselves before death and preferred to dress in white but that might not be the same in London The main 'combat indicator' was more likely to be his or her general body language, maybe an agitated or distressed state, or even a drug-induced trance, or of course, the last warning, praying aloud, as they prepared themselves for that final defining moment, when they screamed '*Allahu Akbar*' (God is greatest) and pushed the button.

Sam had witnessed a couple of suicide attacks; not unusual for an Iraqi and Afghan veteran. She often thought that if the bomber could see what he or she looked like afterwards, they wouldn't give the suicide thing a second thought. When a suicide-vest bomber detonates, for instance, the head tends to pop off skywards while the lower body goes in the opposite direction. After one such incident in Helmand Province, the British Army had found the bomber's head a couple of days later. It had to be rescued from a frenzied tug of war between two wild dogs. Not a good way to end up after death.

*Not exactly Jannah* (paradise)!

Sam's mind was wandering now. She was tired; an hour-long vigil at the screens was about the maximum a normal person could manage before nature takes over and the analytical side of the human brain starts to drift away. She was seeing, but not really observing, as she ran through the present operation in her head.

The return of a jihadi assault team was the ultimate nightmare scenario. The Paris attacks, Manchester and Liverpool, had provided the deadly template, and St Pancras Station provided both a point of entry and seemed like the ideal target but the deadline for the ASU's return to the UK had come and gone. The HUMINT product had dried up, so there was no new intelligence, and therefore no new direction. In other words, the operation had ceased to be intelligence led and had started to just rely on good old dumb-arse luck. More worryingly, it was as if EMNI, the foreign operations arm of ISIS, had tightened all their security procedures. This seemed a clear warning that something was about to happen and that cranked up the tension.

Sam knew, and ISIS knew, that St Pancras was one of the easiest ways to get into Britain because they had tried it before. It was where lax procedures had allowed one of the Paris attackers, a low-life former petty criminal called Mohammed Abrini, to organise a quick trip to Britain. He was the so-called 'man in the hat' caught on the CCTV footage after the Belgium airport attack. He had slipped into England on a Belgian passport to collect £3,000 in housing benefit owed to a jihadist fighter in Syria after a meeting on a Birmingham park bench with some other British-based Islamists. The local council had coughed up the money even though the guy had been living in Saudi Arabia before he went on to kill people in Syria.

*You could not make this shit up,* Sam thought as she glanced at her watch.

She knew the task here was only guesswork. The Security Service had no lock-on. They had no start point for a surveillance operation. The intelligence had indicated that a returning Jihadist cell was on its way, but now that the deadline had slipped, when and where? The original information had indicated that St Pancras was the most likely entry point, so every arrival was monitored with a new set of cameras to augment the existing CCTV systems. The new covert cameras were set up in doorways, walkways, and obvious choke points both at the London end and on the Paris side. They hoped that technology could once again bridge the manpower and resources gap.

Jimmy Cohen, the team's technical guy, had suggested the kit. It was the newest Israeli system. It involved a technique where the suspects' photographs were subjected to computer-aided digital reconstruction until they had developed into a set of facial biometrics. The data was crunched into the cameras. The cameras would then alarm if they got a match. It was the best technology available anywhere in the world.

Sam was the duty silver commander; this was the hot seat at the tactical level and she was manning the Incident Control Point (ICP). All communications were channelled through the ICP where all the operational decisions were made. It was also where, in the event of a catastrophic mass-casualty incident the emergency services response would be managed. Sam had not seen her husband for four days; she missed him, her shifts finished with a full handover to the oncoming silver commander and then sleep.

Sam was feeling the strain and wished she could share the burden. As she thought of Taff, she heard him on the radio.

"Hello, Zero, this is Spartan Zero Alpha, changing now." It was Taff's voice but concise and clipped on the all-stations radio net.

"Hello, Spartan Zero Alpha, this is Zero, roger that," Sam replied.

It was strange, talking to her husband so formally. In just one short hour they were on stand-down together, and she could not wait to see him. This particular job had distanced them. They were on the same team but involved in different tasks at different times. Sam had been engaged in Ops like this on a couple of occasions. They were the opposite side of exciting and sometimes mundane, but always stressful. They required that total concentration be applied at all times to seemingly routine tasks. It was demanding because one lapse of concentration at the wrong time could have disastrous consequences.

*It's more like being a shepherd than a soldier.*

# Chapter Twelve

*Hijrah*

The front of the small boat smelled of diesel and fresh vomit. The four-man team sat opposite each other. They were crammed together at the very front of the bow, hidden by a thin plywood panel, feet interlinked, and slumped forward in shared misery. The weather had deteriorated since they left the small Brittany port of Saint-Quay-Portrieux in France. They could all feel the rise and fall of the slender bow as at first it carved the sea, and then with a bang, crashed, and wallowed into it. The praying got louder as the seas got rougher.

As far as the skipper was concerned his boat was a high-end product and the passengers onboard just another low-end cargo. He didn't know who he was dropping off and it would make very little difference if he did, because the skipper along with his two-man crew would never make another trip. They would be killed before they collected the balance of the money owing to them.

Within the semi-darkness, the monotonous hum of the powerful engine and the endless drone of Sharka's omnipresent prayers intensified the oppressive atmosphere. Rahim could just about make out Sharka's palms upturned in prayer in the dim red glow of the single light.

*He never had any doubts. Or did he?* he thought.

He was wedged in opposite his closest friend, Ali, their knees mutually interlocked in seasickness and despair. Ali Karim had the remnants of his last spell of retching imbedded into the short stubble around his mouth. He caught the younger man's gaze and tried to smile, but failed miserably. Ali Karim and Rahim had been through the IMNE training camp together. Rahim remembered that Ali had nearly cried when Sharka had ordered him to shave his full, chest-length Islamic beard. Sharka had explained that the beard butchery was necessary for the mission. Rahim shifted uncomfortably; his back was aching against the hard fiberglass hull protected only by a thin foam rubber mat, but he had a sudden thought and smiled. The beard shaving didn't actually affect him. *I'm only eighteen and can't grow a beard.* He rubbed his pubescent chin with his right hand as if to check.

*And if I carry on with this mission, I will never see a beard, a wife, children, love, or any normal life, not this side of Jannah (paradise).*

*If it even exists? And from the shit I've seen in Syria I doubt it.*

He smiled nervously as he looked across at Tadge.

Tadge was smiling and gave him 'a thumbs up' with his right hand followed seamlessly by his right index finger pointing upwards towards heaven, the unofficial ISIS salute, the sign of the believer.

Tadge was a believer. He was actually enjoying the excitement of jihad. He actually enjoyed the killing.

Rahim felt an involuntary shiver up his spine.

They all scared him.

The team had been given new clothes more suitable for operating outside the Islamic bubble. They had also received money, time-sensitive code words and had memorised emergency phone numbers. So much to remember in the little window of life his mission had left him.

*How the fuck did I get myself into this?*

He was full of doubt now. It had seemed so exciting when he had told the other lads at the mosque that he was going on jihad. He was full of confidence, knowing that he was doing the right thing. He looked back at the IMNE training course.

*When did I start to have my doubts?*

It was just that nothing they said made sense. It had seemed sort of logical at home in London while being preached at by the local Mullah, but killing somebody is a lot easier to say than to do. It's different when it's up-close and personal. It's not a video game when you can actually smell the blood and feel the man's fear.

At first it was exciting. He remembered the weapons and tactics training. He liked the AK47, stripping, assembling, cleaning and sighting the weapon and the range work. The targets were crudely scrawled outlines against the walls of abandoned buildings. They were painted in all shapes, outlines of men, women and children. They were told by the instructors, "They all must die.". He recalled the instructions they were given.

*In the first minute, kill as many of the Kuffar as possible.*

*In the second minute, search and destroy all the Kuffar that have hidden and hunt the ones that have escaped you. Women and children don't run as fast and are easier to kill. Show no mercy, you are Allah's warrior and you must destroy them. They are not human; they are Kuffar and are like unclean animals that must be killed. In the third minute expect their soldiers, you will fight them, and then use your suicide vest when you can fight them no more. You will be welcomed in Jannah by seventy-two dark-haired beauties and will be able to enjoy them forever.* That bit excited Rahim; he had never been near a girl; they were 'Haram' (forbidden).

When they had finished weapons training they had to prove themselves and be tested by their instructors. Each of the team had to be videoed carving a captured prisoner's head off. This was considered by EMNI as both a rite of passage and also as a 'not so subtle' form of blackmail. He was the youngest and had to go first. He was eighteen and the young man he had to decapitate was about the same age. He was a captured Peshmerga fighter and was trussed up and helpless. Rahim had followed Sharka's shouted instructions. It was like being on remote control. He felt like he was controlled, a robot, just a weapon, not really a person.

The act was just mechanical, part routine and part total horror. He had seen it a hundred times in Raqqa. They had said that it was as easy to slaughter a man as killing a goat or a sheep. They had lied. What made it worse was the Kurdish YPD fighter was brave and didn't cry out. That heightened his own sense of shame and magnified his own personal fear of death. The final horrific act and the thing that made him rethink everything he had been taught throughout his young life was what the senior camp instructors made them do next.

The Mullah had explained that a true jihadist warrior does not corrupt or smell badly after death. The only scent from a dead martyr for Allah was the sweet smell of wild roses. Rahim had heard this before at the madrassa (school) in Whitechapel and thought it true, but the ISIS authorities wanted to prove it. The training team woke them three nights later in the middle of the night and made them dig up the men they had slaughtered in the pitch-black. They had to feel their way through the last few inches of dirt to disinter their individual victim.

The young Kurdish Peshmerga didn't smell of roses, that was true.

In that instant, Rahim knew that his dead body, jihadi or not, wouldn't smell of flowers either. He knew now that death reigned over everything on earth and he realised in that final abject moment of horror that he didn't believe any more. The man he killed was just beginning to dissolve back into the earth like all living things and after three hot days in the ground his putrefying mortal remains stank. He was also a fellow Muslim and he had died with a bravery that Rahim knew he could not hope to emulate.

He actually realised that he didn't want to die.

That might be a big problem on a suicide mission.

The waves seemed suddenly tamed as the boat started to make better progress.

TAP, TAP, TAP.

Maybe the boat had entered a sheltered bay?

Something rapped against the panelling that enclosed them. It was the signal to disinter themselves from their dark hiding place on the boat. The partition was kicked down and there was a stretching of sore bodies. It reminded Rahim of an old horror movie he had seen. Before his dad banned him watching *Kuffar* TV. It was the scene where the vampires had just left their coffins and were readying themselves for a blood-drinking spree.

Maybe it was an accurate comparison. Death was about to rule. Blood would be spilled.

As the team prepared to land onto the Kent beaches of the *Dar al-harb*, or 'The House of War' as it is called in the Koran, there was an excited buzz of low-toned conversation. The team eagerly clawed at the bags containing the weapons and explosives. The rifles were state of the art as far as ISIS was concerned. They were the same AK12 rifles used by the Russian Special Forces, especially adapted and shortened for the task. The rest of the team was excited at the thought of action, death, glory and heaven, but Rahim just wanted to go home; he was worried.

He really didn't want to go. He wanted to live.

But what could he do?

There was only one person that could help him now. It was an older man that had advised him not to go to Syria. He was a respected man in his Whitechapel community and actually a returning jihadi hero himself. He was a guy from the same street and he trusted him. Maybe he could straighten things out. He was still with the brothers. The man's name was Imran, and his street nickname was Barbie. He had memorised his number just in case he needed his help in Syria.

*I will call him when I get the chance,* Rahim thought, as he checked and lifted the suicide vest and placed it into the waterproof bag next to him.

# Chapter Thirteen

*Whitechapel, London, 0300 hours*

Imran, agent 3010, had waited until his wife had drifted off to sleep before he could ring Ahmad. As he waited and observed her untroubled slumber he had time to think. He traced the gentle fall of her chest, still and peaceful. He looked at her face almost luminescent in the thin chink of bright light that streamed from under the bedroom door and he felt shame. Her left cheek still had the red weal of a man's handprint.

Lying there was the woman he loved and whom he had deserted in a fucked-up quest for religion, acceptance, and excitement. He felt so ashamed that he had lashed out at her earlier that day. After he struck her she had just looked at him, held his stare, and in that instant he realised that she was mentally stronger than he was. In that one love-filled, but pitying glance, he had felt both her immense strength and his own pathetic weakness. *I'm becoming more like them every day.* His tears welled up from deep inside and trickled uncontrollably down his cheeks, as if in a vain attempt to cleanse his shame.

*I feel very alone.* He knew he had lashed out through frustration, because he couldn't share his secret with her. He had to wait for at least another hour before it would be safe to phone. His wife slept peacefully now, her innocence shining from her sweet, loving face, just like that old fairy tale, *what was it called? Sleeping Beauty?* He smiled when he remembered that they had banned it at the local government primary school as un-Islamic, because

Sleeping Beauty's face was uncovered, and the story involved a kiss to wake her.

*That could only happen in fucking London.*

It was only an hour before the morning call to prayer. He couldn't sleep as he had something vital to pass. He had to tell his handler that he had heard the Mullah organising something on the phone but he had stopped suddenly and looked directly at him as if he suspected that he was being overheard. The atmosphere between them had changed and it had spooked him.

*The Mullah was suspicious; why?*

Something wasn't right and what did Ahmad say? 'The abnormal is only the absence of the normal'. He had been conversing in shaky Arabic but he usually spoke only in Punjabi or English.

Was this because he knew that Imran's Arabic was weak?

Imran soundlessly opened the bedside cabinet while looking at his wife to make sure she didn't wake. He looked at the glistening blue steel of a Serbian manufactured Zativa factory-produced 'Tokarev' 9mm pistol, the same type that had been used in the attack on Paris.

But ISIS didn't know he had this one. It had a full 9-round mag and there was a new, shiny 9mm 'Fuck-off pill' in the chamber ready to rock and roll.

He had bought it from a greedy, mad Serbian gangster in West London, and only he knew Imran had it.

If the ISIS security guys came knocking on his door, they'd better be tooled up and ready for a gunfight!

He picked up his phone and made his way downstairs to make the call.

*Duty Officer's Cabin*
*Task Force HQ*

Ahmad had lain awake for hours trying to work out what had gone wrong. He was getting pressure at work from people who didn't really understand what source handling was about. To them it was all inputs, outputs, flow charts and statistics but to Ahmad it was far more personal and he was worried about Imran. His agent was 'comms dark', out of contact, and that was bad for a whole variety of reasons. Since 3010 had returned from Mosul he had been in almost daily comms with his handler but now suddenly, nothing. Ahmad had tried the established REVCON (agent re-contact procedure). He had made sure that the surveillance team guys had placed a crumpled cigarette packet under the windscreen wiper of the agent's car. This was his signal to get in touch urgently, but so far it had drawn a blank. Ahmad had also visited 'Sayeed's place', the technical DLB (Dead Letter Box) in a dark Whitechapel back alley, but still nothing.

This was serious; his last source report about the arrival of a jihadist cell from 3010 had been graded 'Alpha 2'. It even had the precise timings of the cell's arrival from Europe via St Pancras, but it had been a complete dud. Ahmad couldn't understand it. The thought crossed Ahmad's mind that maybe the information Imran passed was flawed at source; perhaps it was what they wanted him to pass. In other words, it could be disinformation rather than real intelligence. Had it been fed to him in the knowledge that Imran was an agent? Or maybe Imran was doing a double? Either way, things had gone seriously wrong, and now, at the very time when he needed to know what was happening there was nothing but an ominous, fearful silence.

Ahmad considered the possibilities. Maybe Imran's cover was blown and he was already interrogated, tortured and dead. Or perhaps he was being too closely watched and just could not get free? Ahmad knew that ISIS in London was in the middle of a security shutdown. The feedback from several usually very productive sources had also dried up. Other source handlers were having the same problems. He had started to get anxious about Imran's safety and had just decided to activate a trace on the agent's mobile when Ahmad's phone rang. The iPhone lit up and vibrated on the bedside cabinet. It was 0300 hours in the morning. Ahmad grabbed the phone and checked the number.

*It's him!* Ahmad felt an immediate feeling of relief; he was OK and able to call. That meant that he was at least alive! There was nothing unusual about an early morning call from a source. It was part and parcel of being an agent handler. Agents don't lead normal lives; they have to protect themselves with a screen of half-truths and lies. Imran had to juggle the demands of his terrorist organisation with the needs of his handler while keeping the secret from his family in order to protect them. Nothing was simple in an agent's life; by nature it was always complicated and sometimes just totally fucked up. Ahmad knew that Imran might be under pressure for any number of reasons and he was relieved when his phone finally rang. Agent 3010 had waited until his family was asleep before he phoned.

"Hi, mate, what's happening?" Ahmad answered the phone.

"All good, I'm calling from Uncle Mo's," said Imran in hushed tones.

It was the phrase that Agent 3010 used to let Ahmad know that he was not phoning under duress. He was calling from what had once been an outside privy at the bottom of his backyard.

"Can you talk, old mate?" said Ahmad.

"Yeah, no problems, I have about ten minutes," Imran answered.

"OK, are you sure you can't be overheard?"

Ahmad went through the standard questions every handler asks when he takes a call. Imran had heard this many times and found it reassuring; it seemed this guy was looking after him.

"I've checked, and I'm good," he said, as he glimpsed into the inky blackness.

The back of the house was silent and dark; the only noise the omnipresent drone of city life. Imran flinched. There was a sudden scurrying noise.

"Fuck," he muttered quietly.

94

The silhouette of a skinny-looking black cat fleeted across the small backyard and skipped deftly onto his neighbour's wall. *Control your nerves, you wanker.*

It was a strictly Muslim neighbourhood of London, so at least he didn't have to worry about dogs barking.

"Yeah, I'm OK," he whispered into the phone.

Ahmad detected an undercurrent of stress in Imran's voice; his normally confident tone was muted.

"What have you got for me?" Ahmad said.

"Things are tight here, something big is happening soon," Imran blurted out. "The Mullah is fucking spooked."

Imran paused as he checked the surrounding blackness and then continued at a staccato pace.

"They are blaming London for the security leaks. He thinks someone is reporting straight back to ISIS Europe and his neck is on the block."

Imran stopped as he moved back into the shadows of the outhouse. He felt exposed and was scared.

"I have to drive him somewhere different each day to use his phone. It's always in the open and three of us look after security. He uses a new SIM card for each long call, to Germany, I think."

"Could you hear what he was saying?" Ahmad asked, thinking, *it's strange, this is the twenty-first century with all its technical advances and I am asking the oldest question in 'Spy craft'; what did he say?* Imran again checked the inky blackness.

"It's difficult, he won't talk in the car any more, and he thinks there's bugs everywhere. I've heard snatches of conversation in Bengali, I could just about hear a mixture of Arabic and English names." Imran paused, as if in thought.

"It didn't make much sense, just a jumble of words, but not used in any particular sequence.

One word was, I thought, *'Hijrah'*, in Arabic, and then I heard the number ten?"

There was a puzzled silence from Ahmad at the other end of the phone.

*"Hijrah?"* Ahmad thought it a strange word to find in a phone conversation.

"Yeah."

"Are you sure it was *'Hijrah'*, meant in the Koranic sense?"

"Is there any other way it could be meant?" Imran said quizzically.

The handler knew his Koran:

*Hijrah*, as a word, could be translated or interpreted in different ways depending on both the context and the scholar translating it;

*And whoever emigrates for the cause of Allah will find on the earth many locations and abundance,*

*And whoever leaves his home as an emigrant to Allah and His Messenger and then death overtakes him, his reward has already become incumbent upon Allah. And Allah is ever Forgiving and Merciful.*

Koran {4:100}

"Did anybody else hear that?" he said finally.

"No, mate, I was the only one close enough to the Mullah," Imran said.

"What do you think it means?" asked Ahmad.

"I thought, maybe, the name of a current operation, but no idea, bruv! I had never heard him use that word before except when talking about the Koran, but it was sort of used out of context, as if it meant something else to who was on the other end of the phone. There was no sort of reverence about it."

"What about number ten?" said Ahmad.

The source whispered back nervously. "What about the obvious, Number Ten, Downing Street, home of our newly appointed Prime Minister? Could that be the primary target?"

*Yeah, could be.* Ahmad considered this quickly.

*Maybe, but hard to hit, and after all, there were so many soft targets in London and a hundred ways to get to them and why did only Imran hear these two words? Could this be a tester?*

"Anything else?" Ahmad said.

"No, apart from the fact that just one guy has one of my cars at the moment."

"Have you got a name?" There was a silence as the agent decided what to say.

"No, this man is working separately from the London end. I think he may be the guy that the 'Fat Man' is worried about. He is doing something else, maybe a security review, maybe not, it's the black Merc, and you have the details."

"OK, Imran, listen carefully," Ahmad said, "we need to find out the specifics quickly, a name or even a description would be good. When did he arrive in London and what is he up to? But you also need to be careful. When you get something just phone it in. There will be no actual meets until all this blows over."

"Yeah, sounds good," was the whispered reply.

"But remember if you feel that you or your family are in danger use the distress button on your phone and we will come and get you out."

"Thanks, mate," said a relieved Imran.

"OK, remember, look after yourself," said Ahmad as he stopped the call.

Ahmad had scrawled just two words down after the phone debrief. Just the words '*HIJRAH*' and '10' and a large question mark.

*Why did only Imran hear it?*

*Was he meant to hear it?*

*What was the circle of knowledge? Who else knew?*

A tester is a Security Services term. It was a counter-espionage technique to locate a source within your organisation. It was as old as spying itself.

*Was this a classic counter-intelligence tester?*

Ahmad pulled out his phone, deleted the last call and dialled Tim Broughton's number.

# Chapter Fourteen

*St Pancras*

Taff and the guys had just spent a twelve-hour shift within the confines of a 'gunship'. That was the name that the SCO 19 teams used to describe their covert intercept vehicles. Taff, Scotty and Pat had all operated with intercept cars in Northern Ireland. The Ulster cars were usually up-armoured and specially engineered large saloons. They were then used to get highly armed teams of guys somewhere quickly with the principle aim of capturing or killing terrorists when they arrived. A London 'gunship' served a different purpose and was meant to be reactive rather than offensive.

The twelve contractors manning the cars were called the 'Spartan' call signs. The Spartan operators were all ex-Special Forces and special duties civilians recruited on short-term government contracts. Spartan worked with both SCO 19 and the regular British SF that had been called in to bridge the gaping capability gap. The Spartan cars blended seamlessly into the scenery and like all good covert vehicles they looked like they belonged. Taff 's team was using a long-wheelbase Mercedes Sprinter van. It was a mid-sized van big enough for a four-man unit and its kit. It had the same garish bright orange and black check as seen on police motorway cars. The logo emblazoned on the side 'MEDICARE' explained its function. These vehicles were usually waiting at stations to rush transplanted organs to needy donors but this was carrying an armed response team and a mini operations room.

One side of the interior of the panel van was crammed with TV screens and comms kit. The monitors showed a live feed of the station and all the surrounding streets. The smaller TV screens were linked to the facial recognition cameras. More importantly, after a week of continuous observations the cameras had allowed the team to observe the core 'pattern of life' of the rail station. You needed to know what 'normal' looked like in order to know when things were abnormal. Slowly and painstakingly, the everyday functioning of the station had been observed and recorded. Staff shifts, the opening of shops, train arrivals and passenger foot flow. All this helped to build the picture of the teams' operational space.

The facial recognition cameras were all mounted covertly at pedestrian flow and choke points, starting on the Eurostar platforms and finishing on the exits to the station. The platform cameras were fitted to the inside of the information boards where passengers usually look up to check for their train timings. It was in the best place because the kit needed at least 70% of a face before the recognition data kicked in. Jimmy was in his usual position, serenely studying the displays in a methodical manner, making the odd comment. 'Hold up. We have a likely here,' or 'What's this bloke doing?'

It was the funny, light-hearted moments between friends that relieved the monotony of surveillance.

"What the fuck is this guy wearing? It must be fancy dress."

Sometimes the monotony was relieved by a full philosophical discussion.

"What the fuck are we doing here?" chirped Jimmy as he observed the screens.

"Trying to stop London getting blown to fucking bits," replied Pat. Taff was leaning back in the front passenger seat of the van as he joined the conversation.

"Yeah, so much for fighting them in Iraq and Afghanistan to stop them in Europe. It didn't quite work out that way, did it?"

"That's a big roger," Jimmy chirped. "Because to deal with radical Islam, you need radical methods, some outside-the-box thinking."

"What does the ex-Israeli 2 Para spook suggest?" Scotty said.

"Bomb them all," he said.

"That's a bit extreme. Even for you, mate," Pat said.

"No, hear me out, lads," Jimmy said smiling broadly. "You could 'Love-bomb' them."

"What the fuck is that?" said Taff.

"The E bomb," Jimmy said.

He continued. "It's an important chemical weapon that successfully prevented conflict between warring parties here 'in the smoke' in the eighties and in the even naughtier nineties.

"It's a cunning fusion of an easily available drug called Ecstasy and really loud trance music.

"You should have hit them with the ultimate chemical weapon, not a weapon of mass destruction as such, but maybe a WMP, a 'Weapon of Mass Partying'. You should have crop-sprayed those Taliban wankers in their villages with 'E' and followed up with hardcore 'house and trance' music."

Jimmy winked. "It worked in Bermondsey, it even had West Ham's 'ICF' (Inter City Firm) and those equally mad fuckers from 'The Treatment' at Millwall cuddling each other." He mimed the nineties glow stick thing with both hands. Taff laughed.

"I wouldn't rely on anybody but the village goats getting any love from Terry Taliban, mate, music or not."

The conversation stopped suddenly; there was a loud 'beep' over the communications as the visual recognition system alarmed.

"Hang on, here's a possible." Jimmy zoomed the CCTV onto a young Asian guy and an older man walking together through the main concourse. The philosophical discussion was over for the day and they were back to work in an instant. The camera panned in. The younger man's face filled the screen. He was dressed in a dark red hooded tracksuit and jeans with a black rucksack on his back and he looked stressed.

"Hello, all Spartan call signs, this is Spartan Zero Alpha, we have a possible."

The inside of the van was suddenly alive with activity as kit was checked and gathered at speed.

"He's dark red on blue, slim, five-ten and moving from Yellow One to Red Three."

"Roger that, I'm tracking," Sam's cool, clear voice was heard across the radio net. As Jimmy zoomed the camera onto the suspect another viewing device had also focused onto the young man's head. The cross-hairs of a Schmidt and Bender telescopic sight had also found him.

"Roger that, this is Trojan White One," said an emotionless voice over the radio net. "I have," he stated simply.

"Roger that and hold," Sam replied.

'White One' was a SCO 19 police marksman who was observing the whole expanse of the platform from his high-tech sniper hide. He was seated behind what looked on the outside like an advertising poster for the latest BMW 4 series. He was seated and crouched over his weapon that was pointing downwards from a small table ensuring the correct angle for the shot. He was behind what appeared to be a glass video screen, which allowed him to track all movement on the station. The translucent graphic film not only hid him from view but also allowed him to shoot through the composite plastic with no splash back. The 5.56 Sig Sauer MCX was using adapted ammunition and fitted with a silencer; there would be no noise and the bullet would only hit the target and not a passer-by.

"I HAVE," he said with a slightly more urgent emphasis.

The marksman shifted his position a little and concentrated on his job. The red dot in the centre of the sight was now fixed and tracking the young man's head. The extendable butt of the adapted MCX was locked solidly into his shoulder and pushing the weapon against its biped legs. The policeman controlled his breathing now and slowly took up first pressure on the special adapted 'Geissele' trigger. The red dot tracked centre mass of the young man's head.

"I STILL HAVE," he restated into his radio mike. His job now, was to track the target and await the call; someone else, the silver commander at the ICP would give the GO.

There was activity now on the station platform behind the two suspects. Spartan operators and Box (MI5) A4 surveillance specialists were closing towards the suspects. Jimmy focused the camera again, and took a shot of the younger guy's face and ran it through the face scanner again.

The scan showed NEGATIVE.

"STOP, STOP, STOP, WEAPONS TIGHT," Jimmy said. It was an 'All Stations Call' and it was heard on every radio and in every earpiece.

The SCO 19 marksman exhaled deeply, lowered the rifle and smiled.

He would have to take a life today.

Jimmy had noticed a glint of steel on the young man's wrist as he scanned the camera closer.

"Hello, White One, this is Spartan Zero Alpha," Sam's voice said clearly, with emphasis. "STAND DOWN."

"This is White One, roger that," said the marksman in a quiet voice.

Jimmy explained to the other guys in the van as he again focused the camera onto the young man's arm and brought it into focus. It was a steel bracelet worn by many Sikhs practising and secular. He scanned the camera closer again and picked out a Parachute Regiment badge proudly emblazoned on the regimental hoody.

"We've nearly topped one of our own," he said sadly.

He removed and cleaned his large blue-framed glasses, as if in thought.

"We are going to fuck up here, sooner or later. That's the third time this week."

"Yeah, roger that, Jimmy, that's another young lad we've nearly slotted and a serviceman this time." Taff was replacing the

MCX assault weapon he had quickly picked up when they got the possible.

Jimmy looked thoughtful.

"You know, guys, I think we're on the wrong track here."

"What do you mean?"

Jimmy had been involved in counter-terrorism longer than anybody on the team. He sometimes had an insightful overview that was slightly more nuanced and a lot more left field. He had been an intelligence officer with Israel's intelligence service, 'The Shin Bet', and his opinion was always valued.

"OK, hear me out. We are running this protective surveillance because we had definite processed intelligence valued as Alpha Two, roger so far?"

"Yeah, roger that." Taff acknowledged the thought process.

"Well, now we know that the intelligence for whatever reason, was a dud, a no show, yeah?"

"Yep," Taff said, accompanied by nods of agreement by Pat and Scotty.

"OK. Let me ask you this." Jimmy looked around the van and focused on Taff. "If you wanted to get a team onto the UK mainland, as a former Marine Commando, how would you do it?" Taff smiled, he knew what Jimmy was implying.

"I would use a quiet beach somewhere near to where I wanted to attack," Taff answered quickly.

"Exactly." Jimmy looked around the team. "You can arrive when and where the fuck you like, at a time of your choosing with all your kit ready to go." He paused.

"It's not as if they haven't done it before; the fuckers attacked Mumbai from the sea and that was absolute carnage.

Why bother coming through St Pancras?" Jimmy replaced his glasses.

"It seems like a no-brainer to me." He pushed his glasses back onto his face with his right forefinger.

"If I was them, I would infiltrate somewhere unguarded and unprotected. A nice quiet beach somewhere?"

Jimmy stopped and looked up at the screens. They were filled with thousands of commuters oblivious of the ongoing operation that was trying to keep them safe. The young Londoner, the Asian-looking soldier, blended back into the throng, just another dot in the crowd never realising how the graticule cross-hairs of the weapon sight had hovered over his forehead before a bullet from nowhere could have ended his life.

Jimmy looked at Taff. The thick blue-framed glasses seemed to intensify his very worried look and he shrugged.

"My guess is we're in the wrong fucking place at the right fucking time."

# Chapter Fifteen

*A Beach in Kent*

There was silence apart from the lapping of the surf. It was a pitch-black moonless night, illuminated occasionally only by the odd set of distant car headlights that stitched across the darkness of the beach. The men ducked down to avoid them as they stopped to rest. The four returning 'Lions of the Caliphate' were now crouched in semi-darkness. They were breathing hard after the exertion of dragging the heavy weapon bags over the stony beach and they now waited in the night's shadow for the signal.

Only Sharka knew the signal. It was a closed cell operation and only he knew every aspect of the mission. Only he had control of all the codes and the approximate timings and only he had any means to communicate. He had unwrapped one of the small mobile phones from its waterproof wrapper on the boat and had inserted the SIM card just before they came ashore. He now switched it on and dialled the memorised number. Almost instantaneously the phone buzzed three times quietly in his closed hand. He then immediately turned the phone off.

"They are here," he whispered to the others.

"Wait here," he said to Rahim who was crouching behind them.

The beach was typical of the shores of Kent, a mixture of small pebbles and mini rocks that made soundless movement impossible. Sharka disappeared into the darkness as the other three were left to again drag the heavy, reinforced nylon bags closer to the road. There was no talking now, just the occasional grunt and the tinkling of small stones as they heaved the bags across the last few yards of shingled beach. They peered from the inky blackness of the beach towards the start of a single asphalt track. The men were now waiting, lost in their own thoughts.

Three of the returning Lions of the Caliphate were excited at being back in England. The idea of bringing death into the very heart of the *'Dar al-Harb'* (The House of War) excited them, but the fourth and also the youngest was just scared. His three companions thought only of death, killing, and the promise of that uniquely earthy paradise promised to the martyr. They had left Britain, the place that their parents had fled to for protection and where they had been born, fed, and educated. Three of the lions were back to achieve a religious blood fest in their adopted homeland infected with the same twisted ideology; but one was not.

The youngest was called Rahim, and he was unsure. At that moment he felt emotionally unattached to his comrades and doubted the validity of the mission. He no longer believed and felt as if he had been strapped onto a speeding conveyor belt to oblivion. He knew he was being used and that feeling of helplessness was compounded with the knowledge that he was also being used in another more invasive, intrusive, and shameful way.

As the youngest and as the beardless, he also had to endure the attentions of Sharka, the oldest. At first, it was just a friendly, reassuring touch, and thoughtful hand on his back while advising on the holy book or the best way to pray. That had begun to change as the mission proceeded. The older man had reassured him that there was nothing wrong with intimacy between men, but Rahim felt uncomfortable and increasingly guilty about it. Rahim picked up a small rounded stone from the beach and felt its weight and texture, as he rolled it gently in his hand. He looked at the perfectly rounded pebble and thought.

*How many tides has this pebble endured? How long has it been here?*
*One hundred years, a thousand? One thing is for sure; it will be here*
*long after I've gone. I will be as lifeless as this stone very soon. I must tell*
*somebody. As soon as I can get to a phone, I will ask Imran's advice.*
Noises in the blackness disturbed his dark thoughts.

An engine revved and gears clunked clumsily in the distance.
Rahim squinted into the darkness and could just see the shape of
a transit van outlined against the ambient light of a distant village
before the imminent dawning of an English day. The transit
van's headlights flashed three times; they were ready. There
was a crunch of gravel as Sharka crept back from his recce. He
touched Rahim gently on the shoulder and squatted in front
of him. He turned and was then face to face with him in the
darkness. Rahim could smell his pungent breath as he came close
to whisper.

"Not long now, *Habibti*," he said with a chuckle miming a
kiss.

Rahim felt a wave of revulsion creeping bile-deep from the
pit of his stomach. The older man was goading him and calling
him 'girlfriend' in Arabic.

Sharka then smiled and took out a torch with a red filter
from his right jacket pocket and flashed it three times in quick
succession and the shape reversed towards them. It was then that
Rahim, the youngest, felt a deep sense of dread.

As the back doors of the transit swung open. The other team
members could not see the expression on his face in the red
glimmer of the van's brake lights. If they had, they wouldn't have
seen fear; they would have seen anger.

# Chapter SIxteen

*St Pancras*

Jimmy paused. He zoomed the camera in onto the number plate of an approaching black taxi.

"The old Bill's arriving," he said brightly.

The SCO 19 guys always turned up on time but arrived separately within a ten-minute period, dressed in civilian clothes with only their personal Glock 19's and comms kit but all carrying their nondescript primary weapon bag.

"Thank fuck for that," said Taff.

"It's been a long day."

Jimmy changed the focus onto the door of the black taxi. The SCO 19 team leader transmitted before he opened the taxi door.

"Hello, Spartan One Alpha, this is Trojan One Alpha. Two minutes, over."

Tony, or TL as his mates called him, was the Trojan team leader. He was an experienced firearms policeman of twenty years' experience. TL was fit, in his mid-forties, tall, with a receding hairline and dressed in dark standard street clothes. Tony looked around the station at the start of a rush hour at St Pancras. He knew the station well; after all, this was his patch. The rest of the four-man control team would arrive separately over the next ten minutes.

Tony was a good guy. The two teams had been working together for a week now and that's a long time on a joint operation. The primary barriers and misconceptions of the army/police thing had gone. It also helped that the Trojan team had a fair amount of ex-military guys in their ranks. Both units used the same rugged language, a mixture of black humour and constant piss-taking sarcasm.

"Yeah, roger that, Trojan One Alpha," answered Taff. He got back two squelches of static to confirm that Tony had heard him as he hurried along the pavement towards the RV. He quickly checked behind him as he turned the corner where the Spartan team had parked the Ops van. The side panel slid open and TL climbed in. He smiled and looked around at the four ex-soldiers. He hadn't been sure about the whole 'working with contractors' thing, but he had been pleasantly surprised by their professionalism.

"How's it going, lads?" he said.

"All good, mate, but it nearly happened again," Taff answered.

"Yeah, I heard it over the net, mate," said Tony placing down his weapon bag.

"Thank fuck that didn't go wrong." TL looked thoughtful, colleagues of his had been involved in fatal shootings.

"You are a hero in the Met if you make the right call."

He paused.

"But the bosses hang you out to dry if it all goes pear-shaped."

TL knew that the Met Police gave out awards and plaudits when a gun was used to protect the public and it was maybe an armed robber. But they were a bit more suspect when it came to looking after their own in the subsequent enquiries. The higher the brass got up the ladder the more politically correct the fuckers became.

"Yeah, roger that," said Taff. "It was getting like that in Afghanistan at the end.

They tried to pin a so-called murder on Sam and me before we left.

We should have tried 'Courageous Restraint' apparently, but then we would now both be dead and they would still be alive and killing for fun. You'll soon have to call 'Lawyers are us' before you open fire, mate."

"Yeah, I know what you mean." Tony sort of smiled and shrugged his shoulders as if to say, 'welcome to my world'.

"Policing in London's the same. The same shit every day."

"So what's for the handover, mate?" Tony said, moving on.

Taff launched into his debrief with a torrent of the current operational information.

"Situation, no change, as far as the threat is concerned. We've had no updates and no confirmed sightings of the targets either side of the Channel. The ROE (Rules of Engagement) are the same.

Jimmy will brief you on the technical side."

Taff gestured towards Jimmy who was still looking at the monitors.

Sam was also still looking at the screens and thinking about what might have happened on the platform. She tried to breath more deeply to control her adrenalin. She tapped a biro nervously on the table as she considered what could have happened.

*That was a close run thing. Everything looked like it was one of the targets. A partial facial recognition, the sinister-looking backpack, the worried look on the guy's face. I was seconds away from giving the Go. That young man's life would have been snuffed out in an instant.*

Sam's thoughts were interrupted as she heard a hotel key card click in the room's lock. The door was pushed by Mark's shoulder as he attempted to balance two cups of Costa coffee while simultaneously opening the door. Mark was her opposite number from SO 15, the counter-terror specialists in the capital. He was a smartly dressed and fit-looking guy, mid-thirties, with a receding hairline, with ten years of experience on the 'Thin Blue Line'. He looked across at the still seated Sam.

"I've brought you a coffee, Samantha."

He nearly spilled the coffee trying to retrieve the key card.

"Oops, sorry about that. Substandard juggling skills. I'll take this one," he said offering the intact cup to Sam.

Sam grasped the cardboard coffee cup.

"Thanks, Mark." She looked up. "I need it."

"Are you OK, Sam?" the policeman said. "That stuff can be stressful."

"Yeah, but I guess that's what we're paid for."

She could see real concern in his eyes.

"I'm good, thanks," she said picking up her handover notes. The next ten minutes was a blur of locations, spot codes and actions on. Sam covered each point in turn and waited for questions until she could finally say,

"Right, that's it. You are happy enough with the handover?"

"Yeah, Sam, top notch. You are very thorough. Are you OK after all that? It must have shaken you up a bit. Shall I get one of my guys to walk you towards your pick up?"

Sam smiled. "That's very gallant of you, Mark." She smiled again, a bit more broadly. "But if I can't make it back to the RV on my own, HMG is wasting its money."

"Yes, I suppose so, no disrespect intended," he replied.

"Hey," Sam laughed. "No offence taken, and it's gentlemanly of you to ask," she said with a smile.

He felt a bit embarrassed. It was not only strange for him to work with a private contractor, but she was an ex-Special Forces officer, and also, just about the hottest-looking girl that he had seen for a very long time. Sam was wearing a very smart dark blue business suit with a mid-length skirt. Her shapely body seemed to strain slightly against the light blue blouse that she wore under the outfit. Sam looked more like a fashion model than a soldier. Her blonde hair was braided and hanging to one side in a sort of Viking Nordic mode, and from reading her CV, she was a warrior.

"OK, Mark, if you're happy, I'll see you in four days' time. I'm always on my mobile, twenty-four seven," Sam said as she sat on an office chair and removed her office high heels replacing them with low Chanel ladies' loafers. She placed the heels in her bag and looked up and smiled. He was almost mesmerised by the deepest and brightest blue eyes he had ever encountered. Mark seemed lost in thought; there was a tiny, awkward silence.

"You OK?" Sam said, and the spell was broken.

"Yeah, sorry." He felt his face redden. "I was just thinking about today, shit happens when you least expect it in policing."

"Yes, you're bang on with that, it's the same in my world." She smiled again.

"I'm on coms until pickup," she said brightly.

She took the small Motorola handheld radio from the desk and depressed the send button twice as a radio check. The two bursts of static confirmed that she was on the net. She then took the radio and clipped it onto a belt under her suit jacket on her left-hand side, alongside a black leather clip containing three Glock magazines and the police issue ASP extendable baton.

He also noticed the way that she checked the Glock 19 pistol nestled into a black leather quick-draw holster on her right hip. Sam moved her jacket aside and grasped the pistol grip of the Glock, as if it was the most natural thing in the world. It was more like a muscle memory thing, though, done as an instinct rather than as processed thought.

Mark was impressed.

*This girl has been in the shit before. And I asked her whether she needed an escort home.*

He felt his face redden slightly. Sam turned and slung her very expensive Louis Vuitton bag onto her right shoulder. She smiled sweetly and with a quick, "Have a good one," she was gone.


*Thames House*
*Same Time*


The analyst studied the results of the latest jumble of computer algorithms. He had crunched in the available data on Ahmad's latest RFI (Request for Information), he had overlaid the input supplied by the nationwide ANPR (Automated Number Plate Recognition) system and combined it with some existing tech assets from a car number supplied by the handler. It sounded simple and it was, but some of the existing red tape surrounding the data set wasn't.

Although used on a joint project, the TECHINT stuff supplied by Task Force actually came solely under the remit of MI6. He understood immediately that you could get your fingers very seriously burnt by cross-pollinating the system between secret and nationally available police data. Although the TF 1 unit was created to break down the sometimes overly bureaucratic interface between both parts of Britain's Security Service its rules were all still traditionally entrenched. The car for instance had been fitted with a jark (bug) by A4, an MI5 specialist department, but the asset, Agent 3010, was officially funded by MI6.

*So what have we got?* He pressed the enter key. A digital map of the British mainland reflected on the screen. Two traces, two different colours, of two different inputs that meshed perfectly. The car's travels with the ANPR system superimposed. It showed the traced journey of a suspect car of the registration supplied travelling all the way from central London to the rural Highlands of Scotland. The analyst hit another key and all the CCTV cameras at installations ranging from motorway service stations to banks and post offices in country villages were added to the mix. The computer chimed, six definite hits, the last one on a camera in a place called Fort William in Scotland. He gathered the data and put it into a desktop folder. It seemed that this was some sort of targeting operation. *The data has given us a possible where but how do we find out who the target is and how it's going to happen?*

As soon as he had permission the data would be shared with the TIU (Terrorist Investigations Unit) in Glasgow. They could then harvest information from the hundreds of small, privately owned CCTV cameras installed in small business premises along the route for maybe a photo ID of the driver. He needed immediate feedback on the RFI with Ahmad Talibani and Tim but before he could release the results he also needed to check with the main registry at Six and get permission for the data trawl that he had already completed. *Fucking ridiculous.*

# Chapter Seventeen

*London, Docklands, Task Force HQ, 0500 hours*

Sleep was always at a premium during a research operation and he had learned to grab it when he could, but the call had worried him and the comfort of slumber still evaded him. 3010 had seemed a bit paranoid; was he buckling under the pressure? Source handling is never a precise art. It's sometimes a fucked-up mixture of fantasy, fact, truth and intuition or what source handlers even sometimes called 'SWAG', standing for a 'Stupid Wild-Arsed Guess'. Every report had to be considered through the lens of the handler's knowledge of the source; his strengths, his fears, and his frailties and this agent was a particularly complex character.

Ahmad was worried. He was staring blankly into his rather cold cup of vending-machine coffee as if he was peering into a crystal ball. He played back the recording of the call with a worried expression. The call from 3010 was at times rambling and incoherent. No matter how hard he had tried to reassure the source he lost direction and jumped off track. Imran seemed to be losing it.

The call was unstructured and blurted out in half whispers. Ahmad ceased trying to get inspiration from the cold cup of coffee and turned back to the notepad where he had scribbled. He always found it easier to put his problems on paper. *Number Ten, could that be a possible target?* He wrote down his template.

The actual who, why, what, where and when.

Ahmad worked quickly on his laptop and things just seemed to fall into place. He was just a handler, firewalled sometimes from the head shed that maybe knew more than he did so he gathered everything he had and placed it in a desktop folder and squirted it off to Tim. Tim could then gather everything from the entire TECH and HUMINT spectrum and then all the information would end up with JTAC. JTAC was the Joint Terrorist Analysis Centre and was responsible for trying to work out the overall picture. It was a room in Thames House where information was shared between sixteen different agencies. As far as he was concerned the ISIS team had already arrived but the million-dollar question was, if they didn't come in at St Pancras, where did they arrive and where were they now?

## Kent Coast, ISIS Safe House

Tadge was upset. They had been in the same tiny house on a windswept piece of the Kent countryside for four days. It was an old, isolated and ramshackle farmhouse that literally rattled in the wind. It was worse than being banged up in Wandsworth. The walls seemed to press inwards each day to constrain and restrict him a little bit more both mentally as well as physically, and with every day that passed, the place's custodian, a young Imam straight off the plane from Pakistan was also annoying the shit out of him so there was an atmosphere. He could feel their strong group ethos evaporate a little every day within the walls of the safe house. Everybody was feeling the strain. His young friend Rahim had become very withdrawn and now just spent much of the time in absolute silence. He had caught him, the night before, trying to insert a one-time SIM card into one of the team's phones to make a call. He thought he had stopped him but they had argued and their friendship was now buckling under the pressure of their confinement.

He thought that the entire group felt the same; the initial excitement of being on a mission for jihad had gone. They were allowed no contact with the outside world, no TV, no radio; nothing that the London end of ISIS thought might affect their resolve. Tadge never thought in a million years that after his training in Syria, he would be banged up in a house only a couple of miles from where they had landed. Tadge was a Luton boy and as the boss of a crew called the Gambino family, he had controlled the majority of the local heroin trade locally before he went to Syria. He thought of himself as very much a modern Islamist warrior; straddling the crime/terror nexus like he had invented it. He had used the local jihadist guys to establish links to the drugs networks in Afghanistan and Pakistan and then just reaped in the profits. The local community didn't give a fuck because it was almost an unwritten but mutually agreed law that the shit couldn't be given to their kids, only to the *Kuffar*. There was also a big kickback to the beardies of course, or community elders as the press called them, that they could spend on supporting jihad or bolstering political support on the local Labour council. He was actually a bit fucked off with the whole Islamist thing.

He knew that really, deep down, if it weren't for circumstances and getting nicked he would be happier as a street criminal. It seemed somehow more honest in a fucked-up sort of way. It worried him that he was beginning to have his doubts; the Islamist groupthink was beginning to dissolve with every hour he spent within the corrosive confines of the house. He still prayed four times a day, but that was so the others could see that he was praying not because he really wanted to.

The only noise in the flat was the constant drone of the Mullah and Sharka discussing some *hadith* from the Koran. It was during one of Sharka's long monologues that he had caught Rahim staring at the team leader. Tadge was worried because the youngest member of their group and the guy that would wear the suicide vest was generally brooding and staring at the team leader with a very worrying, hate-filled glare. He had known that the older man had taken a sexual interest in the youngest member of the group but thought that it was a mutual thing; it happened all the time in ISIS circles in Iraq and Syria but was never mentioned. *A lovers' tiff, perhaps?* But if there was one thing Tadge did know about, it was the unpredictability of human nature and how it could prematurely end your life.

*Sharka had better watch his back!*

# Chapter Eighteen

*Renaissance Hotel, St Pancras*

She moved quickly to the hotel lift and pressed for the ground floor. Sam stepped into the elevator and waited until the doors swished closed. She was then alone and between floors. She quickly drew the pistol with her right hand, pulled the slide back with the thumb and forefinger of her left and checked to see the reassuring glint of brass. She quickly replaced the Glock and checked her clothing.

It was just a routine.

It was at times like this that made Sam suddenly think.

*This is London in 2019. I've nearly already sanctioned the taking of an innocent life and now I have prepped my Glock as if I was still working in Kabul, but I'm in London?*

The foyer of the Renaissance Hotel was busy. Sam scanned the crowd. It was operator instinct; she was just looking for something or someone out of place. Her old instructor's voice from Chicksands, the Intelligence Corps headquarters, sounded in her head.

*The abnormal is just the absence of the normal.*

The hotel foyer was also a choke point, where it was much more likely to pick up hostile surveillance. Then she spotted him, what in surveillance terms you call a 'possible'. A smartly dressed young black guy was looking across at her. That wasn't that unusual in London. Sam was blonde and was used to it. It was the way he glanced that sort of rang alarm bells. He was smartly dressed, in a dark blazer and fawn chinos but he just looked a bit too young for the rest of the clientele. It was at that precise time she knew that the guy was watching her; it was an almost primeval feeling, tingles up her spine as eyes focused in her direction. She caught his gaze, not hate, not lust, just a sort of coldness about his eyes, as if he was calculating her worth and just weighing up his prey.

She smiled. *Probably nothing, but...?* As her early intelligence instructors had often said at Chicksands,

*Just because people think you're paranoid doesn't mean that some fucker's not out to get you.*

As she walked towards the hotel's revolving doors she checked her reflection. Sam clearly observed the young guy reaching for his mobile phone.

*Was he phoning in her movements?*

Coco turned on the saddle of the Yamaha and looked towards the hotel to check his back. He always felt a bit hyper when waiting for the action to begin. Although he enjoyed the tingle of adrenalin surging through his system, it reminded him of his boxing days. All those pent-up emotions and fears and then, TING, the blessed relief as the bell rang and you could go to work. He felt his mobile vibrate in his pocket. It was WhatsApp. He pulled up the visor of his crash helmet and said,

"Yeah?"

"Got one, bruv." He recognised the voice of the spotter in the hotel.

"Yeah?" Coco repeated.

"A blonde girl with braided hair, fit looking, dressed in blue business with a black shoulder bag." Coco could tell that the spotter was moving now.

"The bag is a grand's worth and she's on her own."

"You still got her?" Coco said.

"Yeah."

He looked towards the girl and made his appraisal. She didn't look at all like a victim, it was just the way she carried herself.

He noticed that she seemed aware. She had a super confident attitude and he spotted the way that she was running through some AS (anti-surveillance) drills that Lou had taught him on the weekend at Bedford. *She's a cop, this might work!*

"OK, two minutes and where I said, OK?" Coco confirmed the plan.

"OK."

He stashed the phone quickly and tapped his crash helmet with his right hand. Skar got the signal and walked quickly towards the bike from where he had been waiting at a bus stop.

Sam had spotted the guy easily; she was now a bit more convinced that she had a follow and he was not very good at it. He hung back slightly too much, not quite sure whether he had been sussed (spotted) or not. Sam took out an iPhone 7 from her bag with her right hand, turned on the video function with the camera pointed towards him over her shoulder as if she was checking her make-up. CLICK; she could ID him later.

She walked a bit faster towards her pickup location.

*This place is a shithole.* She knew from the police briefings that there were lots of robberies here for a very good reason. It was where London's criminal class could meet the vulnerable, rich tourist of their dreams. It was a target rich environment for a street criminal. The station streamed with a constant stream of travellers, sometimes jet-lagged or travel tired, all confused and therefore vulnerable and sometimes distracted by their search for a hotel, taxi, bus or train.

Sam disliked the Euston Road; it was rough and smelt overwhelmingly of diesel fumes, cheap fast food and was littered with discarded packaging. A small plastic bag fluttered across the pavement, powered by a light gust of wind; even a crisp packet needed to escape to somewhere nicer. The road was just ordinary, with a sort of grey, grainy, stained look about it. It was also crowded, with a complete cross section of the population jostling for space with the incoming tourists. Sam used the crowds to stay unsighted as she ran through some more CS drills. Now she knew.

*He's following me!*

If the young guy on the phone was trying to blend in, he wasn't. She waited until he was unsighted, a blur amongst the throng, and then moved into the doorway of a travel agents. Sam felt the reassuring weight of the Glock against the small of her back and smiled. The young guy now thought he had lost her and began to frantically weave his way through the crowd. Sam casually reappeared and he stopped, transfixed, not really knowing what to do. She walked on, a bit more quickly now, both slightly spooked and quietly confident. She scanned the other side of the road and spotted the black motorbike.

Maybe she was being a bit paranoid?

Maybe she had got it wrong? Maybe the earlier near miss at the station had unhinged her logic. And anyway a young bloke following a blonde in London wasn't all that unusual. *Did he signal to the guy on the bike?*

*Something was going to happen here!*

Samantha stopped and was sort of enjoying the buzz. She appeared to casually check her appearance in the window of the travel agents while studying the reflected street scene. She mentally noted the precise position of the bike while she adjusted her braided ponytail. She reached into her bag to apply some bright red lipstick while still observing.

*With violence, it's always better to surprise your assailant; action is always quicker than reaction.* Sam needed to look relaxed.

She tracked progress and then he stopped and turned around and started to walk the other way. He had his mobile up to his ear again and he was looking across at two guys, in shiny matching helmets on a black motorbike.

These fuckers were going to try to rob her.

She suppressed a smile and took some deep breaths as she felt the adrenaline pump around her system. She was still icy calm and in control, and still observing the mirror image of the street scene. Sam's pulse stayed steady as she watched the bike pull out onto the main road. The bike revved as the rider in front looked for a gap in the traffic.

They are going to mount the pavement.

She snatched her 18-inch ASP extendable from its holster beside the Glock. She held it tightly clenched in her right fist with the rounded steel end protruding by about two inches. Time seemed to slow as the action started. The black scooter was now on the pavement weaving its way through the shouting and screaming crowd that only just seemed to part in time to prevent multiple injuries. The guy on the back of the bike leaned forward. Sam knew what was happening although she still had her back to her attackers. She had spotted the pillion rider's outstretched left arm reaching across towards her in her peripheral vision and felt the sharp tug as his black-gloved hand grabbed the bag as the scooter momentarily slowed.

She pivoted on the sole of her right foot while her attacker was still pulling on the strap of her bag and used her right fist to smash the balled end of the ASP into the pillion passenger's helmet. The visor shattered as he was propelled backwards swatted onto the unforgiving pavement. The scooter paused momentarily and then screeched away with an unintentional wheelie and a cloud of burnt rubber. In an instant the first guy from the hotel was on her. His face was shocked from what he had just witnessed but he couldn't pull back; he had already looped his fingers into a heavy brass knuckleduster. Sam moved fluidly, she looked over her shoulder and swivelled on her left foot, turned and faced her assailant while using the momentum generated by her hip to smash the shin bone of her right leg into the muscle and flesh of his left upper thigh.

"FUCK!"

He screamed in pain as Sam's hardened right shin bone impacted and crashed him to the ground alongside the stunned and moaning pillion rider.

"You've broken my fucking leg," he whimpered.

She reached for the handheld radio clipped to her belt. "Hello, Trojan Zero Alpha, this is Sam. I need assistance at Green Two."

"Yeah, roger that, Sam," came the instant reply.

"We have just watched it on CCTV," Mark said.

The incident had already attracted an audience, a small crowd had stopped in their tracks stunned by the strange and violent street scene, and were staring open-mouthed at Sam trying to comprehend what had just happened. Sam returned the radio to its position on her belt. She reached into her bag and retrieved her ID card.

"POLICE," she said, giving the bystanders a brief glimpse of it. It was a Security Service ID, but shouting 'police' always worked better. Sam had been so focused on the threat that she had failed to assess the bigger picture. Once the action was over, she was aware of a man recording the scene with his mobile phone.

She needed to get away and fast!

The pillion rider, still wearing his shattered crash helmet moaned as Sam grabbed his still semi-conscious form and skillfully rolled him onto his front. She removed the plasticuffs from her belt, pinned his arms behind him, and used her right knee to press him hard into the pavement. He began to groan.

"YOU FUCKING BITCH," he cried out in pain. She bent over his prostrate form and placed her lips very close to his right ear. As her blonde ponytail flicked against his face, Sam quietly hissed,

"Not so fucking brave now, are you?"

The other guy tried to inch away, pushing himself on his back. The man with the phone on his camera focused on the pain in his face.

"The police have broken my leg," he pleaded in the way of an explanation. Sam moved towards him.

"POLICE BRUTALITY," he screamed, as Sam pulled him by his undamaged leg towards her first assailant.

Sam replied in a very quiet whisper, "Guess what, little boy, I'm not the fucking police." She thought maybe her assailant might have gathered that. She then pulled another plasticuffs loop from her belt and attached the pillion guy's ankle to the other robber's cuffed hands.

"Hope you two have a lovely time together," she whispered in his ear. The crowd had grown; everyone seemed to have a smartphone in video mode. *Not good.* At that very instant one of the Trojan cars stopped, mounted the pavement and stopped sharply. There was a blur of activity as the two rear doors opened and two large SCO 19 guys appeared. They pushed through the crowd and formed an ad-hoc cordon on either side of Sam.

"Mark sent us,"

said the burly guy with the longish blonde hair as he pointed his warrant card towards the crowd. The other shorter guy knelt by the two assailants and checked them quickly for their injuries while reciting them a caution.

"What's the plan?" Sam said.

The blonde officer smiled.

"To get you out of Dodge soonest, Sam. Good job by the way."

"Watching these shitheads fuck up has made my day."

His expression changed as he heard something on his earpiece.

"OK, roger that," he said looking towards Sam with a smile.

"In about thirty seconds a dark blue metallic Jag will pull up. That's your lift home. We will clear this shit up."

"Roger that," Sam said.

The Jag pulled up at almost that very moment. An operator sprang out of the front passenger door and immediately opened the rear door for Sam who quickly slipped inside her new leather-seated refuge. She could still see the crowd recording the event on their mobile phones as she slammed the door with a satisfying clunk and they were gone. As Sam clicked on her seat belt she looked across at the other person in the back of the car.

"I thought I might see you here," she said.

"Yes," said Mark, the SO 15 Special Branch officer that she had just handed over to.

"Just thought I'd get the debrief first hand, and make sure you're OK, especially after what nearly happened earlier."

"Like earlier, no damage was done," Sam replied.

"No, not to you, it didn't look like you were too stressed, Sam." He suppressed a chuckle. "I watched the whole thing on CCTV and I'm impressed with your skills and drills, but what a day you're having."

Sam looked across at the friendly face.

"Yeah, slightly stressful, but mostly self-induced. You were right, I should've taken your advice."

"Yeah," said Mark. "Unfortunately, Sam, you now come under the same rules as us poor bastards, and in the Met, there's always an inquiry."

He was quiet as his earpiece got another message and looked slightly worried.

"How hard did you hit him?" he said.

"Not that hard," said Sam.

"Yeah, but hard enough. You've broken his femur. He's in a shit state," said Mark.

Sam seemed completely calm and relaxed.

"He deserves to be, it will stop him robbing other people for a while," she replied in her matter-of-fact voice. "I wish I could've got the other one on the bike."

"Don't worry, we've picked him up," he smiled.

"He was arrested, came off his bike with some assistance from a covert police car." The SO15 guy indicated, looked in the rear-view mirror and changed lanes.

"He's at Paddington Green already. These two will join him later.

He's a bad boy, a gangbanger of repute, they'll be interviewing him now."

Sam was quiet for a moment: the exhilaration had gone and the rush had been replaced with a bone-deep weariness of the soul.

The conversation was partially drowned out by the sound of an approaching ambulance.

"Oh fuck," Sam muttered quietly.

*What a day!*

# Chapter Nineteen

*Paddington Green Police Station, London*

There are many reasons why young black guys end up in a police interview room. Drugs, drink, envy and betrayal are just some, or sometimes, it's just very bad luck, but very few actually plan to get arrested. The prisoner smiled; it was a long shot but it had worked out! Some things had come as a shock though, like the police car ramming him off the bike. The rules had changed. He remembered lying on his back, dazed, winded, disoriented and looking up at the smiling face of the arresting officer and thinking,

*London is one of the very few places on earth where a half-Irish, half-Afro-Caribbean robber could be arrested by a police officer of Chinese heritage.*

He said nothing as PC Wu read him his rights and he kept quiet until he reached the interview suite. By that time his brain had survived the shock of capture and criminal street craft had in turn crafted an explanation. "It was the police's fault!" He after all had tried to aid a mugging victim in distress and after he had tried to courageously intervene the police vehicle had knocked him off his bike only because he had attempted to prevent the crime. He knew he might have problems with this version of events when the cop interviewing him burst out into uncontrollable laughter.

His one phone call wasn't made to a solicitor; it was to his handler.

Lou was duty officer, a job that he didn't like very much; it was a bit like being the Corporal Guard Commander in 45 Commando's guardroom in Scotland after the last Afghan deployment waiting for the whole world to kick off in downtown Arbers, which was what the lads called Arbroath. He always felt a wee bit isolated as the only black cockney in a jock-heavy unit. Not that being black was any disadvantage in the Corps, a green beret made everybody the same, being black was OK, but being cockney and English wasn't. The small Scottish town suffered from a strange love/hate relationship with the young Commandos who were stationed there. The girls loved them, tanned and fit looking and cash rich from a full six months away but the local lads didn't; it often made for an interesting weekend.

What Lou really disliked about being duty handler was the excessive time it gave him to think. The strange world of 'Research Operations' as source handling is euphemistically known is conducted at breakneck speed with the forward momentum of the operation directing the pace. It's a mad collage of meetings, debriefs, assessments and subsequent readjustment. Agents were very seldom logical or reliable; it was a juggling job to try to obtain results from the constantly shifting sands of supposition inlaid with human error. The sources he ran were after all just normal human beings often operating outside their individual comfort zones doing something that was generally totally unnatural to them. Service to your country could come in many guises but the Security Service was the strangest, where the lines between right and wrong, good and bad, black or white were sometimes a blurred shade of grey and that concerned him.. Especially with some of the agents he handled.

Lou's private life was also becoming more complex. His relationship with Fatima was becoming ever closer with marriage being the most natural progression for him but significant problems stood in the way. He thought it strange that even in twenty-first-century London, which was sometimes more progressive than even he would have liked it, she had again refused to tell her parents about their relationship. She was sort of living a double life herself, a modern MI5 officer when at work or with him, but a dutiful daughter expected to marry within her religion and definitely not get spliced with a burly black bootneck. He sort of understood, but it sometimes depressed the shit out of him.

He was walking out to make a coffee in the small kitchenette when source line number 3 sounded with a shrill bleep that resounded throughout the binner. He rushed to the phone. The heads-up display indicated the source number, name and location of the CHIS.

The phone said *CORKSREW* and the location said *Paddington Green Police Station*; the prefix *B* came up next to the agent number, indicating that it was an online cyber source.

"Oh, for fuck's sake," he muttered.

He picked up the phone after five rings and said,

"Coco, what's happening?"

The voice on the other end of the phone was definitely CORKSREW, Bravo Agent 1099, and he was speaking clearly and concisely without any of his usual street jargon.

"Help obviously, Lou, I think there has been an unfortunate misunderstanding."

Lou was used to this voice, it was the tone his source adopted when passing complex information in a very short time.

"OK, explain," he said, pushing a button to record the conversation while picking up his MI5-issue moleskin notebook and cheap MI5-issue Bic biro.

Coco explained and Lou smiled.

"And that's what you've told the old Bill? Mate, you are in the shit."

"Can you help me?" There seemed to be a hint of desperation in Coco's voice now.

"Yeah," said Lou. "But you will owe me big style, pal." Lou knew that his agent was looking at a five stretch for his next offence.

"Yeah, I thought I might." Coco knew how the game worked.

"Right, I will send our duty legal rep. Do not speak to anybody until the brief arrives." Lou was already speed-dialling the number on the other line.

"She will come and find you."

"Thanks, Lou."

"Thank Her Majesty's Government, mate, because that's who's sorting this for you!"

Lou placed down the handset and stopped the recording. He held the iPhone to his ear and on the eighth ring a girl answered.

"Hi, Sheena, one of ours is inside, aggravated assault and robbery, we need him out soonest."

"Yeah, OK," she answered. "Where?"

"Paddington Green."

"Has he any form?"

"Yeah, lots: gangbanger, drugs, robbery; can you still swing it?"

"We'll see, secure text the details and I'll get onto it."

"Thanks, Sheena."

"Always a pleasure," she said as she rang off.

*Coco's Place*

Coco had been bailed at two o'clock in the morning. The legal girl that Lou sent was both businesslike and efficient, and he was now looking towards the Thames from the kitchen window of his high-rise. He had the lights switched off so he could pick up the ambient lights towards the river. The new waterfront apartments crowded the right side of his view, their lights twinkling in the urban equivalent of a starlight sky. He thought how his life had differed from the rich, liberal elite that now occupied the new riverside properties. He imagined them explaining to their dinner party guests how, 'We actually get our cocaine from that council estate area over there but one should never try to fetch it oneself.'

It was strange, part of him wanted to be just like them, or at least how he imagined them to be, but the other part of him hated them. They were the ones who actually created the demand, the people that supplied the local motive for murder and it was young guys from areas like his that actually died making sure their next dinner party night went well. Their pleasure had caused what the press called the 'postcode wars' and that's why he probably knew as many people who had died from gunshot wounds as a soldier returning from Afghanistan. He actually never liked drugs very much. He had of course tried them and enjoyed the buzz, but he soon realised that a young working-class guy like him who might enjoy a good night on the odd line of coke could end up an addict in a heartbeat. He just didn't have the disposable income that the people 'nearer the river' had and it was as simple as that; no disposable income plus addiction equals crime and junkies, and junkies are really shit criminals.

He had time to think now. The rather pretty-looking MI5 brief who had managed to work her magic with the cops had also said that she could do very little to help him when he eventually came to court. Coco sort of knew that; he couldn't tell the girl that he wasn't really that worried.

*Prison is temporary but death is forever!*

And then the phone rang. He looked at the number; it was his handler. He waited the required rings and answered.

"Where are you, bruv?" said Lou. "Can you speak?"

"Yeah, I'm home, just got back this morning," Coco smiled.

"OK, cool." Lou paused slightly as if thinking. "OK, listen up, you know I said you owed me?"

"Yeah," the younger man responded.

"Well, son, I have some good news and some bad news; what do you want first?"

"Bad."

"Well, that's easy, you are going to prison at your remand hearing." Coco wasn't surprised at the revelation. He was resigned to it, he had planned it; he was a pro and knew that it was his time to leave the streets.

"Tell me something I don't fucking know, bruv."

"Ah, that's the good news," said Lou. "You play the game and you will get paid a shed-load of dosh while you are there." Lou waited for the information to filter in.

"Four thousand a month, you interested?"

"What do I have to do for that?"

"Easy, son. Use your brain while talking to brainless wankers and let me know what they are saying."

"I'm in," Coco smiled.

The plan had worked out better than he could have ever envisaged.

# Twenty

*Waterstones, Oxford Street*

Ahmad was waiting for his agent but trying not to seem like he was. He was waiting for a couple of buzzes in his earpiece that would let him know that the A4 surveillance team had picked up source 3010. Paul, the A4 team leader, was providing close cover as the other A4 watchers boxed off Leicester Square Tube station to trigger the source. Ahmad was inside Waterstones bookshop in Oxford Street and was purely by coincidence in front of the spy novel section. He had only three minutes' walk to the Box DBC at a hotel on Carlisle Street in London's Soho area. The DBC (Debriefing Centre) was an ordinary hotel room in an area of London that was well used to nefarious assignations, some of a sexual nature. Suspicious activity very often becomes the norm when everybody is at it.

It was a last-minute arrangement and it was an emergency meet called by the source, unusual on HUMINT operations. MI5 always had nominated hotel rooms that could be used for agent meets. It had only taken two hours to organise with Tim and Paul's team of A4 watchers who were now on overtime.

Imran, source 3010, had waited until just before the Tube door closed to step out onto the platform. His tradecraft had needed to evolve just to outpace ISIS's constantly improving security procedures. He stepped out of the Tube station just in time for one of those typical London downpours. He quickly turned and stepped back into the shelter of the station. Imran checked his watch, *plenty of time*. He was ten minutes early.

A voice sounded in Ahmad's earpiece.

"Hello, Ahmad, Alpha 4, 3010 stopped at Blue Two." The surveillance team was keeping him in the loop. Ahmad clicked his coms twice in response and continued to browse the bookshelf and then it suddenly occurred to him and he smiled.

*I'm browsing books devoted to all things 'Spying' while waiting to debrief a spy; how weird is that?*

He turned his head towards the front window just in time to recognise his old friend from training, Paul, as the A4 team leader walked past the shop to clear his back. Paul was dressed as a scruffy-looking council worker.

The rain stopped, almost as quickly as it had begun, and Imran left the station with twenty other likeminded Londoners in a sort of controlled rush. The air now was fresher, but still smelt of that inner London mix of diesel fumes and fast food. The sound of car tyres hissing through rainwater accompanied his progress, as he used the occasional skip around a puddle to check his back. Imran knew he was being observed, nothing at all positive, just that weird thing that you sometimes feel in the centre of your back when someone is watching you.

*It must be part of the human condition and maybe a hangover from when man had animal predators instead of the present day human type.*

He also knew that Ahmad would not call him to what was known in intelligence circles as a 'fixed point meet' unless he had all the safety and security side covered. Ahmad had explained it to him. 'A fixed point meet' was a meeting arranged at a specified time at a specific place. A sort of 'Meet you under the clock at twelve' or versions of it, and was almost never good tradecraft. Imran knew that because his handler had given him a start time and a meeting place he would also have organised a team to clear him down and look after his close security.

*Yeah, probably I'm being followed, not that I can pick them up.* He looked around the crowd jostling for space on his journey to the RV. *Maybe that guy in the hoody? No, too young. Maybe that guy there? No, much too old.* He played the spot-the-watcher game for a while but really couldn't identify anyone. *But they're very good at what they do.* Imran looked again at his watch.

*Bang on time.*

Imran spotted his handler as soon as his eyes left his watch. Ahmad left the doorway of the bookshop, looked around, seemingly oblivious to his agent's presence and walked off in the direction of Soho to the DBC. Agent 3010 noticed that his handler held his black pocket umbrella in his right hand; that was the signal for 'All Clear'. If he had no brolly or if he had held it in his left hand that would have been the no-coms signal for 'Abort'. Imran waited and checked for any hostile surveillance while tracking the MI5 man in the reflection in the bookshop window before he locked on to Ahmad's back and followed at a discreet distance. It was a short walk to the hotel.

The walk gave him time to think. Just a couple of stops on the Tube and it was like he was in a different country. The place was crowded and busy. He brushed past people just beginning to queue for theatre tickets. The bright neon lights on a theatre had just started flashing, a musical called *The Commitments*, and the source really wished he had fewer. The weight of his commitments had drowned him in worry. He checked that he still had Ahmad's ever receding back in sight and remembered his tradecraft lessons. He tried to zigzag through the ever-increasing crowd. He glanced at the reflection of a chemist shop window to clear down and check for a double sighting. He thought he spotted a guy that he had seen outside the Tube station. It didn't worry him. He sort of knew that his handler would provide a counter-surveillance box around the walk in.

As they got nearer to Soho, and the theatre district yielded ground to the seedier side of London life, the more religious side of Imran started to fight back. He was still conflicted over the so-called freedom that a western liberal society insisted upon. He found London's non-judgemental blatant disregard for morals both deeply fascinating and slightly repulsive. His eyes searched the crowd forward again and tagged Ahmad as he disappeared into the foyer of a small but upmarket hotel. A large art deco angel in dark bronze with outstretched wings and twinkling with small lights guarded the entrance. Imran spotted the guy inside making sure he wasn't followed. The same man brushed past him and left the hotel while skillfully palming an electronic door key into his hand as he left. He waited by the empty concierge's desk looking through the tourist stuff and he felt the muted buzz of his mobile in his jacket pocket. He checked the message. It just said,

*Room 8, Conference room, second floor*

He made his way to the shiny steel lift just to the right of the hotel desk. He swiped the card key and pressed 2 and Ahmad was waiting as the lift door tinged open. He turned and smiled. Both men shook hands.

"Welcome, mate, we are in here," the handler said as he turned towards a white door and opened it for Imran to enter. A menacing-looking large man loomed at the bottom of the hall.

"Don't worry, he's with us," Ahmad said as Imran entered the large meeting room.

Bright magnolia walls made the focal point of the room a large oval dark wood table prepared for a larger gathering than just an agent meet. Tasteful dark wood chairs were spaced evenly around the table with notebooks and pens. Eight glasses and two large bottles of water took centre stage. The end wall had a flip chart and stand; a large TV monitor was fixed to the wall.

"We are expecting company?" Imran said.

"No, bruv, just us. What have you got for me?" Ahmad answered. The start of a standard debrief was almost routine now. Imran knew the sequence those old-time handlers called 'the four fingers'. It was a trainee agent handler's check chart. It always followed the same order. First question, what's vital, any time-sensitive intelligence that he should get as a priority, then the greetings, 'How are you?', 'How's the family?'. And then the time assessment, 'How much time have you got?' and finally the fourth finger, arranging the next meeting in case it gets interrupted, 'When can we next meet?'. The two seldom followed this sequence any more the burgeoning friendship made it a bit too formal.

"I have lots," said the agent. "But I need something from you first."

"Shoot, bruv."

"It's big, and I'm fucking blown, fucked, once I give you this. I need out with my family with me, once you get it. Can you swing it with your bosses?" Ahmad sensed the fear in his agent's voice; he also knew that he was not a man who scared easily.

"I will try my best." Ahmad was sincere. "The more you give me, the easier it will be."

Imran knew that made sense.

"OK," he said. "Remember the training you gave me on the circle of knowledge?"

"Yes." Ahmad knew what was coming.

"Well, the circle of knowledge for this information is the Mullah, the guy I'm going to tell you about." The agent paused for effect. "And me! The minute this is acted upon, they will be trying to kill me and my family."

"I fully understand," the MI5 man said in a measured tone. "And your life and the lives of your loved ones are my organisation's highest priority." Ahmad knew he was both reassuring his source and lying to him at the same time.

Imran took a deep breath and told Ahmad everything. It was as if the ex-jihadi needed to unburden himself. Ahmad frantically made notes, only sometimes saying the odd 'Where?', 'When was this?' or 'What time?' to clarify a point. The information flowed from Imran in a verbal torrent with the agent barely stopping to take a breath. Ahmad scrawled the points in biro on one of the hotel-supplied notepads. Some points were known but some were new.

One of his new Mercedes taxis had been away for a week and was back with miles on the clock and a dinged wing.

The Mullah suspected him because he was finishing a conversation whenever he was in earshot. The guy who used the car was setting something up.

The technical override on the satnav had worked, he had checked and it had been to both the safe houses he had previously reported in both Luton and in Glasgow.

He had received a strange phone call from a young man called Rahim. He had gone jihad a year ago but had phoned him out of the blue three days ago.

The handler stopped the outpour of information to clarify the last point.

"What is his full name?" said Ahmad.

"Rahim Akhtar Amadi," the source answered quickly.

Ahmad knew the name immediately, but couldn't show surprise.

"I gave him my number a long time ago, before he disappeared. His family lives close to mine, it's a really strict Wahhabi family so not much fun in his life. Even less now, I should think."

"What do you mean?" Ahmad asked.

"Last known at a training camp in Syria and now he's back."

"I have the number here." Imran wrote the memorised number on Ahmad's notepad.

"I'm pretty sure it's a burner number, but it was phoned from somewhere inside the UK." The source let the information sink in. "That means they're back!"

"OK, great work," said Ahmad glancing at his watch. He needed to make some immediate calls on this one.

"But listen very carefully, I want you to just carry on as normal at the moment for your own safety." He spotted a momentary spark of fear in Imran's eyes.

"If you move out or change your pattern of life they will know immediately and your life will be in real danger. I'm going to ask you to just carry on as normal." Ahmad was thinking quickly. He placed his hand on his heart, a typical Arabic gesture of sincerity.

"I will guarantee your safety and the safety of your family."
He reached across and grabbed Imran's hand to doubly reassure
him. "I will make sure that we have a team always near you,"
the handler lied. "No harm will come to you, but we need you
to carry on as normal while the SAS team looks after you."
Ahmad knew that they just didn't have enough assets to cover
his promises, there was no SAS rescue team, but he had to stop
the whole operation being blown at this late stage.

He looked at Imran directly and caught his worried gaze.
"Trust me, I won't let you down." He knew by the look in his
agent's eyes that he had convinced him.


*MI6 Vauxhall Cross, London*
*The Secure Room*


Collette Brown knew enough about persuasion and coercion to see
that she was being totally coerced. She was looking across at the
CIA man who was her rank equivalent. She was the operational
controller for almost everything that Six planned worldwide in an
ever more perilous world and he was the London head of station for
the Agency. She was used to working with other people's versions of
the truth and trying to convince them of hers but after nearly thirty
years working her way to the top of one of the world's premier spy
agencies only a quote from the cold war seemed to amply sum it up;

*The world of intelligence is a wilderness of mirrors where truth
and falsehood endlessly reflect and refract one another and nothing
is quite what it seems!*

She was a woman of that world but she had never been
propositioned in such a forthright manner.
"If this ever becomes public knowledge my agency and yours
are properly fucked," she said.

"I understand, but I'm asking on behalf of the Government of the United States of America and I suggest you guys comply," the bullet-headed man replied.

"Remember this shit coming Uncle Sam's way all started in your backyard." The big American was making his point forcibly.

"And this is the only way that our two countries can stop extremely bad shit happening for the next two years. The game has changed; the enemy has adapted and has come back stronger. We need to get on the front foot and start punching back. It's the archetypal 'ticking bomb scenario'."

Collette had studied law at Oxford and was very familiar with that particular ethical conundrum. It went like this, a *terrorist bomber has been captured having already planted a bomb that will kill hundreds of people and the clock is ticking; the question is 'Can you use torture to find the bomb and save those people?'*. She knew that a good interrogator generally wouldn't because real torture meant that people will say anything for the pain to stop, but she also knew from historical case files that extended 'EI' or 'Enhanced Interrogation' did work. She remembered the case of Khalid Sheikh Mohammed, the man who organised the 9/11 attacks and who had been arrested in Pakistan and rendered to Guantanamo; the EI produced results that had not only prevented multiple attacks but also supplied the clues that led US Special Forces to Osama Bin Laden's hideout.

At the moment things were unproved, but if this man's identity was confirmed, he had direct control and solo access on everything that ISIS was planning for the next two years. He was a fanatic, and a confirmed murderer, and his rendition and interrogation were really the only ways to unlock the secrets that could eventually save thousands. She had made her decision.

*It is the only way to stop the carnage.*

*He's got a circle of knowledge of one. There's no alternative.*

"But this is a rendition from the United Kingdom, heads will roll and governments will tumble if this ever gets out," Collette said.

"It won't," the American said as he fixed her gaze and went into reassurance mode.

"Yeah, I suppose, you're right, it's a calculated risk but the stakes are high and the rewards are higher. It could mean your job, my job, your agency, my agency and one of those human rights lawyer types could tear us to pieces, but the threat against us is not as bad as the possible loss of life and the human rights of maybe thousands of innocent victims worldwide."

"OK, explain it to me again," said Collette.

"OK," said the bullet-headed man. "And remember this guy is officially dead!"

# Chapter Twenty-One

*Millbank, The Next Day*

Millbank had been the London-based home of Britain's homeland Security Service, MI5, since 1994 and was, at best, a rather poorly kept secret. The building, built in the 1930s, was in what architects like to call the 'Imperial Neoclassical style'. DannyMac had always liked it. It was smaller and a bit less 'in your face' than the larger MI6 building just along the river. The MI6 building at Vauxhall Bridge was impressive but just reminded the old history and architecture buff of a huge, ugly art deco cash register getting ready to slide into the Thames. He far preferred the look of Thames House.

He loved the finely carved exterior detail. He always took the time to look up at the 'Britannia figure', resplendent in Portland stone looming above the main entrance. Danny knew the backstory. The sculptor Charles Sargeant Jagger had been both a talented artist and a decorated war hero. He had volunteered at the start of the First World War and had served with distinction both at Gallipoli and on the Western Front, where he had been awarded the Military Cross for bravery. He was originally a Territorial Army officer in 'The Artists Rifles' the unit that eventually, in more modern times, became 21 SAS, a reserve Special Forces unit that used to be at the old Chelsea Barracks before they sold it to the Arabs.

History was everywhere in London; you just had to look for it.

Danny glanced up, to pay his respects, but that was not the reason he was visiting. The joint Task Force that kept his company employed met alternately at either of the agencies' buildings for intelligence updates and case conferences. It was the Box's turn to play host. He knew from the edge of urgency in Tim's voice that things had changed.

*Maybe they are going to pull the plug on the St Pancras task?*

*Maybe the HUMINT element has an update?*

*Maybe they have another task?*

Danny realised that information arrived in many different forms. It was collected around the clock from a complex web of human sources, intercepts, and technical means. The ever-whirring intelligence machine never slept. Information was gathered and processed into actionable intelligence on a twenty-four-hour basis. He had been at MI5 just before his last tour in Afghanistan. He knew that the complex machinery of operators, agent handlers, technical experts and analysts was all interconnected by the perpetual motion of intelligence collection, and it was here where that magic happened.

Danny approached the main entrance to start the rigmarole of gaining access. Security precautions were always tight. Danny looked up at the CCTV camera, and there was a buzz as the massive bombproof side door clicked open and he walked straight into the small security room. Thick ballistic glass lined the room. The security staff team recognised him with a wave and beckoned him over to the intercom. Danny handed in his passport through a small metal hatch that snapped shut as soon as he dropped it in. Thirty seconds later another door opened, and a uniformed security guard appeared with a metal detecting wand.

Danny knew the routine; every visitor went through the same procedures, no exceptions.

"Shoes off please, sir. Place your briefcase and coat onto the scanner, sir," the polite voice said.

After the security checks were over Danny sat to retie his shoelaces.

"Mister Broughton is on his way to escort you, sir."

The guard held Danny's phone.

"You can collect this on the way out, Colonel. It will be kept securely here until you leave."

As Danny looked up, another electric door swished open and Tim Broughton, the task force's MI6 boss, appeared. "Welcome back to Thames House," he said with an outstretched hand.

"What's happening, mate?" he added as an aside.

"Lots, pal, follow me through the tubes to X3." The tubes were the electronic scanning security pods used by all the staff at MI5 and X3 was the Task Force office on the fourth floor. As DannyMac entered the tube, it whirred, scanned and opened as Tim led the way to the lifts.

*I guess that today is the day when I get to know exactly what is going on.*

Danny followed a seemingly preoccupied and worried-looking Tim at a scurrying pace from the fourth floor lifts to the conference room. Danny could feel the energy in the air as they passed other preoccupied people along the bright, modern corridor. An intelligence agency gets a real buzz about it when everybody is working on the same task, a sort of communal lock-on to the target. Danny nearly collided with a girl in a hijab carrying some files. He noticed that they were red in colour, the same colour for source files that his old army agency had used. The girl looked up and flashed a smile by way of an apology and then hurried on.

*Something is happening, and Tim knows something that I don't.*

Tim reached the conference door, scanned his card and tapped in some numbers on the key code and the steel door whirred and opened with what seemed like a wheeze of air. As Danny entered the room, he recognised some of the men and the one woman seated around a medium-sized Scandinavian-looking table. The table was adorned with the detritus of the collective thought process. Four coffee cups, four Chinese-bought MI5 issue biros, guaranteed to self-destruct when needed most, notepads, scrawled notepaper and a colourful collection of whiteboard markers. A whiteboard was the centre of the group's attention; it was like a mad Dali drawing, covered in arrows and circles, some connected, but some not.

*It looks like all the decisions have been made then.*

The American broke the silence.

"Danny, how the devil?" said the big Texan in a mockney Mary Poppins accent that he thought nailed the way English people spoke. Danny immediately recognised the resident senior CIA officer in London. They had last met in Baghdad in 2006 during what was loosely referred to as the 'Death Star' days. It was called OP TRIDON; the operation where the combined Special Forces of all the 'Five Eyes' nations had waged a campaign of eradication against the upper and mid-level leaders of Al Qaeda. The specialist source-handling unit of the British Army known as DHU (Defence HUMINT Unit) had supplied some of the targeting for the raids. The big Texan's affable manner hid a steely core.

Tom O'Neill, nicknamed Tip, was bald-headed. Ex-Special Forces Delta Operator long before being recruited by the CIA and still thought he was one.

"Lovely to see you, Tip." Danny was looking around the rest of the table. It was a high-level meeting.

Ahmad, his old friend from the kidnap extraction operation four years earlier, beamed a smile. He was standing silhouetted by the glow of a large presentation monitor and he raised his hand in greeting.

"I think you know most people here," Tim said by way of an introduction. Danny looked around and didn't but thought that maybe he should. The only person that he knew apart from Tip and Ahmad smiled up at him. Still a striking-looking woman in her fifties, Collette Brown was stylishly dressed and impeccably made up as usual. She flicked her expensively styled auburn hair and smiled. Collette was also a colleague from the Baghdad days but now the director of the special operations arm of the Special

Intelligence Service, MI6. Collette was known for two things, as far as DannyMac was concerned, her uncompromising attitude to Britain's enemies and her loyalty to her friends.

"The famous DannyMac, good to see you again." The smile continued, "Kabul last time, wasn't it?"

Danny smiled back, faintly remembering a boozy British Embassy party just a year after the fall of the Taliban when Kabul was still an OK place to be.

"Great to see you, Collette." And then there was an awkward silence as Danny tried to place the two other men looking up at him. Sensing his confusion, Collette helped.

"Danny, I don't think you know the other two gentlemen here, allow me to introduce you." Collette glanced to her right. "They will be working with us on some phases of this project," she said gesturing towards the two hard-looking military types still seated at the table.

"Danny, this is Lt Colonel Robert Mayne, the current Commanding Officer of 22 SAS."

Danny nodded in his direction and the SAS man glanced up and gave a standoffish polite nod. SAS officers were generally suspicious of intelligence types, so it didn't faze him. The burly guy looked unlike anyone his men would consider a typical 'Rupert'. He was of medium height, a thick-necked, broad-shouldered man, who had gained a broken nose and a slight cauliflower ear by playing army rugby once too often. A thick scar indented his forehead, the result of an RPG frag in Afghanistan. The injury had permanently raised his right eyebrow and gifted him a sort of quizzical look. He had joined the Paras as an eighteen-year-old and had been commissioned as an officer while serving as a Corporal in 3 Para. Bob had had some hard soldiering under his belt both in Iraq and Helmand before he passed selection in 2010.

Collette flicked her hair back with her impeccably painted nails and directed her gaze to the other man at the table.

"And this is Major Howard Watson, the Ops Officer of the Special Reconnaissance Regiment who is attached to DSF

(Directorate of Special Forces) at the moment." Howie Watson stood to his full six-three and shook Danny's hand.

"Great to have you onboard, mate, just call me Howie," immediately indicating that he was both an ex-Royal Marine and from Newcastle. "We did meet once, Danny. It was in Baghdad during the 'Death Star' days just before an OP, and you gave a quick Int brief on the helipad before we smashed a place in Fallujah. I was working with C Squadron (SBS)."

"I apologise, Howie, I'm usually much better with faces," Danny said secretly wincing as he returned his vice-like handshake.

"I wouldn't worry about it, I was wearing a Nomex balaclava at the time."

"That might explain it," Danny replied. The brief outbreak of laughter finished as Tim spoke up.

"Danny, we have just finished a discussion on the way ahead, mate." Tim had his serious face on again. He looked towards the whiteboard at the scrawled Dali sketch that represented four hours of combined mind mapping. A thought flitted across Danny's mind.

*All that's missing is the melting clock face.*

"As you see we have new information and we have been wrestling with a solution. Everything, including some new TECHINT and some HUMINT, and we have also had considerable input from the cousins." He looked towards his American guest while inadvertently using the MI6 slang for the CIA.

"Sorry, Tip," he said.

"Don't worry, Tim, I've been called worse," the Texan said as Tim turned back to Danny.

"Ahmad will bring you up to speed on what's happening and then Collette would like a private chat after we leave. We've got another meeting to go to." He glanced towards the SF guys.

"I will leave you in Collette and Ahmad's capable hands." The two men seated rose when prompted and left quickly, with only a quick wave and a half smile. Tim turned and smiled. "I will ring you later, Danny, I know you will have questions." And then the steel door wheezed open, and they were gone.

# Chapter Twenty-Two

There was a brief halt in conversation as the steel door sealed itself closed. Ahmad shifted nervously in his seat as he waited for the MI6 woman to speak. Danny knew exactly what was happening. It was called in intelligence terms a 'de-confliction' strategy. It was a system to ensure that the collection part of an operation would never bleed into the operational side. It was developed during the long war in Ulster to ensure that the two main elements of counter-terrorism remained firewalled from each other to prevent cross-pollination and possible collusion. It was a natural development of the 'Need to Know' doctrine that kept the circle of knowledge as tight as possible.

In the latter days of 'The Troubles', the organisation that had over-watch was called TCG or Tasking and Coordination Group. Operations were now overseen by a multi-agency organisation called the Joint Terrorism Analysis Centre or JTAC.

The thought suddenly occurred to Danny.

*I'm going to be told something that they don't want the operational end to know or even JTAC.*

"So, Danny, you are probably wondering what's been happening," said Collette.

"I have a feeling that you guys know a lot more than I do?" Danny shot back.

"I'm not sure," she said. "You know the framework I think, but some of this is bound to be new to you." The large TV monitor clicked on.

"We've had significant input from our American friends augmented by some TECH and HUMINT gains, so I will just take you through what we have so far and we can discuss it afterwards and maybe ask your help with some aspects of it."

"Sounds like a plan," Danny said. The chair scraped awkwardly on the tiled floor as he sat down. Ahmad sat directly opposite him.

Collette continued, "Things have been moving quickly over the last couple of days." She absent-mindedly picked up one of the discarded pens and pointed it towards the mad mind map.

"And this is as far as we've got." A slight smile appeared on her lips. "It looks a mess but I think we've worked out what's happening." She seemed to sense Danny's doubt.

"We have two different plots driven by an individual who we think is a top ISIS operative trained by EMNI, their Security Service. He is a former British citizen who has re-entered the country with a mission to plan and execute two distinctly separate operations.

"Via St Pancras?" said Danny. *Maybe my guys missed them?*

"No, that option is out, we think the main threat will come from the sea, and that means that our current operation at St Pancras, if you'll excuse the pun, is therefore 'dead in the water'." She paused and leaned forward in her chair.

"Before we go on, I have to remind you that the security level of this conversation is TOP SECRET." A slight smile formed on her lips.

"But also, and I must stress, this is also UK eyes only, so it is solely between us and is not to be discussed with Tip or any of the cousins, is that understood?"

Danny nodded. "Of course, totally," he said, wondering why. The MI6 girl continued.

"First of all, Danny, Tip was here because the CIA has a current high-level asset working in Hamburg."

*That was where the 9/11 plot was hatched; coincidence?* Danny shifted in his seat. *So that's the US connection!*

"Intelligence indicates that a team of British jihadists are on their way home, or could even have already arrived. HUMINT indicates that St Pancras is no longer their intended access point. Reliable multi-source intelligence informs us that they intend to arrive with all the means to conduct an attack on a government target." Collette paused and sought out eye contact with the older man.

"And secondly, and this is more personal to you," she said thoughtfully.

"We believe that there is a kidnap plot against an ex-Special Forces soldier in your employ."

Danny seemed temporarily shocked. He took a minute to refocus.

"Who?"

"Sam Holloway," she quickly answered.

Danny shot a worried look. "How do you know?"

"We have confirmation that her house in Scotland has been targeted."

"TECHINT or HUMINT?" he said.

"Both" Collette said " and it's cross referenced and confirmatory"

"Let me explain why we think Samantha Holloway is a target."

"And what do you intend to do about it" Danny shifted nervously in his seat.

"Ahmad's agent supplied the lock-on for what we are about to discuss. So I will let him fill in the details"

Ahmad reached across the table and picked up a remote for the large TV monitor. He caught Danny's gaze and could sense his concern.

"I will try to answer all your questions Danny, but can I start with a question of my own?"

"Fire away" DannyMac snapped back.

"Do you recognise this POI (person of interest)?"

He pressed the remote and a face appeared on the screen. It was very much like any other photo on a source file or target pack. Just a young man smiling for the camera that Danny couldn't immediately place.

He said. "Are you familiar with this guy?"

"Vaguely, from old reports maybe?" The photograph featured a young man of Middle Eastern appearance with the beginning of a wispy beard and dressed in an Arsenal football shirt.

"This is an early photo when he was a fairly normal kid. He was a typical young Londoner then. But you are probably more familiar with his later persona." The next picture was taken from a YouTube video featuring a hooded man dressed in black brandishing a lethal-looking black combat knife standing behind an American journalist.

"Jihadi Joe," said Danny. "The guy who died in the team's hostage rescue."

"Yes, precisely," He confirmed as he pressed the remote again and another image appeared.

"And what about him?" Ahmad asked. The photograph showed another similar looking man, maybe slightly older, dressed in London Islamist chic, white robes and sandals at a demonstration outside what looked like Finsbury Park Mosque, standing beside the unmistakable hook handed figure of Abu Hamza.

"That was what he looked like in 2004," he said, "but this is how you probably remember him."

Danny did, and he had been a tier-one target in Iraq before he had been taken out by a predator air strike. The MI5 man flicked the remote and another more official photograph taken from an intelligence montage flashed up. The image was obviously taken from the targeting pack. The name CYCLONE was emblazoned underneath the full-face photo. A thick black diagonal line intersected the photograph indicating that the target had been terminated.

"Yes, I remember him, Jassim Emwazi, reported as the British jihadist with a computer masters who was tipped for senior leadership in the *Dae*sh"

"And, as you might remember, actually Jihadi Joe's elder brother!" Ahmad said.

"Yes." Danny frowned. "Where's this leading to?"

"Just a theory at the moment but if you remember there was a lot of speculation at the time to whether the air strike had actually killed Objective Cyclone as most of the evidence was circumstantial and the US troops on the ground couldn't positively confirm DNA because there were six other people in the burnt-out Toyota truck." Ahmad then clicked the remote again.

"Here's another photo taken last week of the guy targeting Samantha Holloway." The picture was freeze-framed from some fairly poor CCTV footage.

"This guy was buying cigarettes from a garage in Scotland."

A similar face partially shielded by a black hoody now replaced the targeting picture. The image was grainy with poor resolution. The face was partially blurred and he was looking up, with a slightly shocked look as if he had just spotted the camera.

"It could be him, I suppose," Danny said.

"Yeah," he said, "but the facial recognition software is inconclusive and we need to know whether this man is actually still alive."

Ahmad laid the remote down gently on the desk between them and looked towards Collette.

"Thanks Ahmad" she said "I think that brings Danny up to speed on things, excellent brief and thank you"

Ahmad smiled, stood, turned and started towards the door and looked towards the old cold war warrior.

"Sam's safety in very important to me" he said with real sincerity.

"I know" Danny replied as the door swished open and Ahmad left the secure room.

Danny was now alone with Collette and the circle of knowledge had just constricted a little further. The discussion was now just between the two of them. Danny understood that the de-confliction strategy had again removed another witness from any possible post operational enquiry. There was a brief moment of silence before he spoke.

"And is that why Tip O'Neill was here?"

"Yes" Collette replied and that's why we need to talk privately and totally off the record."

"Why involve the Americans in our business?"

"Because, if it is the same man, the cousins want this guy really badly," Collette said.

"Dead?" Danny quickly responded.

"No, not dead." Collette turned to look at the CCTV image. "No, they want him alive, he's too important to them to die, because they want what what's in his head."

"So rendition?" Danny made the logical assumption.

"No, we aren't allowed to do that any more," Collette smiled. "But your team could." Her smile faded.

Danny paused for a little as he experienced a moment of clarity.

"So that's why you employed my company, because you knew they were coming after Samantha." *Everything suddenly makes sense!*

"You knew she was under threat and you wanted to use her as bait, like a tethered goat, as a trap for Cyclone if he's the man in the picture." He fixed Collette with a cold stare. "There shouldn't be any complications when the life of a British subject is at risk," Danny said briskly. Collette continued with a slightly more combative edge to her voice.

"Danny, let me explain. Of course we didn't know at the beginning and our first priority will always be Sam's safety. I can assure you that she will not be in any danger. Major Watson's guys have the specific task of keeping her safe."

She caught his gaze with a sort of steely look. "I can see that you are worried about this, but we have come up with a plan that suits the unique dynamics of the situation. Can I explain it to you?"

"What, a rendition from the UK, by an independent agency, without any strings?" Danny was intrigued.

"There is a reason and remember if it is the same man, Jassim Emwazi, or Objective Cyclone as we know him, he is already officially dead."

"Why do they want him so much?" Danny looked at the screen as Ahmad hit the button again and spoke.

Another picture flashed up, a still taken from an ISIS propaganda video. It featured three men sitting cross-legged, smiling for the camera against some sparse greenery and a bullet-scarred wall, all lovingly cradling AK47s.

"Let me explain. The guy in the middle is Abdul Ismail."

"Yeah," Danny looked puzzled. "The man executed by ISIS."

"Correct, you know the story."

"Yeah, hard not to, it was plastered all over the *Times*."

Danny had read the tragic story of the zealous seventeen-year-old Islamist from Coventry who had gone to fight for ISIS in Syria. The article had reported his demise. He had been interrogated and executed as a spy just before the fall of Raqqa.

"Was he actually one of ours?" he asked.

"No," Collette snapped back.

Danny understood immediately. "CIA."

"You know I cannot either confirm or deny that," she said as tacit confirmation.

"But I can tell you that our American colleagues are really pissed off and they are wanting some serious payback from HMG."

"Why?" Danny was intrigued.

"Because, Ismail had been leading them to the personalities that are presently running operations against the US with a multi-billion pound fund solely financed by the British taxpayer. HMRC had failed to report to us that over eight billion of taxpayers' money had been siphoned off by certain Asian businessmen and politicians using multi-identity fraud, tax evasion, VAT fraud, and by money laundering from the drugs trade."

"I know, I read that on the same front page," Danny said in a matter-of-fact type of way. "The cousins still call this town Londonistan behind our backs." He smiled.

"You couldn't really make it up, could you?"

"No." She looked solemn, almost sad. "The money is laundered through the Islamic *Hawala* money transfer system worldwide, and only Cyclone has all the answers.

The man who was killed told his handler that Cyclone is the main stakeholder of a fund in Hamburg worth many millions of British taxpayers' money and that he is the only one entrusted with the operational planning for ISIS operations for the next two years." She paused.

"Following the technical successes that we have enjoyed in the past the *Daesh* have adapted their security procedures. Most information is now passed either strictly on a one-to-one basis or by coded messages on encrypted social media sites.

"If the man in the CCTV footage is Objective Cyclone. He wants to kill Sam for personal reasons. His motivation is purely revenge, it's solely an honour and shame society thing and it only has tacit approval from the ISIS leadership."

"What do you actually want, Collette?"

"First of all, we need to confirm that the POI (Person of Interest) in the garage photo is actually Cyclone. We need DNA that current service directives make it illegal to collect without a court order. We know where traces may be and I want your team to collect them."

Collette turned towards Danny and sighed.

"Here is the real problem, I can't get anything constructive done under the current service guidelines. We have no spare capacity and an operation doesn't even get sanctioned without a sign-off from some faceless bureaucrat in Whitehall and a full risk assessment. Your guys are my only adaptable assets."

Everything suddenly dropped into place and Danny suddenly understood why the Security Services had employed his company. Hedges and Fisher was the final and unofficial firewall that could work in a particularly murky area of government direct action tasks while also guaranteeing the right amount of plausible deniability. The pieces of the jigsaw had finally clicked into place.

"What do you need?" Danny almost whispered.

"I need proof that Cyclone is alive and I need you to get it."

"OK, give me the details and we will see what we can do."

Collette reached into the pocket of her classically cut Chanel jacket and palmed a USB stick onto the table.

"Everything you need is on this, I will send you the activation code once you have confirmed you can carry out the task."

"Roger that," the old cold war warrior said wearily as he picked up the device.

"When?"

"As a matter of urgency." The MI6 woman turned and looked again at the target photograph. "We need to know whether this fucker is alive and kicking, and if he is, we need to snatch him."

"OK, I will let Sam know and she will deliver a plan."

Danny needed to see Sam and let her know what she needed to know. He felt bad that he wouldn't be able to tell her everything straight away. She would eventually understand, he hoped!

Danny tapped in Sam's number as the doors of Thames House closed behind him.

Sam answered.

"Danny, how did it go?"

"Interesting," he answered. Danny stopped under the Britannia figure and casually checked the space around him before he asked the question.

"What do you know about collecting forensics including DNA for analysis?"

"Lots," she said. "I've watched CSI LA on Netflix and I'll google the rest."

"OK," Danny smiled. "I have an urgent job for you to plan."

"Roger that," said Sam.

# Chapter Twenty-Three

*Whitechapel 0100 hours*

The team was once again operating in this particular part of London. It was a strange place to work and it made Sam uneasy, especially at night when its old red walls seemed to reflect its blood-spattered history. This was where in Victorian times the mad serial killer Jack the Ripper had stalked and slaughtered women and in the swinging sixties where the notorious home-grown gangsters the Kray brothers had exceeded his body count. Source 3010's lock-up was situated on the extreme edge of the cultural interface between the hip, trendy and multicultural Hoxton and, as it was known locally, the 'Islamic Emirate of Whitechapel', a seriously monocultural part of the city.

Hoxton and its relaxed, enlightened, open-minded 'hipster' movement abutted and affronted the frostiness of an unofficially sharia-controlled neighborhood. Most of Hoxton's pubs had been converted into coffee shops, art galleries and wine bars catering for arty types and students while some of Whitechapel had been reinvented as mosques and madrassas. The interface had therefore produced two sets of bizarrely bearded men, in strange garb, competing for space both physically and ideologically.

The source, Agent 3010, had reported where the car was parked and it had returned with an extra 1000 miles on the clock. The fat Mullah's friend had gifted the expensive Mercedes a full ashtray and a dent in the offside wing. Imran's taxi cars were always in the same place when not working. Car parking in Whitechapel was at a premium and the drivers knew that leaving an expensive motor on the street was just tempting fate. The target car was one of two that were waiting to be cleaned, valeted, and refueled. The garage was a commercial premises tucked under an old red brick Victorian railway arch at the end of his street.

He was annoyed as he dropped the Mercedes key fob into his jacket pocket. He already disliked the mysterious driver who'd misused one of his cars. It had already cost him four days' taxi income and added to that, it was dirty, dented and generally in a shit state. Imran was seething as he sent a text to Ahmad on Telegram. It just said *Now*, and he immediately received a thumbs-up emoji. His handler needed the keys for this car, and since he was the guy that had supplied the funding for it, he knew not to ask too many questions. He had been on the other end of his handler's 'Need to Know' lecture before.

Sam and Taff were parked facing away from the target location that they called X-ray One. Both sat in a camera surveillance van borrowed from A Branch sporting a BT logo emblazoned on the side. She wore her burglary gear; dark jacket, jeans, and black CrossFit trainers. Her bright blonde hair was hidden by a black silk hijab. The burly bulk of Taff occupied the driver's side, and Jimmy crouched in the back. Sam studied the monitor mounted in the centre of the dashboard. She moved the small joystick towards an adjacent railway arch opposite the start point. The OP van rear doors were facing the target as both operators studied the small screen linked to the hi-resolution night-vision camera. She could clearly see Scotty in a spectral white glow and 'eyes-on' X-ray One lurking in the shadows to give the trigger.

Scotty looked towards where a single street lamp illuminated the doorway of the workshop reflecting a slight shimmer of light across the rain-sodden pavement. It was the only splash of colour on an otherwise soulless dark night in Whitechapel.

161

He watched as Imran pretended to lock the outer door of the garage. The ex-SBS man casually leaned against the nineteenth-century red brick wall in the deeper shadow cast by another Victorian railway arch. He was dressed in his Ops kit for that area. Both hands were tucked into a simple dark blue zipper jacket, the send button of his radio in his left hand with a heavy brass knuckleduster reassuringly weighty in his right. The coat was reversible and ideal for surveillance serials, and the look was accessorised with slightly worn training shoes and dark jeans. It captured the non-aligned, nondescript look that you needed in this part of London.

Scotty depressed the radio button three times as Imran turned to walk towards his home.

Ahmad turned the corner thirty seconds later and approached his agent on the same side of the road. Ahmad made sure he was on the inside of the pavement as Imran brushed past him while his agent expertly palmed the key fob of the Mercedes from his right hand into his. It was a perfect brush contact drill from the old-school tradecraft playbook; no eye contact, no conversation, and the MI5 man had the car keys. As he turned the corner, he spotted a rear view of the van where Sam waited with Jimmy and Taff. Jimmy wound down the window only seconds before Ahmad lobbed the Mercedes keys into the driver's side of the van. They landed directly in Sam's right hand on the passenger side more by chance than design. She looked towards Jimmy, nodded and opened the door while testing her coms with three distinct bursts of static over the encrypted radio. Pat Patterson, the ex-Para and blade, observed the operation from the end of the street and returned the three bursts. The Op was on.

"All Clear," Pat whispered into his coms.

"All Clear at Red One," Scotty confirmed. The street was still deathly silent.

"Foxtrot to X-ray One," Sam said as Jimmy opened the rear door of the van and removed a bag of Ops kit. Both walked around the corner towards the target, Sam with her eyes focused downward, slightly behind Jimmy, as was the custom in this part of London. People in enclosed communities notice the slightest thing out of place, so the bulky form of Taff hung back to provide rear cover. Scotty was providing the close protection and Sam heard the reassuring sounds of three beeps from his coms, which meant 'I'm eyes-on and covering your approach'. Scotty knew the 'actions on' for any hostile interference from a local 'sharia patrol'. If they were stopped and questioned, and if they couldn't explain themselves sufficiently, Scotty would use his CS spray and then the knuckleduster and he and Taff would just beat the locals up, very severely.

This old part of London was quiet after dark; it was an enforced 'enjoyment-free zone'. The only other noise was the distant sound of young people in nearby Hoxton enjoying some music. This little bit of Londonistan they now inhabited had a totally different vibe and very little happened here after the last call to prayer. The dreary red brick walls seemed to amplify its joylessness, a little bit of Wahhabi Islam sealed inside a city where liberalism was being soundlessly strangled.

Jimmy passed the entrance to the lock-up and observed to the front as Sam tried the door. It was open of course, as planned, and she tapped Jimmy's shoulder as she moved inside. Jimmy followed through the door and locked the door behind him. They stood silently by the entrance as they waited for nature's night vision to kick in. The garage smelled of damp brick, oil, and eau de petrol. Both operators listened intently trying to tune themselves into the moment, using the earliest sensors that humans possess. The only thing that broke the silence was the gentle ticking of a wall clock. Sam scanned the area as her eyes decoded the dark; the inky blackness faded as the dark outline of two parked cars became apparent.

Jimmy took the NVGs from the Ops bag and handed her a set. There was a slight buzz as she hit the toggle switch on the NVGs and the garage was instantly outlined in a stark spectral white as she scanned the room. The inside of the brick-built arch

163

had seen happier days. It looked like it had been a thriving garage once, the sort that had once been the lifeblood of London's economy before sky-high commercial rates and the change of demographics. The NVGs' white glare suddenly jumped out old signs from a bygone era that lined the red brick walls. A slightly rusted large white Michelin man, with a smiley face, beamed out from the darkness, both spooky-looking and unnerving.

The working part of the garage appeared to have been abandoned in haste. An old 80s BMW, probably a classic, was crammed into the darkest recess of the old brick arch where the engine dangled helplessly over the bonnet on an ancient rusting pulley. The two Mercedes 280s had been parked near the entrance of the lock-up and were easy to access. A cursory scan of the area checked for anything that might impede progress. The worst risk was probably a slip on the stained concrete floor that shimmered with ingrained oily dampness. Sam then took the Merc key fob from her jacket pocket and a high-pitched beep and a flash of interior light confirmed the target. Sam quickly removed the NVGs and handed them to Jimmy who in return handed her the evidence bags and an ultraviolet lamp. She now had all she needed to conduct a DNA search of the vehicle.

A working taxi was a treasure trove of unexpected DNA of all types but what Sam was looking for was DNA solely specific to its last driver. A latex gloved hand opened the car door. The UV light scanned across the light grey leather. The driver's seat headrest yielded the first piece of evidence, a couple of dark hairs that stood out and maybe a trace of hair grease smeared over the surface. A strip of sellotape was quickly used to pick them from the leather and seal them in an evidence bag. The smell of stale cigarette smoke inside the car indicated her best chance of success. The overflowing ashtray had three distinct types of cigarette ends. Sam carefully selected two of each and sealed them into another bag. As Jimmy tapped her on the shoulder to remind her of time constraints she had already collected all the evidence she needed. The DNA samples would be delivered to a private laboratory were they would be processed immediately after the two shadows left as soundlessly as they had arrived.

*The Company Safe House in Essex*

Danny had waited until the DNA sample was confirmed before he decided that he could not leave Sam and the team out of the loop for much longer. He now knew that the man who had used the Mercedes was actually the long dead Objective Cyclone. He now needed tell Sam that this was also the man that wanted to kill her so badly that he was willing to risk both his life and his present mainland Operation to do it personally. He was a twisted personality of a type familiar to DannyMac. After thirty years of exploring human nature's darker side he fully understood the blackness that could corrupt and infect the human soul. He had seen things that nobody should ever see and had witnessed first-hand the savagery that a twisted ideology could sanction. He now consciously tried not to think about it too much for a very good reason. The words of the German philosopher Fredrich Nietzsche's sprang to mind.

*He who fights with monsters should be careful lest he thereby become a monster. And if you gaze long into an abyss, the abyss will also gaze into thee.*

Maybe the old Danny Mac, the FRU guy, and DHU Colonel would have done things differently. His service to his Queen and country had demanded compromises as he attempted to keep Britain safe. He had always tried to make the right decisions, but he knew in his heart of hearts that he had made some bad ones. He had done some very dark things for his country and had also persuaded others to do the same. He knew though that he was right to give Samantha the final choice before it was too late. The only problem with this disclosure was that MI6 and the 'cousins' had given him a time-related caveat. He couldn't let the team know until the Anglo-American operation had started rolling. It was one of the most audacious and morally dubious he had ever been involved in and the operational clock was beginning to tick down; as each hour passed elements of it phased in. It was dark and devious and probably illegal under international law, but he knew that it was the only way to deal with Cyclone and it could save thousands of lives. He checked his watch; he needed to talk to Sam after 14.30. He picked up the mobile and flashed up Sam's Ops number. Sam answered on the fourth ring.

"Hey, DannyMac, how did that work out?"

"Well, top notch." Danny paused as if thinking what to say. "He's definitely the guy we are after, the results are positive, good job."

"What's next and when is the team going to be included in what's going on?" Sam exchanged glances with Taff who was listening intently.

"When can you get to Dominic's? I'm there now."

"One hour?" Sam recalculated the distance. "Maybe one and half if the M25 is busy."

"Can you bring the team?"

"Why?" A perplexed look fleeted across her face.

"Because it's something time sensitive that involves all of you," Danny said. "And 14.30 is the earliest time I can discuss it with you."

An even more perplexed Samantha replied.

"OK, see you soon."

Danny flashed a glance at the Edwardian carriage clock that adorned the mantelpiece. It was 1300 hrs.

He caught a look at his face in the mirror behind the clock. The strain of thirty years trying to do the right thing had changed him both physically and spiritually. The young Intelligence Corps Sergeant who had played cat and mouse games with the KGB and the slightly older officer who had penetrated the upper echelons of the Provisional IRA in Belfast had grown old. Some of the horrors of the past flooded his memory for a horrific instant. The broken children killed in a Taliban suicide bomb in Kabul, the carnage of the Sunni and Shia civil war in Baghdad, a hundred headless bodies. Suddenly, he knew it, the truth.

*I've stared into the abyss for far too long.*

166

# Chapter Twenty-Four

## *The M25*

The Volvo V70 indicated right and flashed its emergency lights to get a break in the dense traffic on the London Orbital. It nosed out letting the ambulance creep behind it into the heavy traffic; it was a typical day on the M25.

"Hey, mate, fuck all changes," said Bill the police driver. "The great British public are being as cooperative as ever, we could be an ice cream van as far as they are concerned"

Davey, the co-driver made a quick assessment, the traffic was literally bumper-to-bumper and inching its way forward at a snail's pace and the flashing lights and the occasional blast of the sirens of the seemed to make no impact at all.

"It's gridlock mate, we need to use the hard shoulder or this guy in the back will die of old age" But it was the drivers call, as he was the nominated vehicle commander that day.

"What do you think?"

"Yeah, roger that," said the driver "Call it in Pal"

Davey picked up the handset.

"Hello, Control, this is Blue Tango Zero, permission to use the hard shoulder to make progress." He looked towards his colleague and smiled. "We have made a full risk assessment." And he awaited the reply. "What a load of old bollocks and PC shite," he said grimacing. He had been a police officer for ten years, and the libtard-speak still grated his inner being.

"Yeah, I know, but you get strung up if you don't play the game, mate, you know the head shed."

"They are..." he said.

"WANKERS," they both said in unison as if rehearsed. After what seemed an eternity, the answer came back.

"Hello, Blue Tango Zero, this is Control, you have permission to make progress."

"Roger that," Davey answered. "Right, bruv, let's go." The Volvo revved hard and screeched away with the ambulance in its wake.

At that exact time, Rahim's eyes opened slowly. It took him a second to realise where he was. He was physically drained, first by the boat crossing and then by his lack of sleep at the farmhouse. He had fallen into a deep, dreamless slumber as soon as the transit van's doors had rattled shut. The back of his head now ached. It had been resting on the pistol grip of the AK that was stowed away in the large reinforced nylon grip on which he had slept and for once he had been spared the flashbacks of Syria, jihad, and death, but as his eyes opened his living nightmare flooded back. He smelt the fetid closeness of unwashed others and heard the snoring of his friends. He recognised again, the dark outlines of the equipment bags they had dragged up the beach and he knew that he was back in the situation in which he had placed himself.

All four of the returning jihadists were now lying in the darkness on cheap foam rubber between the various bags of weapons and equipment. The transit van was hardly moving. It would rev slightly, move forward, and then stop. For Rahim, who had been born in Whitechapel and had once had a gentler life working for a mobile phone shop in Brick Lane, local knowledge had given him both the possible time of day and location. He thought he might be on the M25.

*The M25, the largest car park in Europe, even after the rush hour.*

He glanced at his watch, the luminous green hands said two and another dark thought flashed across his mind as he studied the ticking second hand sweeping around the face.

*That's the seconds of my life ticking away.*

He could not feel any more downhearted than he did and then he realised things could get worse. He felt the damp groping hand of his team leader wandering along his thigh towards his genitals. The hand belonged to the one who was charged with keeping him spiritually strong and focused on jihad and its promised place in *Jannah* (heaven). He was again reminded of his other burden, his shame and his other nightmare.

"How are you, sweet *Habibti?*" he whispered. He was close, with foul breath that made the young man gag. He fought hard not to be sick. And then there seemed a brief moment of silence before they all heard it. It was quiet at first but became louder and louder the closer they got; it was the unmistakable wailing sound of emergency sirens.

Then there was a frantic, blind panic in the darkness.

"COPS," the driver shouted.

"It's the SAS!" another voice said.

"Get the weapons!" said Sharka, as the four jihadists clawed frantically at the Ops bags. As AKs were snatched from the bags they seemed to snag on anything and everything. There was a yelp as the hard steel barrel of one man's rifle collided with the soft fleshy scalp of another's.

FUCK!

Rahim was starting to pull at his bag to free the suicide vest, as the police sirens got louder.

"RAHIM, get the vest!" shouted Sharka. Rahim felt strangely calm, almost disembodied, as he found himself obeying Sharka's orders.

"I've got it," he said calmly, as he pulled it onto his lap from its reinforced nylon resting place, and almost without thinking slipped it on and quickly removed the thin wire safety device, as trained. He was now wearing ten kilos of commercial plastic explosive, it was armed, and he was holding the firing mechanism in his right hand.

ISIS in Europe had recently changed the system from a press button one to a release switch. It made it harder for you to change your mind. The bomber now had to keep constant downward pressure on the device with his thumb. Rahim held the spring-loaded plunger down and waited for his death. The sirens became louder until they were almost ear-splitting and then stopped. It was suddenly quiet and virtually silent apart from Sharka's mumbled prayers. The praying stopped, as he placed his hand around the pistol grip of the AK and whispered nervously.

"They're here."

They held their breath in their darkened refuge, the flashing emergency lights reflected on the shiny dark blue interior of the transit as they waited in an almost ghostly silence.

The two policemen assessed the situation and could immediately see why their rapid access up the M25 had been stopped. An ageing Ford Mondeo blocked the hard shoulder with bilious clouds of smoke drifting up from its bonnet as a distraught-looking Asian family of four peered over the motorway crash barrier at their family transport. The driver waved to the family behind the crash barrier as the co-driver undid his seatbelt and leaned forward to release the passenger door.

"Hang on, mate; something's not right here."

Davey had two tours of Helmand in the Rifles under his belt and felt that strange sense of apprehension again. He didn't know why but he thought that there was danger nearby.

"Let's see what's happening."

He casually glanced over his shoulder at the transit van on his right. It was dark blue and battered-looking.

"That van doesn't look right." Bill followed his gaze.

"You might be overcomplicating things here, buddy, it's just a breakdown." There was no response; the driver was thinking.

""Wait out,"" said the ex-Rifleman using army radio procedure in his everyday conversation.

The driver of the transit was a young, fattish guy of Middle Eastern appearance, with a straggly-looking beard. And as he looked, the guy looked away.

*He's avoided eye contact, he's crapping himself, and he's terrified; something's wrong with him, but maybe that's more to do with the police sirens than anything else?*

He scanned the blue transit van.

*The tyres and wheel arches are covered with sand; maybe been to a beach? The suspension is under stress and it's running heavy. I'm pretty sure it's up to no good. The driver looks shifty. Maybe the van is heavy with drugs, cigarettes, dodgy gear, or even people-smuggling? That guy in front looks nervous, almost too scared to look across, but here we are in vehicles with flashing blue lights; not that unusual if he's feeling a bit nervous,* he reasoned.

"They are dodgy as fuck, mate. Do you want to pull them?" he suggested to his colleague.

"No, mate. We need to get this ambulance moving. Maybe we'll call it in."

"Yeah, sounds like the right call, too much paperwork if it is people-smugglers anyway."

"Yep, you got it, mate," he sighed. "Doesn't pay to be involved in a contentious crime like that any more. Their lawyers will rip you up for arse paper."

Then, a distinctive sound from the past.

KAT-CHING

Was that the sound of an AK47 being cocked or just bad memories?

*No, it's your imagination, mate.*

"Did you hear that Bill?"

"What?" The driver was now looking towards the slightly smoky Ford Mondeo.

"That sounded like a weapon being made ready."

"Fuck me, mate, not another war story. I'm going to get you checked out for PTSD, mate," he laughed. "Let's get past this old scrapper and get moving."

"Yeah, sorry, buddy, probably nothing." Davey drew a line under the conversation. He was embarrassed;

*I probably have got PTSD because I can't sleep for shit!*

But the driver of the transit had also heard the sound of the AK cocking, very loudly, from behind his head and it had scared him, and his face betrayed his abject fear. Sharka whispered quick instruction to the two brothers nearest the back doors to check their weapons. He looked in the rear-view mirror. Tadge had placed his left hand on the internal handle and was ready to open it.

Rahim had closed his eyes and felt strangely calm, almost trance-like.

*So this is it. Is this how it ends, ten miles from home?*

His right thumb was still on the firing device for the vest.

"If they leave the vehicle, Rahim runs out with the vest, waits until we get clear and takes them out," said Sharka. "We will try to continue the mission." A sharp collective intake of breath and surprised expressions reflected the change of plan. Sharka was willing to sacrifice Rahim within a heartbeat.

*Surely they should all go to Jannah together if God willed that they should die?*

The driver looked across nervously. The brothers in the back prayed in hushed tones that became more intense and fervent with each repetition of the prayer.

*Allahu akbar-Allah akbar-Allahu akbar (God is great)*

Just at that moment, the police car in front of the ambulance started to move. It pushed out into the nearside traffic, creating a gap, and aggressively nosed out and created a passage for the ambulance and then they were past the still smoking Mondeo and away.

"*HUMDULLALAH!*" The driver turned in his seat.

"It's OK, it's an ambulance," he said in a relieved voice to the guys in the back. The passengers seemed to exhale in relief as Sharka whispered collectively.

"Quiet, no noise. What can you see?" he said to the guy in the front.

"It was a police escort for a medical move," the driver said. "But they are gone now."

"OK, fix the vest," Sharka said, in a panicky voice.

Rahim felt composed. He calmly searched for the wire strand that he had dropped onto the van's floor. His thumb was beginning to ache with the pressure of the plunger and he couldn't locate it.

"Can't find the safety pin," he said.

"Fucking find it," whispered Sharka, his voice quivering with panic.

"I need some light," Rahim said in an icy-calm voice quietly relishing his tormentor's discomfort. One of the brothers struck a match. Sharka also shone his torch but nearly dropped it as he removed the red filter. Eventually, after what seemed an age, he flashed the ex-British Army right-angled torch into the gloom of clutter and bodies in the back of the old transit. The torchlight shimmered with the involuntary shaking of his hand. Rahim finally spotted the shiny piece of wire; he picked it up carefully and rethreaded it into the firing mechanism and released his right thumb. The vest was safe again.

Sharka muttered, "*HUMDULLALAH.*" His facial expression switched from full-on terror to relief in a second, his hands were still shaking uncontrollably.

At that moment, Rahim knew he had broken the spell that Sharka had held over him. He had proved himself to the team, he had shown no doubt, he was willing to die, but in complying, in giving up to it, by accepting it, he had also realised the total futility of that decision. Sharka and his friends had been willing to sacrifice him in a heartbeat. He had also witnessed how the older man had panicked. When the bravado was gone he was just an empty shell and the same as everyone else, an ordinary man grasping for life, trying to hold on to it. It suddenly became crystal clear. He knew now that he held his fate in his own hands.

Rahim closed his eyes. He mentally pictured the horror he had endured. He shuddered when he thought of the abuse he had suffered at the hands of the older man. He made two quick decisions.

*Firstly, I will steal one of the mobiles and phone Imran.*
*Secondly, I need revenge; I need to feel like a man again.*
*I need to kill Sharka.*

# Chapter Twenty-Five

Sam was on the M25 at the same time but driving in the opposite direction. Taff sat next to her and the team occupied the rest of the Ops van. She tapped the wheel rhythmically in time to some reggae song from the seventies called 'More Questions Than Answers' which is exactly how she felt as she drove towards the safe house. She had racked her brains and tried to work out exactly where everything fitted in. She knew that Danny was holding something substantial back and she had also guessed that 'the something' was maybe to do with her. She also knew that what was happening was also 'Need to Know' for a reason.

Maybe she just didn't need to know until now?

Her years in the Intelligence Corps, however, had honed her analytical skills and taught her to investigate and question everything. In the hazy half-light of intelligence collection the truth was often found by groping away in the shadows.

Almost nothing was exactly as it seemed and things got particularly hazy when the CIA and Six were involved!

Her experiences working with 'the cousins' had been both good and bad, but the higher up the agencies' food chain you went the harder the going got. Operators at the tactical level worked well together although, as a Huminter, the Americans over-reliance on technical methods sometimes totally confused her. But maybe that was a direct result of the debacle of the

Khost job, where their over-reliance on a single source that turned out to be working for the Taliban had led to the death of seven Americans in a suicide-bomb attack. Whatever the reasons, it was always difficult working on a joint operation with the American friends. They still had a hangover of mistrust from that awful time when Kim Philby and the rest of the Cambridge Four had spread their virus of betrayal throughout MI6's 'Old Boy Network' during the cold war. Things had never quite been the same since that.

Things were also worrying her on the domestic front. She was still not sleeping and the bad times from Iraq and Afghanistan were back more vigorously now especially after she had beaten up the two muggers. She knew she had overreacted and she also knew that she had almost wanted it to happen. She had actually enjoyed it. She had felt that familiar emotion of coldly focused battlefield rage and suspected that she was developing an almost unhealthy lust for violence. She actually enjoyed the buzz of it.

Maybe she was losing it? She always felt that she was being watched; maybe this was the start of it, when a healthy respect for risk management was slowly turning into paranoia.

Deep down the emotional scars of combat and the death of friends clawed away at her daily and made her feel like she didn't really deserve any happiness. She was jolted from her thoughts as the music stopped and was interrupted by the voice of the newsreader from Capital Radio.

"A government injunction to ban an ISLAM4UK march planned for the weekend has been refused by the High Court. Activists and civil rights campaigners have called the decision 'a victory for free speech'. The new Prime Minister had stated that he was, 'appalled by the outcome'."

"Only in the fucking UK," Taff muttered under his breath.

Sam checked the rear-view mirror, switched off the satnav and prepared to do a counter-surveillance loop before arriving at the house. She made a mental note of the cars behind her and hooked right at the roundabout. She would be at Dominic's in ten minutes.

The clock ticked behind Danny's head as Sam and Taff sat together on the leather Chesterfield sofa and the remainder of the team draped themselves over the remaining furniture. Danny stood in front of the fireplace in his country squire pose, the four fingers of his left hand in the pocket of his expensive tweed sports jacket. He wore his usual Breitling spear ocean automatic watch that the unit had commissioned. He almost ceremoniously lifted his hand and in a very military manner drew it chest-height and pulled up his cuff to look at the watch. It said 14.30.

"Firstly, I must apologise to all of you," he said as his left hand returned to his pocket.

"What I am about to brief you on couldn't be disclosed until this precise time for operational reasons." Danny looked towards Sam for eye contact.

"Samantha, I have to inform you, through my duty of care both as an employer and as a friend, that you have a death threat against you." Sam looked across at Taff.

"Nothing unusual about that," she said calmly.

The remainder of the team shrugged in agreement.

"People have been trying to kill us for a long time."

"Yes," said Danny. "But what I must divulge to you is a very specific threat that's already in play." He rocked slightly on the thick carpet as his hands moved to behind his back.

"I couldn't tell you everything until now," he rocked on his heels again, "and for that I apologise.

The threat is credible and the terrorist plot already in progress as are the operations for countering that specific threat." Danny glanced again at the clock.

"Governmental approval for this operation was received at 14.30 and consequently as of last light this evening, Samantha and Taff's cottage in Scotland will become an 'Out of Bounds' box for a Special Forces operation."

The team exchanged surprised looks and shifted uneasily in their seats. Samantha felt across and placed her hand on Taff's. He returned her gaze as she spoke.

"Are we going to be involved?" she asked.

"Of course," Danny nodded. "But I need all the team's assent before I can explain your possible role."

"I'm in." Jimmy was the first to speak.

"Yeah," said Pat Patterson. "Nothing else on for tomorrow."

Scotty smiled. "Me neither, I'm in."

Sam felt a squeeze on her hand from Taff's big paw.

"I'm in," he said.

Sam announced the verdict.

"Yes, we are all good to go."

"Excellent," Danny smiled. "I thought you all might be. Please follow me into the library for detailed orders." He looked again at the clock. "We have one hour for orders and you have two hours before you all fly from RAF Northolt," the ex-DHU Colonel said as he led the way.

# Chapter Twenty-Six

*The Highlands*

It was nearing the end of a long, hot summer in Scotland and the nights were cooler. Major Howie Watson moved soundlessly through the Highland mist over a tactically challenging mixture of bracken and heather. *No ambient light and blacker than a witch's tit.* It was a perfect night for covert work with only the occasional sliver of a crescent moon to guide his progress. He crawled the last twenty metres over the pleasantly smelling wild heather and got his first view of the objective. He looked through the thermal-imaging binoculars that had been stowed under his combat smock. The moisture in the atmosphere had beaded the optics. He wiped the lenses with the fingertips of his right black Nomex glove and raised them to his eyes again.

The destination was defined by a green spectral glow. He was about 300 yards away on the slightly higher ground looking down onto the target house. He carefully scanned the row of small dwellings. He was looking at the rear aspect of six single storey, neat, tidy, white-painted croft cottages. A long, low wall ran along the length of the back gardens.

*About four-foot high, as in orders.*

He clicked on the thermal imager and it gave a slight buzz as it started to register heat sources.

The target house was cold and seemed empty. The only source of heat was a slight orange glimmer from what looked like the gas boiler.

The occupant's vehicle, a mud-spattered white BMW X5, was still warm with the engine glowing with a deep burnt orange. It was parked in the usual place; hugging the cottage, nose out into the lane. It had been collected from where the owners had left it in London.

*Glad they dropped it off in time, everything has to look normal.*

He scanned the area for movement. All the houses apart from the end one registered cold.

*Holiday homes, maybe?*

The only inhabited cottage was the end one. The optics showed the small end cottage aglow with varying levels of warm orange light. In the front of the house, the silhouettes of two adults shimmered in a warmer green. They were lying close.

*Looks like they are in bed.*

The thermal imager picked up a slightly darker line of burnt orange indicating an increase in heat source between the two shapes; maybe the heat generated by embracing lovers?

He knew from the target pack that the end house would be occupied.

*That's the doctor's basha, with his wife, I suppose?*

There were also two smaller shapes in the next room at the back of the cottage.

*The doc's kids in bed,* he guessed.

*All good, we're good to go.*

He replaced the thermal imager back around his neck under his camouflaged windproof. He glanced over his right shoulder at Gaynor and gently tapped her shoulder. She looked towards him. As he made the hand signal for FRV (Final Rendezvous Point), her big eyes, framed by the circles of the black balaclava, registered her understanding. Gaynor tapped the two other guys and passed on the information. They had both been in the kneeling position with their weapons protecting the patrol's rear. The team leader snapped down his NVGs (Night Vision Goggles), adjusted them, placed his weapon firmly in his shoulder and led the covert entry team on the last leg to the target house. They stopped with their backs resting tight against the wall facing the rough ground they had just traversed and waited, listening for movement in the soft drizzle. The team leader checked his watch.

*Stacks of time.*

He tapped Gaynor's shoulder again and gestured towards the back door of the cottage. Gaynor gave the thumbs-up and slithered over the low wall and regained her balance soundlessly on the other side. She knelt on one knee, waited, and listened. The only sound was the gentle tinkling from a small highland spring that served as a natural water feature. The back door was only five metres away and she had a covered approach. She waited, listened again and then adjusted the weapon onto her back, barrel pointing downwards. She pulled the NVGs onto her face with a slight click and waited again until her eyes adjusted. She moved towards the back door with the set of lock picks already selected. She had done this many times in training.

As the instructors at Hereford had said,

'Covert entry is a unique cross between advanced infantry skills and burglary.' And she was a natural.

She knew what type of lock it was from the target pack. It was a Chubb 4L67 deadlock with a ten-disk cylinder.

*It would take her maybe ten seconds.*

She inserted the two lock picks and heard and felt the telltale clicks of the lock opening in five.

"I'm in," she whispered into her chest mike.

Gaynor eased the back door open looking for alarm contacts.

*There are three.*

She moved to the alarm box, waved a small black plastic box over it and neutralised the alarm.

Gaynor quickly scanned the room with her NVGs. She crouched on the floor, listening intently.

*Just the ticking of an electrical wall clock from the kitchen.*

She studied her new surroundings through the green tinge of the goggles.

*A comfortable front room, very upmarket and modern-looking for a cottage, but it was beautifully decorated and expensively furnished, with a white leather L-shaped sofa on one side, and a flat-screen TV mounted on the other, low ceilings, lots of white. The small kitchen was open-plan and at the back of the house. There was a bleached white wood, fitted bookshelf against the wall, neatly lined with books. It was mainly military stuff, with some crime, fiction, and classic novels. In one alcove there was a group of family photos. A little blonde toddler cradled in a soldier's arms. A family picnic on a sunny beach; looks like Cyprus?* Gaynor's eyes lingered on one in particular. Gaynor loved weddings. She recognised the bride.

*So that's the famous Sam Holloway,* she thought.

*At least we are in the right place.*

She scanned again; *all good!*

She depressed the radio send button twice and heard the noise in her earpiece. The team leader replied with a double tap of the same squelch on the net and the rest of the four-person patrol flowed through the back door, weapons up, to clear the house.

Then whispers on the coms.

"Left clear."

Different voice.

"Right clear."

Another voice.

And then...

"All clear, stand down," from the team leader.

As the team leader moved towards the main wall-mounted light switch, a wooden tripod-type lampshade suddenly flooded light into the small living room.

"They had the lights on a timer. That wasn't in orders, or the target pack," he whispered, removing his NVGs and stowing them away.

"Yeah," said Gaynor. "That could have been embarrassing."

"Yeah, roger that," he said looking across and removing his face protection.

Gaynor was the newest member of the team. Howie Watson had already worked with the other guys in Iraq, Afghanistan and in London. Gaynor was fresh out of the box, a Special Reconnaissance Regiment newbie, but she fitted in, she was a real professional, and he liked working with her. She would do OK.

# Chapter Twenty-Seven

*Inside the Luton Safe House, Same Time*

There was a buzz of excitement throughout the house. Sharka had announced that they were going to get operational orders that night. Everybody now was focused on what they needed to do to get things ready. Tadge had stripped down his AK and was cleaning it at the kitchen table. The rifle had a very short, stubby barrel with a folding plastic butt and was designed for concealment. Sharka was checking the communications equipment; four small Motorola radios, and the four little beat-the-boss super-small mobile phones on the table in front of him. Rahim was loading a magazine for the AKs while occasionally staring at Sharka with a slight smile and a steely glint in his eyes that betrayed his inner anger.

He observed his abuser with a weird detachment. He could see things clearly now. He realised that throughout his short life, he had always been used in some way or another, especially now on the verge of his death, and just a day before his nineteenth birthday. He now realised that modern society was divided into two distinct groups, the users, and the used, the predators and the prey, and up till now he had always been part of the latter group. He was actually angry at the system for letting people like him fall through the ever-expanding cracks in British society.

What chance had he ever had?

He had never felt included. He was born entombed in a Salafist family in Whitechapel and therefore placed by society on a conveyer belt to failure. It started with a mosque-run childcare arrangement and finished in a London-based and government-funded 'faith school', which was 'London-politico-speak' for an extremist religious madrassa. He had completed school well versed on Koranic scripture, intelligent, but semi-literate, and was therefore left rudderless in a modern liberal democratic society for which he hadn't been adequately prepared. His father didn't even let him watch television at home, because it was un-Islamic. He had been beaten continuously, at the mosque, and at home, and consistently bullied throughout his childhood. The punishment was particularly severe when he couldn't memorise some part of the Koran by rote memory. His father always reminded him that he had been able to recite it, word perfect, in Arabic, at the age of ten, *but he still couldn't speak English or speak Arabic properly either.*

The social services had been notably absent from his life, the bruises and broken bones accepted because of cultural sensitivities. He remembered that his parents were quietly proud when he had gone jihad because it had brought them special status in that particularly cloistered ultra Islamist community. He had been brought up, preached at, and educated on a diet of hate. It was kill the Jews, kill the *Kuffar* and the glorious jihad, but they didn't know what killing was really all about. Rahim did, and he knew that when you killed a man, a little bit of you died as well, and it was far from glorious.

He had a plan now and he actually wanted to die. Life for him had been thoroughly miserable. He had been living in a black hole of grief since he had killed the young man in Syria. He knew that when the time came, he would push the button without a second thought, but he would take back control by doing it at a time and in a place of his own choosing.

He looked at the equipment laid out on the threadbare, faded green carpet in the main living room. The pride of place went to his suicide bomb and his exit strategy. It was made of thick black nylon and filled with Semtex and shrapnel, and it lay with two Czech Skorpion machine pistols and two AK12 assault rifles. Alongside the vest were eight Russian hand grenades. The four large silver kitchen knives glittered evilly in the light of the single high-powered LED light bulb that hung from the ceiling. Beside them lay the props to access the so-far unconfirmed target. Rahim placed the magazine he had filled with the others next to the AKs.

He then stood, arms folded, studying the props for the mission while he tried to work out where their lives would end. There were some Dayglo council donkey jackets, two road-sweeping brushes, and a crumpled pile of what could be a lady's black silk abaya and niqab. A smart black, man's raincoat overcoat hung off a kitchen chair with a folded flat tweed cap protruding from its right-hand pocket. A black furled umbrella lay propped against it.

His eyes widened as a thought registered.

*It's Downing Street.*

# Chapter Twenty-Eight

*Driving Towards Parliament Square*

The old black Zafira people carrier was in heavy traffic as the rain started to fall. The worn windscreen wipers screeched annoyingly and added to Rahim's discomfort. It was hot in the car, and the thick, explosive-filled vest made him sweat profusely. Sharka had given him some Captagan, saying that it would make his decision to die easier, but it hadn't worked yet. It had just crammed his racing mind with thousands of 'what ifs' and 'if onlys' and made his heart seem like it was going to beat itself out of his chest. His dark eyes framed by the niqab were large, dilated and watering. His unseen tears moistened the silken fabric. Rahim was scared and nineteen tomorrow, but he knew that birthday would never come. The end of his earthly misery was fast approaching. The abuse would be over. The time around him seemed to slow and with his final acceptance came clarity. *Maybe Sharka was right about the pills; they did make it easier.*

He had noticed that as soon as he had put on the black silk abaya, the sort that only a very rich Arab would give to his wife, he almost seemed to have become invisible. Sharka and the driver had stopped talking to him as if he had ceased to exist and maybe he had? It was as if he had become a nonentity when he had dressed for the attack. The crowd was beginning to thin, protesters with crudely drawn signs and the odd unarmed policeman walked in front of the car as it nosed into Parliament

Square. It was at this precise point that everything he had been thinking about became clear.

Death was his only option. He knew what he must do!

The jihadists unloaded their equipment under the blind glare of Winston Churchill's statue on Parliament Square. The square was busy as the attack was arranged to coincide with a demonstration organised by Islam4UK. The police, as usual, had been told not to interfere with the demo. Many of the protesters displayed banners glorifying the feats of the 'Glorious Nine' 9/11 terrorists to celebrate the anniversary of the attack.

The passenger door of the Vauxhall Zafira opened, and a smartly dressed man in a black rain mac and wearing a flat peaked cap climbed out and moved around the car. He extended his hand to help his heavily pregnant wife climb out. She was dressed in the all-encompassing black abaya as she struggled to negotiate the step down onto the pavement from the rear passenger door. He then opened the rear door and lifted a collapsible child's pram from the back and placed it on the ground.

He struggled with the mechanism and pressed down with his right foot to adjust it for use. His enshrouded wife then moved back to the inside of the car and lifted a small bundle and laid it in the pram.

The man smiled and whispered to his wife, "Yah, *Habibti*, we've nearly made it. We will enter *Jannah* together, and *ishtishhad* (Martyrdom) is our path."

The other person said nothing; the black covered Rahim was thinking and planning. He knew he would die that day and accepted it but it would be on his terms.

*Parliament Square*

If there was one thing that Ahmad, the ex-soldier, British patriot, and MI5 handler never thought he would be asked to do as part of his job, he was doing it now.

He was holding a placard demanding:

# SHARIA LAW FOR UK

And he was shouting in unison with a crowd of black-garbed Islamist fanatics in the city that had sheltered his family when they fled Iraq. The A4 surveillance team that the covert camera had triggered on Luton's Bury Park Estate and A4 realised that they didn't have enough Asian operators to operate within this particularly partisan crowd. He had watched the Zafira pull up and observed the terrorists prepare to attack Downing Street. He heard his handler colleague Fatima over the radio net, although he couldn't have identified her. She had also been called in to help as a watcher. She was dressed in a full black abaya, niqab, and accompanying elbow-length black gloves, and was carrying a placard saying *ISLAM4UK* as she moved closer to the targets and transmitted.

Her life partner, Lou, was also dressed in the latest London Islamist fashion chic and with his beard looking almost biblical. He was holding a placard featuring the Twin Towers attack, and the ex-Marine was looking distinctly uncomfortable. Fatima triggered the suspects.

"Gulf Two Zero, Alpha Three Bravo, that's two X-ray One and two towards Red Three, descriptions, no change."

She observed Sharka and the woman pushing the pram attempting to cross the road while weaving through the crowds and towards Downing Street.

"You got them?" she said.

"Yeah, the guy with the black coat and umbrella with the YooBow (UBO-Unidentified Black Object) and pram, I have eyes on," answered the burly member of B Squadron 22 SAS.

"That's a roger," said Fatima.

The blade was wearing a worn-looking waxed Barbour jacket that concealed his Sig Sauer MCX carbine with suppresser suspended on a bungee cord around his shoulder. His right hand was in the pocket of his coat holding a Glock with a short Gemtech 'Aurora' silencer. Then Ahmad heard the call that changed the operation from surveillance serial to armed intervention. B Squadron's boss transmitted.

"Hello, all Stations Alpha, we'll take it from here, we have control."

Once he heard the call Ahmad knew that the operation was now beyond his remit; B Squadron would do their work. His thoughts turned back to his own responsibilities. Agent 3010, codename KEN, was his most pressing priority and he was blown, compromised, and in danger after the information he had given to stop both attacks. The circle of knowledge was just too tight and the ISIS security team would know that his agent was the organisation's weak link. His accurate and timely information had undoubtedly saved countless lives, but now his own life, and the lives of his family were in danger.

*The agent that he had recruited two years before who eventually had become his friend wouldn't be abandoned.*

The SAS had switched channels to its encrypted communications. The senior SAS officer checked the net.

"Hello, Gulf Sierra One, radio check." The SAS Major was talking to the pre-positioned sniper team on the fourth floor of a red-bricked, four storey, grade 2-listed building on Parliament Street that was being refurbished and was temporarily a building site.

"Gulf Sierra One, Lima Charlie (Loud and Clear)," confirmed the sniper.

"Gulf Zero Alpha, you got eyes on?"

"Gulf Sierra One, that's a big roger," whispering into the headset.

The sniper adjusted the scope of the Accuracy International .308 AW covert rifle with a sound suppressor. The wafer-thin graticule of the Schmidt and Bender MK 2 sight moved over the head of the female suicide bomber dressed in black. The soldier rested a finger on the 'Geissele' trigger and the stock of the weapon nestled snugly into a shoulder. The weapon's biped legs pushed against the sandbag that had been placed on the deep windowsill.

"Hello, Zero Alpha, I have," the shooter said with emphasis.

"Roger, wait out," said B Squadron's boss. Intelligence had confirmed that the person pushing the pram was a terrorist with a suicide vest. He was nearly one hundred per cent sure that was the case, but the rules of engagement were still strict. His sniper could only engage when a weapon was visible, or when the bomber had committed to the Downing Street exclusion zone. Alongside the sniper, the number two spotted with a strange type of optic. It was a Canon EOS C200 4K camcorder fitted with the extendible black plastic butt from a C8 rifle. This addition was very much in the sniper's interest. In the military environment of the litigious twenty-first century, the video footage would record that he had done the right thing. It would save the soldier being dragged to court at a later date and accused of murder.

"You got this, Max?" The sniper was crouching over the weapon sitting on a chair intently tracking the target.

"Yeah, I'm tracking," he replied.

"OK, boss, we are good to go," said the expert as the cross-hairs of the sight's graticule continued to track the black-robed primary target.

*Whitechapel, Same Time*

Imran was at peace with himself, and he had prepared himself for the worst. He had dressed in his cleanest white robes and completed his ritual ablutions. He was ready to deal with them. Imran Sarwar, the criminally inclined cynic, the pseudo-Islamist, former murderer and British MI5 agent had prayed to his God, and for the first time, it had felt like it meant something. He had been on his own, in silence, without the comfort of other worshippers around him for support. For the first time, the prayer rituals hadn't been just an automatic reaction, a response for the sake of others. This time the experience was genuinely personal, and he felt liberated.

Imran was at home. He fully understood the consequences of the information he had passed. He knew that the circle of knowledge was so tight that if the London

attack failed, he, and he alone, would be held solely responsible by the ISIS spy chasers. He had never been frightened by anything or anybody, and they didn't scare him in the least. He knew many of them by name and not one of them had ever seen a shot fired in anger. But maybe they would soon. As he had lifted his hands to his face in prayer, he had again remembered his parents' mild Hanafi form of Islam. The Islam they had taught him. It was a teaching that believed that your relationship with God was deeply personal and should not be controlled by governments or others. He had again listened to his long-departed Dad's voice in his head.

*Now, look at your hands, Imran, turned upward in prayer. Look at all the individual creases in your skin, look at your fingertips that are unique only to you. Allah has created you with the ability to think for yourself. You are the only person in charge of your thoughts and acts. You can choose – good or evil, darkness or light – only you can choose your path.*

He had now chosen his path. He had sent his wife and children away to safety. He would deal with this himself. He had done things in the past that he was thoroughly ashamed of, but saving innocent lives as a British agent wasn't one of them. He had weighed up all the options and arrived at his decision. Alongside him lay the Serbian Tokarev 9-mil pistol resting on the arm of the sofa, loaded and cocked and good to go. He was much better with an AK than a pistol but the Tokarev would have to do. When they came for him, he would try to kill them all. He knew he couldn't betray Ahmad, the guy who had become his only real friend. He had seen an ISIS interrogation. Therefore, he would do what he could to protect himself and his family, and then if he failed he would point the pistol at his own temple and hope that his God and his family would forgive him.

# Chapter Twenty-Nine

*Whitehall, London*

The CCTV camera situated on the top of the eastern side of the Foreign and Commonwealth Office (FCO) faced south. The operator picked up the couple with the pushchair early walking on Parliament Street in front of the building and had just passed Derby Gate on the opposite side of the road. At first he detected nothing unusual about them. The woman shrouded in the all-encompassing abaya was slightly worrying from a security angle but it wasn't the first time he had seen that in this part of London. A large elm tree momentarily obscured them and then they loomed back into view. The operator zoomed in again, and now the man was holding an umbrella protectively over the woman even though the rain had stopped. Again that rang alarm bells. All the CCTV footage was now automatically fed into the latest facial recognition software, but the combination of the abaya and the sizeable, and temporarily unneeded black brolly, effectively put a spanner in that works. The security man was now concerned and looked with the other camera that faced the square.

Bystanders were now beginning to break away from the demonstration. A couple of council road sweepers with Day-glo donkey jackets and a Westminster council cart moved along the road beside the pavement at a relaxed pace. He then zoomed onto the big guy in the green Barbour jacket that seemed vaguely interested in the family's progress. He was looking up towards Downing Street and maybe 200 metres behind them. Then he saw something that again seemed a bit strange. The man with the brolly stopped and started having a long conversation with the two road sweepers.

*I wonder what they are saying.*

Sharka had stopped and was talking to Tadge and Ali, who were pretending to sweep the inside of the pavement on Parliament Street. The orders had stated that they would not even exchange glances until they were within striking distance of the Downing Street barrier, but Sharka had changed the plan. Tadge had only just lifted the lid of the council cart and checked both AKs were ready to go. There were also six Russian F1 fragmentation grenades with the pins prepped and a Russian RDG smoke canister to add to the confusion. When the suicide bomb went off, it would be their mission to use the vital element of surprise that Rahim's sacrifice gave them, to storm Number Ten. The two guys looked at each other nervously, in a sort of embarrassed way, as the team leader spoke.

"Brothers," said Sharka, "the time has come, and all our struggles are now over." He paused. He had thought about this speech for a very long time and had mentally rehearsed it on many occasions.

"Allah has led us here, and from this point onwards we are the *shaheed* (martyrs) and blessed. The Holy Koran, Chapter Three, verse 169 to 170 says, *Think not of those who are slain in Allah's way as dead. Nay, they live, finding their sustenance in the presence of their Lord and they rejoice in the bounty provided by Allah.*"

Tadge, probably the most streetwise of the group, scanned back towards Parliament Square. He noticed the big guy halted on the other side of the road. He was looking towards a black Range Rover that had suddenly emerged from the crowd at the end of the street. He interrupted Sharka's sermon with quiet venom and almost spat out:

"Leave that for the mosque. Let's get moving. We are being watched."

The group started to move again, and the plan was back on track, but the group had almost subliminally just elected a new leader. The incident on the M25 in the van and the endless preaching in the safe house had slowly eroded Sharka's credibility, and they all knew it. They were now 300 metres away from the primary barrier that blockaded Downing Street. By moving towards the target, they had confirmed their objective and intention.

The CCTV operator zoomed in again on the group. The couple and the pushchair seemed to pick up speed and walk a bit faster. The two council workers and the cart moved to the other side of the street. Soon, they would enter the area designated as the 'Red Zone' under earlier protocols designed to thwart an armed attack by the Provisional IRA. The CCTV man reached for the buzzer on the central console and pressed it. An alarm sounded in all Whitehall's government buildings.

A red phone rang on the Prime Minister's desk. There was a murmur of conversation from the other end of the phone. The PM was silent for a moment; after nearly a year in power, he was becoming used to making hard decisions about Special Forces operations, but that had been in Syria and Afghanistan, not in London.

"OK, wait for my call." He held his hand over the handset and looked towards the wise and experienced face of the private secretary.

"You have no choice, Prime Minister," he said.

"I know, we've both studied the intelligence, and we can do nothing else."

The Prime Minister spoke into the handset.

"Get the police to step down. The Special Forces now have primacy," he said with a resigned tone. "They have the GO," he confirmed.

The SAS immediately had the green light. B Squadron, 22 SAS's OC, then sent the message that would change the dynamics.

"Hello, all stations and Golf Sierra Alpha, this is Golf Zero Alpha," he said very concisely. A deliberate pause and then:

"All stations – Standby-Standby."

The sniper who was still scanning the primary target prepared to take the shot.

"You got that call, Max."

"Yep, you've got the Go, and I'm recording."

The cross-hairs focused on the target's head and the shooter took a deep breath and slowly squeezed the trigger and then stopped.

"You seeing this, Max?" the shot said in an amazed voice.

"Yeah, still rolling. What the fuck's going on?"

Rahim had stopped; he had calmly removed the abaya. He was now looking at his panicking abuser, his suicide vest visible to all, as he showed Sharka the detonation plunger and smiled.

"What are you doing?" Sharka screamed.

"Taking away your earthly life and your chance of heaven," Rahim shouted.

The sniper had seen the suicide vest and pressed the trigger, but the target suddenly moved. Rahim darted towards Sharka and grabbed him tightly in a death embrace and laughed. He shouted just one word "REVENGE" and released the button.

BOOM!

The sniper team ducked down as the overpressures from the huge blast roled over their heads and rattled the windows of their hide. The blast peppered the walls of the FOC with shrapnel and then there was a momentary deathly silence and then the screech of car alarms and the screams of the injured, and then another sound, the unmistakable high pitched crack of AK rounds.

BANG, BANG, BANG.

The sniper scanned again. The two road sweepers armed with AK74s were moving on the final 200 metres towards Downing Street in what the army calls 'tactical bounds'. Ali was firing his weapon in short three-round bursts from the shoulder in the kneeling position, in the direction Downing Street as Tadge sprinted towards Number 10 with his weapon held in both hands.

"SHOT", the sniper said to the number two. The cross-hairs of the Schmitt and Bender moved onto the first target, the man who was kneeling.

PHUT!

The weapon was almost soundless as the sniper skillfully reworked the bolt, ejected the empty cylinder and placed another round into the chamber.

"ON," Max said as Ali smashed forward onto the pavement, dead.

Tadge had just frozen in his tracks as his covering fire stopped. He looked back and saw Ali's lifeless form. He was smart, and he had quickly worked out that they had been set up. He wanted to drop his weapon and put his hands up, but he knew it was too late. He could almost feel the malign influence behind him boring into his back. He screamed and fired one last long burst at Downing Street until the magazine emptied.

"SHOT." The cross-hairs switched targets.

PHUT! The weapon fired again.

"ON," said Max.

Tadge screamed when the bullet impacted entered his back and exited his chest.

He had wanted to shout *ALLAHU AKBAR*, but it came out differently.

"Oh fuck," the boy from Luton murmured as he died.

Two minutes later a black Range Rover weaved its way through the dazed civilians and pulled up outside the house on Parliament Street. The large man in the waxed jacket opened the rear right-hand passenger door of the car as the sniper left the house with an oblong green plastic case. The slightly built figure was wearing a black NOMEX facemask and a hooded combat jacket. Max, six-foot tall and stocky, was dressed the same way and carrying the camera when he finally closed and locked the front door behind him. They climbed into the vehicle's peaceful refuge of grey leather and dark tinted glass.

The large guy who opened the door was B Squadron's Sergeant Major (SM) who joined them in the back of the car. He was smiling; he hadn't been at all sure about using a specialist from another unit. The sniper wasn't one of his but a late replacement from the SRR. The option had been forced on B Squadron by DSF as part of a new cross-agency approach, but the operator had done a brilliant job. The SM shook the sniper's hand. The marksman's hand was small but strong.

"That was one hell of an explosive first shot. You must have hit the detonator on the vest."

The SRR soldier pulled down the combat jacket hood and removed the black Nomex facemask. A cascade of dark brown hair fell to her shoulders. She deftly gathered it up into a ponytail and tied it back.

"Strangest thing," she seemed relaxed, "Max can back me up on this," she looked thoughtful, "it wasn't me." There was a moment of silence within the Range Rover. "The bomber blew himself and his mate up."

"Yeah," Max said. "I've got it on tape. He clacked himself off. He was a suicidal suicide-bomber if that's at all possible." Max looked puzzled. "I think 'Ruperts' (officers) would call that an oxymoron or is it a tautology, a contradiction in terms, yeah?"

"No, those words mean you've skived off on too many education courses, Max," the SM said smiling. Max continued, really trying to confirm what had happened.

"No, Tania's right, and it's weird, it was the strangest thing. He deliberately killed himself and the guy in the black coat."

"Enough chat," the Squadron Sergeant Major counselled.

"You are now going straight for a debriefing with the regiment's flying lawyer. Remember everything, every tiny detail of what happened but only discuss the incident when you are with him. We have four dead terrorists, and there will be an inquiry." And then as if to contradict his instructions he turned to the SRR girl with a puzzled look on his well-worn face.

"I wonder why the fuck he did that?"

"I guess they didn't get on," said Tania, without even a smile.

*Scotland*
*In an SAS FOB*
*The Day Before*

The SAS forward operating base was a cavernous aircraft hangar within twenty miles of Sam's house and another sniper specialist was working. He had stripped down and examined his weapon and it was a different piece to anything he had seen before. He had been an apprentice toolmaker before he joined the army and he admired the finely tooled engineering. His game was weapons and he knew he was looking at a good one. As the other G Squadron men busily prepped their equipment for the job that had just got the green light, they occasionally looked across at the sinister-looking weapon on the bench in front of him. It was painted in a mottled green and brown camouflage and looked pretty deadly but actually it was designed to be non-lethal.

It was an Evanix ML pneumatic rifle of a 'bull pup' design with the magazine and breech at the rear of the weapon. It was a glorified air rifle that was usually employed in tranquilising large game on conservation projects. It had a 9-mil calibre and a rifled bore with a maximum range of 100 metres. The ammunition was unlike anything that he had seen before. It had a standard SF issue Trijicon low-level sight but mounted underneath was something truly special. It was the latest kit for digital imaging and called a Hale and Parker 'Visual Imaging Sensor', or VIS site. Both the weapon and the optic had been supplied by the tech department at Six and was of course totally untried.

His mates called the twenty-year veteran 'Smiles' not because of his particularly rosy disposition but for the opposite reason. His face carried a permanent frown on the right side of his mouth caused by a poorly timed door entry charge in Iraq. He had been chosen because of his experience and proven track record at the sharp end of counter-terrorism. He was the SAS 'go to' guy for difficult shoots. He had once waited in a hide for three days before killing down a tier one HV (High Value) target with a Barret Light 50 at over a mile in Iraq. He worked diligently on this new piece of kit and smiled.

*This is the first time I've done this without the intention of flat-packing some fucker! Life is strange, sometimes.*

He had quickly worked out that at one hundred metres with a slight wind it was achievable but that was at the optimistic range for this kind of ammunition. The shot had to be precise and the range was important. The rifle could be charged up to 2900 PSI, far too much for a shot under a hundred. He knew from his practice rounds that with that compression the dart would pass through the soft tissue and kill the guy stone dead. Not the desired effect in this case as the dart had to stick into the target but not go through the soft tissue.

He picked up one of the two operational rounds and inspected it and whispered,

*Beautiful.*

The dart was aerodynamically perfect and rifled for accuracy and a technical triumph for the Israeli micro-engineering firm that had designed and manufactured it. The point of the dart activated a drug-filled reservoir that instantly pumped its contents into its new home. It had been operationally tested by Mossad, the Israeli Intelligence Service and had apparently worked. The drugs inside were specifically loaded to affect a man of the same height, weight, and age group of the target. When delivered in the right place, the blend of Valium and Ativan with a supercharged spike of Ketamine-concentrate should render the target senseless instantaneously.

He lifted up the dart round and examined it again under the desk light.

It occurred to him, *it's the first time I've held ammunition designed to save a life.*

He smiled. *How weird is that? Fucking amazing!* He knew he could place the dart in the right place at over one hundred metres even in a decent wind. Then the chemicals would do their job.

*Hope the fucker works because you can't debrief a floppy one.*

# Chapter Thirty

Cyclone had spent the whole day preparing for the arrival of the other brothers. The house had to be cleaned, food provisioned, bedding arranged and a prayer room organised. After he had finally finished, he rechecked the equipment. Everything he had gathered for the mission. He held a crumpled piece of paper in his hand, and occasionally squinted as he deciphered the scrawled Punjabi script and mentally listed the equipment.

There were four small Motorola radios, four mobile phones with separate unused SIM cards. A local hardware superstore had supplied the large roll of black plastic sheeting, the strong tape, and the cable ties. There were also some brass knuckledusters and four small lead-filled leather coshes. All this hardware lay on four sets of black overalls with a pack of latex surgical gloves and some black cotton balaclavas.

The four AK47s were propped up on the roll of plastic sheeting. The wooden shoulder stocks had been removed to make them easier to conceal. Each had a thick bungee cord where the shoulder stock had been, so that it could be hung from a shoulder. Alongside each weapon lay two of the AK47's distinctive banana-shaped 30-round magazines that were now bound together with green tape, reversed and positioned end to end, to ensure a quick mag change. The three large silver-bladed carving knives glistened under the light of the front room's single light bulb alongside a black carbon-steel combat knife and one small Sony video camera lying on a large black *'Shahada'* flag neatly folded in two, showing one half of the white scrawled Arabic script, that when unfurled would say:

There is no God but Allah. Mohammad is the messenger of Allah.

He looked and rechecked the equipment. He placed the list in his pocket and then picked up the large black 'Bowie' style combat knife almost like he was grasping a sacred object. This was the martyr's knife, the knife his brother had been holding when he died in Mosul. He felt the weight of it and assessed its balance. It was a foot long and made of cold black carbon steel. He turned the knife almost lovingly, appreciating its form and considering its final function. The serrated edge glinted under the front room's single light bulb.

*The woman who killed my brother will die with this knife in front of that holy banner and the entire world will know.* The man's eyes glittered with an icy stare that mirrored both hate and his inner desire for revenge.

*And now all I have to do is wait. The dark will be here soon and the brothers will arrive to drag the she-devil to hell.*

The camera was triggered at 0300hrs as they opened the shiny red front door of the three-storey house on Maxwell Road. A2 Branch had fitted the switch on the same night the source had identified the safe house. It was a quiet enough area with a lot of Asian doctors and professional types that minded their own business, so it was a good place to hide. The Pollockshields Estate nearby also kept unwanted visitors to a minimum; a local Asian drugs gang called the 'Shielders' had an excellent deterrent effect. The estate was effectively a no-go zone for the police and was left exclusively to what was called 'Community Policing'.

As soon as they opened the door to load the equipment, they were being watched and the high-tech camera had night vision and recorded everything. The large roll of plastic sheeting caused some cursing in Punjabi and Glaswegian before it finally fitted into the back of the transit van. The rest of the equipment followed. All the necessary accoutrements needed to murder Captain Samantha Holloway and record her suffering were placed inside. The four-man team then climbed into the van. They were followed as soon as they passed Eglinton Street and had three-car surveillance follow by the time they accessed the M8 at Junction 20. It was about two and a half hours to Sam's cottage and 115 miles.

Gaynor looked at her watch and it was four thirty. She had the middle stag on the camera observing along the pathway of the cottage. She was playing with the zoom facility; it was an expensive piece of kit and it had night vision and a thermal capability. The first inklings of dawn were becoming apparent. Sunrise on a thermal camera is an interesting experience. The burgeoning sun was transforming the darkness into a mad blue and orange collage-like image. Almost like an Impressionist landscape painting.

*Get a grip, girl, you're not here to experiment with the ambient colours of a thermal camera, it will either be today that the bad guys come, or the INT has been a dud. Not too bad for us, but shit for the G Squadron lads who have been in an ambush position all night.*

"Hey, Gaynor, how's it going?" said the voice of the team leader.

"OK, I'm just about to radio check to the blades," she said. Everybody was fully alert now. The sun was just beginning to bring a hazy light to the Highlands, and it was the time soldiers call 'Stand-Too'; since time immemorial first light was supposed to be the most likely time for enemy attack.

"Hello, all stations, Gulf Two Zero this is Romeo One, over," Gaynor transmitted.

"Yeah, that's a roger, Romeo One," said a bored-sounding male voice. Gaynor turned and looked towards her boss.

"I bet it was a cold one last night," she said.

"Yeah, don't worry, kid, they're well used to it," answered the big Geordie Major.

"Ambushing and generally killing bad guys is what they do!" As he smiled, his encrypted phone rang. The TL recognised the number and picked up the mobile. It was the team leader of the MI5 A4 surveillance team.

"Hello, is that Howie?" the A4 guy said in a matter-of-fact way.

"Yep, send, mate," and then the message they had been waiting for.

"X-rays, your location ten minutes. They are four-up in a blue Ford transit. Registration is Sierra-Gulf-One-Five-Romeo-Uniform-Gulf. I will call when they have finally committed to Red One."

"Roger that, Alpha," he answered, and then, "OK, Gaynor, you're on," he said with a sense of urgency. Red One was the brevity code for the house they were occupying.

The team leader transmitted.

"Hello, all stations, we're on. Ten minutes to Standby." The SAS call signs answered with a businesslike and sequential 'Roger that.'.

Gaynor stood up; she was dressed in an outfit that she had chosen from Sam Holloway's wardrobe. A short dark blue waxed 'Barbour' jacket and jeans. She placed on her blonde wig and adjusted it, picked up a brush and combed its length. She applied some lipstick and checked her appearance. She smiled.

"All dressed up and nowhere to go," she said to the TL. "I'm OK and prepped for work."

"OK," said the TL. "But remember, you're the bait not a human sacrifice, Gaynor. As soon as it goes noisy take cover," he smiled. "Just let the blades do their work and keep yourself safe."

"Yeah, OK, boss," she said calmly, as she removed her Glock from its right rear hip holster and checked for the glint of brass inside the breech. Gaynor picked up the keys for Sam and Taff's BMW and said, "Just tell me when. I'm good to go."

Howie's phone went again. "They've just committed towards Red One." There was a long gravel drive up to the cottages; they had two minutes until they arrived.

"OK, Gaynor, you're on. Be careful, no heroics, girl. Just flash by that window a couple of times, nothing too obvious. Hopefully they will come to us," said the senior SRR man.

"Roger that," said Gaynor adjusting the blonde wig in front of the hall mirror.

The old blue transit rattled along the single-track road. High walls and highland hedges channelled it towards Sam Holloway's house. The driver turned towards the cell leader who used to be Objective Cyclone. The rest of the team were all townies and had never been this far out of Glasgow before. The driver felt lost.

"Ya ken this is the right place," he said. The passenger was holding his phone in front of him and was using Google Maps.

"Yeah, we should be there soon, look for a row of cottages." As the transit rocked into a pothole a single row of white-walled croft cottages appeared on the road lined along the bottom of the hillside. The vehicle stopped; there was no other traffic on the road.

"Which one is it?" the driver said. Cyclone ignored him and opened the front passenger door and climbed out.

"Hamid, you will find out when the others do," he said, picking up the binoculars that he had bought from a second-hand shop in Paisley three months before. He moved stealthily to the end of the lane and used the cover of a hedge. The blurred image came into sharp focus. He could clearly see the target house and caught a glimpse of a blonde head flit by the front-room window. He was excited now. He moved to the back of the transit and rapped on the double doors.

"We've got the bitch!" he said quietly to the rest of the team who were climbing out of the van.

"No weapons yet," he said. "Let me check out the area first."

The leader had needed to be a cautious man; his careful approach had kept him alive in Syria and Iraq while he waited to avenge his brother's death. He was worried because the rest of the guys were local lads with no military experience, but he had plenty. He used the binos to scan the slightly higher ground either side of the straggly hedge contained by a green-topped derelict-looking wall. He was looking for anything out of place.

"Hang on here and get the gear ready," he said, as he climbed the loose stone wall and dislodged a part of it that thumped into the undergrowth. The thick green moss was still retaining the early morning dew. He spotted that the moss had been scraped in a couple of places and a few of the stones were also missing. Those marks made him scan along the top of the wall.

*Maybe someone else has crossed it? I'll check out the area.*

He scanned the sparse woodland again with the old binos and then moved through the brambly undergrowth looking for tracks. He walked slightly uphill struggling to keep his footing, and he then stopped and listened. All he could hear was the first twitter of birdsong. He studied the ground, first the immediate area he was standing in and then a bit further out. It looked all clear, and he turned and returned to the van. He walked across to the only building, a tumbledown cottage.

The sniper could have reached out and touched his foot. He was dressed in his warmers kit, a layer of thermal clothing covered by his camouflaged uniform with an extra windproof smock. Not that he considered it cold. He was ex-Mountain Troop and had known it a lot colder. The camouflage was then improved by what was known as a ghillie suit, a strange-looking smock-like over garment attached with strips of green, brown and tan material that perfectly matched the late summer foliage. His position was near the left hand wall. The weapon was veiled in an outer camouflaged net embellished with local vegetation. He had a view down to the end of the track and the killing area. That's where the troop's three Minimi Light MG with 200-round box magazines intersected the track forming the perfect geometry for death.

The sniper whispered into his throat mike as the terrorist turned away and out of earshot, "That's X-ray One back towards the blue transit." He paused as he squinted through the ACOG sight on the weapon at the ever-diminishing target of the back of the terrorist that almost stepped on him.

"It looks like they are good to go," and then he said with emphasis, "Standby, Standby."

Gaynor was calm as she heard the Standby on the radio net from the small bean-sized receiver in her right ear. She listened to a quick succession of 'roger thats', from all the call signs involved until it came to her turn.

"Roger that," she said concisely, her voice steady, but with the adrenaline slowly starting to pump around her body. This was her first live operation but all her training had led to this moment. The kidnappers would have to show their weapons before the SAS unit could engage. She reassured herself by placing her hand on the butt of her pistol and checking that it could be drawn quickly. She adjusted any clothing that might snag on a combat draw and then satisfied that her personal weapon was unencumbered, she then heard the call to her TL from the blades.

"Yeah, I have," said Gaynor in a matter-of-fact type of way as she grabbed the car keys in passing and opened the front door of the house. She knew what was required. She walked towards the BMW and quickly checked the underside of the car and climbed in leaving the driver's door open as she started the vehicle, exactly as Sam would have. She started the vehicle and was rewarded with a blast of pop music from Nevis Radio. She then closed the door and placed the automatic gearbox in drive and waited. Her heart was beating loudly now in sequence with an old country and western song by Billy Ray Cyrus called 'Achy Breaky Heart'. Gaynor mouthed the words soundlessly as she waited.

*'But don't tell my heart*
*My achy breaky heart*
*I just don't think he'd understand*
*And if you tell my heart*
*My achy breaky heart*
*He might blow up and kill this man'*

208

*Won't be long now.* Her heart was still hammering away.

"It's all clear," the Syrian jihadist said as he lowered his binoculars and scrambled back to his team. "But, she's getting ready to leave," he said with an urgent edge to his voice. There was a flurry of activity from within the vehicle as weapons were grabbed and then all four of them stood by the back doors.

"Right, leave the other kit in the wagon, we will drive that up to the house as soon as we have her."

The four men split up, two on each side of the small lane. Each had a collection of implements to subdue the victim. The runaway from Syria was carrying his brother's black combat knife and a means of drugging his brother's killer so he could take his time and enjoy using it. It was the powder form of a drug called Scopolamine. It was a powerful sedative that made people do what you wanted. It would ensure that the execution was controlled and filmed. Each man had an AK hanging by his side under his outer clothing, but these were only to be used as a last resort. The team hugged the ragged hedgerow, and they moved slowly towards the house. They could see the white BMW X5 as they reached the end of the gravelled lane.

"Wait," the Syrian veteran whispered as he removed the binoculars from under his coat and rechecked the target. Gaynor tapped her right hand on the leather of the steering wheel in time with the music as she looked towards the end of the lane. There was some movement from the edge of the hedge line and then she spotted a glimmer of the early morning sun reflecting off a set of optics.

The sniper studied the target intently; the terrorist lowered the binoculars and let them hang around his neck and reached into his right-hand jacket pocket. Smiles identified the object as the target paused momentarily to adjust it before covering his face.

*It's a ski mask; once he puts it on the VIS won't work.*

PING.

The tiny earpiece sounded, the VIS was positive and locked on, but all four terrorists were still short of the optimum range of the sniper weapon and what was known in military terms as the 'beaten zone' where all the troops' machine-guns and rifles intersected. The terrorists had stopped and were scanning the area nervously.

*Maybe they've spotted something.*

The VIS pinged once again before they all pulled on the black ski masks. He kept the Trijicon locked on to his target's upper body.

"Hello, Gulf Bravo Zero and all stations, I HAVE," he said with urgency, in the hope that he would get the go. "But X-ray One is fifty metres too short for shot."

"Roger that and wait out," came the instant reply from his patrol commander who then called the SRR call sign in the house.

"Hi, Howie, this is Gulf Bravo Zulu."

"Yeah, send," said the SRR team leader.

"Gulf Bravo Zulu, they are not moving, mate, they need some encouragement."

"Mike, that's a roger, you got that, Gaynor?" he said with a hint of concern in his voice.

"Yeah. Moving now," she said as she put the BMW into gear and pulled out of the parking space.

The moving vehicle had an immediate effect. The four terrorists ran forward to where they could clearly see the X5 travelling towards them. They scrabbled under their coats for their AKs and brought them up on aim.

Smiles the SAS sniper, actually smiled as he smoothly depressed the trigger. He heard the quiet PHUT as the dart left the barrel. The dart impacted the upper left shoulder, the target turned and looked in his direction with a slightly shocked look as the dart pumped the drugs into his system and he fell. The three remaining terrorists exchanged a quick, confused glance from hooded head to hooded head, their eyes wide in fear.

He said "FIRE," into his chest mike.

Objective Cyclone fell onto the gravel path as if lifeless just split seconds before the deafening sound of rapid fire shattered the silence. The high velocity zipped in from the surrounding SAS ambush and crashed into their arc of death. It was the ambush sweet spot. He felt no pain as he crashed to the ground, but he could hear everything; his senses were still operating. He could smell the cordite and hear the screams as machine-gun fire jerked into his comrades. He waited for the pain of bullets smashing into his own body but none arrived. And then he heard it.

A whistle blew and then silence. And then another loud shout from that seemed to echo around the small valley.

"Watch and Shoot – Watch and Shoot."

The other G Squadron sniper now zeroed in on the other shapes that lay on the ground. The driver from Glasgow cried out and tried to push himself upwards.

"Help me," he said, just before a .308 Lapua Magnum round impacted his head.

Gaynor had stopped the vehicle just in time to observe the ambush to just after the last bullet was fired. There was a long moment of complete and utter silence after that last pitiless shot. No sound at all, not even the twitter of birdsong; it was as if nature was suddenly attuned to that moment of death. The early morning sun was just beginning to dapple the broken piece of woodland by the track. She then witnessed a scene that seemed straight out of a ghoulish horror movie. Amongst the jagged jungle of ancient sallow trees and weirdly angled willows, the SAS soldiers slowly began to move. Strange arboreal creatures emerged from a low-lying haze of gunsmoke. Previously inert and man-sized pieces of foliage loomed to life as the undergrowth stood up and became apparent. Ghostlike green figures stretched to their full height and then crept out of their ambush positions away from where the terrorists were lying within the ever-spreading pool of blood.

Those few seconds of kinetic violence would now be indelibly etched into Gaynor's memory. This was her first contact and the carnage had just confirmed her opinions on the fragility of life. The potential kidnappers had been thrown together by multiple bullet strikes into a gory tableau of death. Twisted bodies and their AK47s were chillingly intertwined, biodegradable software and soviet hardware haphazardly mixed, the wreckage of a failed terrorist attack. There was only one body that seemed to be untouched. She thought she detected the rise and fall of his chest.

*Strange…*

"Howie, this is Gaynor, one X-ray still alive," she whispered into the concealed chest mike as she pulled her Glock 21 free from its holster. She really didn't know whether she would be asked to kill him and she didn't really know whether she could.

Howie answered immediately, loudly and nervously.

"Gaynor, walk away NOW! Let the blades handle it." Her team leader's voice had an urgency that she had never heard before. She glanced up from the carnage and noticed that the SAS ambush party had disappeared.

*They've just turned and walked away, something's going on!* she thought as she turned to walk back to the house.

Gaynor took a final look down the track at the place the locals called 'The Weeping Willows'. She noticed the coldness of the place for the first time, no flowers, no colour, just an atmosphere of evil conjured up by the twisted half-dead willow trees and dead bracken.

"Fucking spooky", she whispered.

Sam and the team were parked in a small lay-by alongside the only navigable minor road that led onto the track. Everything was totally quiet in the van; there was no conversation, none of the usual good-natured banter. Sam looked at her reflection in the rear-view mirror framed in the background by the team dressed in ghostly white forensic overalls in the darkness of the back and she posed herself a question.

*Is this the strangest job I've ever been involved in?*

She knew it was not the first time that she had felt strangely uneasy about a job, but in the past she had always felt on the side of the righteous, but this was different. It was effectively a UK government sanctioned rendition organised by the CIA. She was getting ready to replace a live terrorist with the very dead body in the back of the transit. She rationalised and resolved;

It was morally dubious, probably illegal but absolutely necessary!

The crack and thump of high-velocity rounds finding their target stopped the internal moral audit. The contact was sharp and heavy, but quick. It ended with the shrill sound of a whistle, and a shout, and then total silence.

"Standby, Standby," Sam said and then the silence descended again. Two minutes after the last single gunshot the radio squelched into life.

"Hello, Spartan Three, this is Gulf Zero Alpha."

"Yeah, send," Sam responded.

"Gulf Zero Alpha, two minutes."

"That's a roger," Sam said as she turned to the guys in the back of the van.

Blood seeped from the plastic bag as Jimmy unzipped and what was left of the cadaver's ashen face stared back at him.

"Nearly show time, mate," he whispered and smiled.

Sam pulled the transit van onto the track and rolled slowly towards the ambush site. An SAS man was waiting down the track standing beside the first willow tree. Sam stopped the transit by where he stood and wound down the window. The G Squadron Major looked at his watch.

"We've got under five minutes," he said pointing towards the human remains one hundred metres further on. He was business like. "Our guys are away, there are no cameras and no witnesses. I'll walk you in," he said, as he turned to lead the way.

He noticed one of the operators dressed in the white forensic suits was a woman.

"It's a bit of a mess, I'm afraid."

"Thanks," said Sam, knowing that he couldn't realise that she had seen much worse during service to her country.

The switch had been rehearsed; the main problem was untangling the bodies that had fallen over the objective. It became apparent that the coolly applied professional violence hadn't been kind to them. High-velocity rounds and their entry and exit wounds made a mess, and hundreds of them shred bodies very messily. The white coveralls were soon splashed with blood as the team tried to free the only living thing in that pile of death. They picked up Objective Cyclone and laid him on the track. His body was unmarked but slippery with blood.

Taff and Pat had his even bloodier replacement on an army-issue green canvas stretcher. Sam supervised as they tried to place him in exactly the same place under the three other bodies. The SAS Major used a picture he had taken to make slight adjustment here and there while he placed Cyclone's AK47 on the body then looked at his watch.

Jimmy quickly went through Cyclone's jacket pockets. Two AK47 magazines, six loose 762 rounds. Three sets of black plasticuffs and the plastic bag of Scopolamine powder he intended to use to disable his victim. Inside his left-hand jacket pocket, wrapped in a black silk wrap, he found the jagged-edged black combat knife. He then turned his attention to the trouser pockets; a bloody packet of American cigarettes, a battered Zippo lighter, an old receipt for fuel.

The ex-Mossad guy suddenly stopped. He noticed that the subject's eyes had flicked open. Jimmy picked up the knife and held it up to the prostrate man's face.

"Didn't quite work out the way you expected, did it, mate?" and smiled.

He quickly moved all the collected items and transferred them to the unknown man, the FNUSNU, in the pile of bodies.

The SAS man rechecked his watch.

"Two minutes," he said as the stretcher now burdened with the objective moved towards the van.

Jimmy and the blade stayed behind to camouflage the transit's wheel tracks as Sam slowly reversed the V8 transit. In two minutes they were gone.

It was dark in the van, he was awake but unable to move, and he sensed white-covered entities looking over him. Jassim Emwazi, alias Objective Cyclone, thought at first he was paralysed. He remembered very little about what had happened. He knew his limbs felt heavy, immovable, as if individually pulled down by a hundred demon hands. He fought to open his eyes again while slowly trying to assess his injuries. He remembered the gunfire, he remembered the shock but he felt no pain, he felt nothing. Maybe he was on his way to *Jannah*. His eyes flicked open; just darkness at first and then a beautiful face with blonde hair with a halo of light outlining the face.

He was dead. Had he died a martyr and this was the afterlife he had been promised?

His body rolled with the movement of a vehicle and jerked him into reality. He studied the face and hit his moment of horror.

*It was her!*

The face smiled and held up a syringe.

"Remember me, Jassim?" He felt the needle in his arm.

"Welcome to hell," the radiant angel said.

# Chapter Thirty-One

*Whitechapel*

Imran was still waiting for them to arrive. A few tell-tale signs of his diminishing prospects for life had already become apparent. He had seen a couple of the local Muslim patrol guys looking intently at his front door, and they didn't do covert surveillance very well. And then came a bizarre phone call from Mullah Rahman to try to set him up. He casually mentioned that some brothers would like to meet him to talk about a family member that was last seen in Iraq.

Would he mind chatting to them? the Mullah had said. Imran had rechecked the pistol lying on the settee beside him and answered: "Not at all."

*He must think I'm stupid.* Imran was smiling sadly as he stood and squinted through the front-room blinds. A slight adjustment to the wooden slats had the ISIS watchers reaching for their mobile phones. The news of the failed attack would be out by now and they would have worked out who was responsible for the leak. He operated the remote for the TV and the first news reports were soon coming through: Breaking News, 'failed terrorists attack' in London with civilian casualties. Sky had released a short news item of some jumpy phone footage of an explosion and the ensuing scenes of panic amongst the protesters in the vicinity of Parliament Square, but nothing else so far. Imran knew they would now be making plans to snatch him and he sort of accepted that his game was up. He thought about his life's whole misadventure, he felt at peace with himself and viewed it through the prism of bitter experience.

Imran's life had been like a series of interconnected dominoes, the game you see the old white guys playing, but his dominos had been standing in one long, unbroken line all just a bit too close for comfort. The chain reaction had led him to where he was now. One domino falls and hits the next and then they all come tumbling down, and twenty-six years later you are waiting for some murderers to knock on your door. He looked back, without any anger now!

He was solely responsible for a series of events that had accelerated beyond his control and taken him to where he was. In a society where everybody glories in victimhood it was always easier to blame other people; his parents, his area, the police and the Government. He knew though, that in the final analysis, he had lived in a free country and that he had made his own decisions. They just happened to be the wrong ones. He had to pay the price, not for what they considered his treachery but for what they had made him do. He had hoped that maybe he had redeemed himself. He was a realist though and realised that no matter what he had been promised, that once he could no longer fulfil his function as a covert agent, there was a distinct possibility he would cease to be useful and therefore, he was on his own.

And then the phone rang. It was Ahmad's number, Imran answered.

"Hi, Imran," said Ahmad.

"Hello, mate, I'm at Uncle Mo's," he said using his agent compromise code indicating that he could speak freely.

"I know you are, mate," said Ahmad. "I have my guys looking at the guys who are looking at you," he said with a laugh.

"That's good to know," said Agent 3010 with a smile.

"OK, listen, Imran, very carefully." Ahmad talked quickly and with a sense of urgency. "Your family has been safely collected and is now comfortable and at one of my organisation's safe

217

houses. In precisely five minutes' time your phone will ring four times and then ring off. Immediately after that, a team of armed officers from Special Branch and SCO 19 will break your door down. You will be forcibly arrested, handcuffed and taken from your house. You will be with your family within one hour. You have my word."

Imran looked slightly stunned. All he could say was, "Thanks, Ahmad."

Imran immediately looked at the pistol lying next to him. He quickly unloaded it, stripped it down and carried it to the kitchen and then opened a kitchen cupboard and tipped the various components into an already opened packet of his kids' breakfast cereal.

*Snap, crackle and pop.* Imran smiled.

He would tell Ahmad later. He wouldn't need the gun now. And then his phone buzzed the first time. On the fourth ring, he was just walking back into the front room when the door came crashing in, and then he first heard the shouts from black-uniformed figures that were already inside the house.

"GET DOWN, ARMED POLICE!"

At the same time, Mullah Rahman's door and five others were smashed down in separate areas of London. The Government's big clean-up of ISIS elements had begun. Imran lay on the floor obeying instructions. As his hands were pinned behind his back, the officer applying the quick cuffs whispered very quietly in his ear.

"Don't worry, mate, Ahmad sent us. You will be with your family soon."

# Epilogue

*Canada*

Distance, Speed and Time are calculations that are often grouped together in the military. It is possible to find any one of these three values using the other two, which is really handy when map reading the old-school way. Samantha Holloway's sanity had also benefited from the equation. Time had proved to be a great healer, and the distance between herself and the source of the trauma had also dramatically helped the healing process. Rural Canada had ticked the box on all fronts. Sam was sleeping better. Much better now, and after some professional help, she had finally managed to put the thoughts of Helmand and Iraq back in their box. They would always be of course part of her inner sadness.

Taff taught trainees in a Canadian Special Forces unit known as JTF 2 or the Joint Task Force Two based in Ottawa. They had left their beloved Highlands and their croft cottage within two days of returning from the last job. They were under a death threat and had been incorporated into an intergovernmental resettlement package. The press had again ensured that they couldn't stay. They had been 'outed' in several papers and news channels when directly linked to what the tabloids were calling the 'Spean Bridge Massacre'. The inquest into the deaths had concluded with a final verdict of 'Lawful Killing'. The DNA samples that Sam supplied for the initial identification of Objective Cyclone had been covertly recycled at the coroner's office and now the name, Jassim Emwazi, had been officially recorded as one of those killed in the ambush and EMNI now thought their future plans were safe. The small highland croft and 'The Weeping Willows' was now the scene of an annual all-night vigil organised by London-based political activists and Islam4UK to both commemorate and to mourn the four men accompanied by the inevitable counter protests.

Imran, Source 3010, had to push slightly against his front door to open it. The recent fall of crisp snow provided little resistance, especially when a doting dad has to take his kids to play in the strange white stuff that they loved. Imran now called himself Ahmad. He was given a choice of the name when they moved him to Canada, and it seemed a natural choice, and the family was now living just outside Toronto. The resettlement people had arranged for him to study computer programming and software development, and he had secured his first well-paid consultancy. He worked from home so he could look after the kids. His wife was now reading modern languages at Toronto University, and he occasionally lectured on the subject of Islamic Radicalisation for the Canadian SF.

His family loved Canada, and he was happy for the first time in his life. The house was modern, large and full of joy. Both his children were thriving outside London and Whitechapel's Islamic bubble. Religion was never discussed at home. It was no longer safe for them to be around religious gatherings of any type as Canada was now starting to have its own Islamist problems. His god was personal to him, and only him, and was nobody else's business. His children would make their own choices. He only kept in touch with the UK by watching Sky News. He smiled when he had heard that Mullah Rahman was doing thirty years' minimum in Belmarsh, part of the same prison system that used to employ him as a Muslim prison chaplain.

There are many ways a young Jamaican-Irish ex-boxer and former gangster could end up in prison. Drugs, drink, envy and lust are just some, or sometimes it's just bad luck, but none is actually paid a decent wage to do it. Coco had played the long game inside and finally made it. At first, he evaded and avoided them, and then slowly, he let them think that they were influencing him. This was aided by the fact that being an Islamist in prison was considered cool and even sensible. You got more time on your own, better food and the screws were shit scared of being considered religiously intolerant, or worse still, racist. So on this wing, the ISIS crew he was part of pretty much ran things. Of course, there were the downsides; the constant droning of idiot fanatics that you just wanted to tell to *'Shut the fuck up'* but couldn't. No drink, no drugs, no girls, and the pungent breath of the government-supplied Mullah during Ramadan when he was the only fucker that was fasting. And of course, there was the internal loneliness of being the sole MI5 agent in Wandsworth Prison, as far as he knew?

Coco looked across towards the mirror above the single washbasin framed against the standard magnolia wall. He could see his reflection in the shiny but severely scratched steel. Coco hated what he saw, he hated the stupid-looking hat, and he detested the beard. The worst thing was, that his mum could never visit him here as she was banned at his request. He had to pretend to give her up, as she was a practising Christian that had refused to convert. It had broken his heart, but he hoped he would be able to explain it to her one day. Those were the minuses of being an undercover operator in prison, but there was an upside.

The money was excellent, and he had already saved up £40,000 in the overseas bank account that Box had set up for him, and it was tax free. There was also the fact that as an agent, he had been very productive. He had been able to infiltrate planning sessions and was trusted, and so he had prevented some very heavy shit going down outside. Lives had been saved. He also supplied the smuggled mobile phones and provided the drugs that kept the prison anaesthetised and oblivious of reality. He also timed and organised the drone flights that arrived at certain cell windows during the dark hours. And finally, he was doing an Open University course in political science. He had been promised a life-changing opportunity. He had been offered the chance to put his old life behind him and actually become a Security Service operative. He would start his training as soon as he was released.

Now, he needed to find a quiet place for a phone call to pass something on to Lou, his friend, mentor, handler, and maybe, in the future, fellow operator. Some of the guys were talking about a big operation that 'would make the Twin Towers attack look lame'. It was probably a fable, prison talk, usually generated by some wanker trying to make himself interesting, but it all got reported. He was learning that nothing in his new profession could ever be dismissed out of hand; as Lou had once put it, in a quotation that had lodged in Coco's memory:

*Large streams from little fountains*
*flow*
*Tall oaks from little acorns grow.*

# The Author

W.T. Delaney is the pen name of an ex-Royal Marine Commando who now writes books. he joined the Corps in 1973 and served for twenty-four years. During his time in the military, he was attached to the Special Boat Service and served as a special duties soldier. A second career on London's security *'Circuit"* led to a variety of tasks ranging from body-guarding an Arab Royal family to providing security advice to both Fox News and NBC News while they covered events in Iraq and Afghanistan. Delaney retired to write books in 2016 after a ten-year contract employed as a US contractor teaching intelligence collection to both the Iraqi security services and the Afghan National Army. He started writing intelligence-based action-adventure books in 2014 and published the first book in his Sam Holloway series in 2016. 'A Shadowing of Angels' was followed in 2019 by 'A Falling of Angels'; these are also available as audiobooks. The final book, 'An Evil Shadow Falls', has just been released. The author is currently in negotiation with a major film production company to make 'An Evil Shadow Falls' into a film. Delaney is married to Marion and father of five, a grandfather to four and a prospective great-grandfather to a little girl who is approaching fast and will be with us soon.

Author Web Site wtdelaney.com

Thank you for reading 'A Falling of Angels' and I really hope you enjoyed the second book in the Sam Holloway Trilogy. If you have enjoyed it, please take the time to leave a review and let others know how much you liked it.

Thank you once again.

Bernie Plunkett MBE MSc MLitt (AKA W.T. Delaney)

*An Evil Shadow falls*

An Evil Shadow Falls is the next and final book in the Samantha Holloway Trilogy.

Sam is once again pulled from retirement for the team's most dangerous mission yet. A nuclear warhead has gone missing in Pakistan, and terrorists are planning a mass-casualty attack that can only be measured in the metrics of madness.

Sam and the team must work with Britain's secret intelligence services to make sense of a complicated jigsaw of clues, technical intercepts, source reports, and inputs from foreign intelligence agencies to prevent Ground Zero 2.

The last book in the series reaches a very bloody conclusion on a stormy night in mid-Atlantic, with the Special Boat Service on standby from a Royal Navy warship to rescue the team.